SECRETS OF AN OLD VIRGINIA HOUSE

TARA COWAN

TEA & REBELLION PRESS COMPANY
110 North Tatum Street
Woodbury, Tennessee 37190

Secrets of an Old Virginia House

ISBN-13: 978-1-7332922-8-3 (paperback)
ISBN-13: 978-1-7332922-9-0 (ebook)

Published by Tea & Rebellion Press Company

Book cover and interior design by *Hannah Linder Designs*

For S.

SECRETS OF AN OLD VIRGINIA HOUSE

ONE

I t is a maxim in the South that when death comes, it comes in threes. Fight superstitious tendencies as I might, I have never known this saying to be wrong.

For me, the deaths were as follows: my career, my relationship, and my dog. I could have dealt with one. Two, I might have managed. It was the dog that finally did me in.

Oh, there was me trying to pick up the pieces, salvage what friendships I could, and carry on in my apartment like I knew how to be single after five years of being *not* single. But the dog? That was what had me on a plane flying out of Boston. Heading toward Virginia, contemplating a bizarre new chapter. Virginia. *Rural* Virginia.

In fairness, I had grown up in the South. I had acquired my dark humor there. A certain grittiness. My preference for quiet evenings over night life. My conviction that macaroni was a vegetable. And probably, disastrously, my predisposition for taking a stand. Sticking to my guns in the face of overwhelming resistance. Letting the cookie crumble. Letting *everything* crumble. The thing was, I hadn't even agreed with the kid I had defended.

This, all of it, was what Bradley had said when he had stormed out of the apartment. I had known then that the proposal wouldn't be coming at Christmastime. I hadn't known he was finished with me completely. I had thought we were just having an argument.

In fairness, he had lost his job, too. Had his name associated with mine in every news or social media story which had run in the immediate aftermath. Received ugly messages.

I was *sorry*. I really was. I felt like the lowest form of humanity. I wasn't sure it was worth it, all that we had lost. If I could have just been *silent*. I didn't know what more to say.

Bradley didn't want me to say anything else. It was over. Thankfully, I had gotten the toaster. Also the griddle. Silver linings...

And then I had walked into the living room, found my dog dead, and thought, "*Ah!! Hahahahahahahaha! I'm crazy. We're all crazy. Who am I?*" That was when I had begun seeing an online therapist. And then there were the bills, the rent, the ostracization...all of which Bradley had just *left* me with—!

In fairness, I was being a little dramatic. For every six bad newspaper articles run, there was one which was mildly, cautiously supportive. For every fourteenth catty video made, there was one person privately messaging me (begging me not to disclose their name) and whispering that they had agreed with me. For every four-hundred online trolls, there was a single colleague assuring me he or she would stand by me in everything except taking public stands. I was truly blessed.

I had been, in another life, a well-regarded historian. I had acquired modesty in Alabama, too, but it's just a fact to say that I had two tenure track offers from Ivy Leagues when the ink was barely dry on my dissertation. In a land far away (Boston) and in a time now distant (four months ago), I had been the queen of early American studies. I was publishing a book a year. I was called regularly for interviews by news outlets. I had one hundred thousand followers on Twitter. My students learned things. They pondered the deep questions of life. There was jockeying for the crowded seats in my classes. I loved spilling over into the auditoriums so more could join. I got to go to a dark-paneled, musty office every day. I had loved the must.

I had loved a lot of things about my life. There was a certain high-brow intellectualism that suited me to a T. That sounds snobby. On the other hand, there was something distinctly, ruggedly American about the open discourse, the free exchange of ideas, the experimental philosophy that could happen, seemingly, only in those beautifully paneled, musty halls.

Open discourse. Ha.

That had landed me straight on a plane to Virginia. Without a clue as to where I would live or what I would do for the rest of my life.

I knew I planned to hide there for the next few months. I was clinging to this plan, my new plan, with everything in me, determined that it *would* happen. It was just a bonus that I wouldn't be a social pariah there, miles from anyone. I massaged my temples.

I had nowhere else to go. Well, there was Alabama. My home. I had a couple of very distant cousins there, a friend, my dad's best friend who had always been very sweet to me...

In fairness, there were reasons I didn't want to live in Alabama. I had gotten out when I was seventeen. I didn't want to look back. I hadn't.

But one thing was certain: I couldn't stay in Boston. I wasn't even sure I was completely safe there anymore. The death threats on Twitter were mounting, and I didn't know how seriously to take them. I had broken my lease. I had packed. I had said goodbye to the two people in the city still speaking to me.

I had admitted that there was no fairness in life anymore. No one was interested in it. And I was headed to Middle of Nowhere, Virginia.

WHERE WAS I?

Oh, yes. In bed.

You know that feeling when anxiety and lack of sleep and the headache from the night before combine like a hurricane first thing in the morning? I had that. Pain in my body that was a manifestation of emotions; but I intended to continue shoving them down. I didn't see any other way to keep going.

My name is Madeleine Apkarian, and I have suffered three losses. My therapist told me to say that to myself, given that I am still in the denial phase.

I had spent the night in Richmond at a plush hotel. There was a part of me that knew my similarly plush bank account would only last so long, given that there was the slight problem of no income. This thought—money—made me sit upright in the massive, soft, exquisite bed.

I crossed the beautiful carpet (which annoyed me because of its obvious price tag) looked up at the soaring ceilings (which made me roll my eyes in exasperation with myself) and quickly opened my purse. From it, I fished out my phone.

I tapped the banking app. A reassuring number met my eyes. Thank goodness Bradley and I had kept separate accounts for our paychecks, even if we were technically co-owners. I didn't think he would steal my money, and at least I had the reassurance that everything that was there was morally mine. But I needed to contact him about taking each other's names off our respective bank accounts. Something to look forward to. I could hear my grandmother, long dead, telling me that I was a fool for ever giving him access to my own account in the first place.

Anyway, looking at the account, I could afford a few months of researching without pay—just barely—especially in furtherance of a stubborn determination to save my career. My circumstances had changed. I had lived frugally before. I could do it again.

But no more opulent hotels.

And I really shouldn't have rented a beautiful BMW. I sighed, looking at it as I emerged into the parking lot. Popping the trunk, I tossed my (expensive, of course) suitcase in and slammed the trunk. Getting in, I buckled up and headed out toward the Tidewater region of Virginia.

The drive was pretty but uneventful, quite rural, and I had time to think.

My destination was Hayden's Ridge Plantation. Don't let the "Ridge" fool you into thinking it was a rustic or folksy site. On the National Register of Historic Places, it had been the original land grant of George Richard Hayden, who had settled in Virginia in 1644. Tobacco was a successful endeavor for Hayden and his sons, to say the least. The site was known now as the largest surviving colonial plantation in the country. The Hayden family had acquired thousands of acres and hundreds of slaves pre-Revolutionary War. To say that it contained a wealth of resources pertinent to early America was an understatement.

That was where my interest came in. I was, primarily, a historian of colonial studies. But my area of specialty within that discipline was the study of the enslaved of early America. Hayden's Ridge had so much to tell us. Countless historical treasures—not only of the tangible kind, but also of the information kind—were locked away within its walls, waiting to convey immeasurable knowledge about colonial slavery that we hadn't yet found.

I say "locked" because the Hayden family had retained ownership of the property throughout history to this day, and only limited portions of their archival collections had been made public. The parts that had been released from Hayden's Ridge were vast and rich in terms of the things we had learned. But not even a fraction of the treasure trove had yet been tapped, according to legend.

I got chills thinking of the primary sources tucked away, unseen by any historian's eyes. Colonial documents, architectural history, and possibly antiques or artifacts we had never accessed... Books had been written from outside sources about the family's history, the house, and the slaves there. Hayden's Ridge was as much a part of early Virginia history as any other colonial plantation, so it was very famous and quite thoroughly explored academically.

But the family records had never been seen.

The house itself was Georgian in appearance. It was older than that, but the original structure had been consumed within the later mansion. There were wings on the brick house which were actually quite elegant. The structure was an imposing one if the pictures I had found were any indication.

Apparently, decades back, there had been several days when the family had opened the grounds to the public, and a few people had posted pictures online. They were often grainy and discolored photos, but the row of extant brick slave cabins visible in one of them made my breath catch. What could their walls tell me? What could archeological digs down that avenue find about the lives of the people who had lived there?

I wondered (as I navigated my rental through the swampy terrain and turned onto a dirt road that would take me to the plantation) if I had been too optimistic in my determination. If the Hayden family had resisted turning their collections over to a historical foundation, why would they open them up to a random Ph.D.?

The current owner was a descendant—a testament to the ability of the family's male line to reproduce itself, if to nothing else. Since my social ostracism had begun, I had sent the man three different letters asking (begging) for access to his collections. All had gone unanswered.

He was a professor-historian himself, a fairly well-regarded one if what I heard was true. I understood that he was on sabbatical. Word was that he had divorced, with some drama attached, and then his father had died, and he had taken time off to focus on Hayden's Ridge.

I was skeptical. A sabbatical was what they called an emotional breakdown for an acclaimed scholar. A paid sabbatical was when you were so good that they didn't care, and they wanted you back at all costs. That was what he had. Meanwhile, I had nothing. Except a plan and a prayer.

My heart accelerated as the house rose in the distance. The thought that it wasn't open to the public made me want to gasp with outrage. A Revolutionary War movie could be filmed here without any major alterations. Think Colonial Williamsburg meets...Colonial Williamsburg.

I put my car in Park, glancing up at the imposing structure.

I drew a deep breath and slowly released it. I was a fool. I had come all of this way. What was I, crazy?

Getting out, I hitched my purse strap on my shoulder.

Just as I was about to climb the steps, the door opened, and a man and a chocolate Labrador exited. A dog was kept in this house, and oh my God, I didn't even know what to say about that.

I refocused to the man. He was in some sort of an L.L.Bean coat and a ballcap, with a literal shotgun cracked open over his arm. He sort of jumped when he saw me (flinched might be a better word). Obviously, he hadn't heard my car.

"Can I help you?"

I tucked my hair behind my ear. My breath clouded around me in the cold air. I met his eyes. He sniffed, looked away, reached down to pat his dog. The dog looked up at him worshipfully, so obviously they had a connection thing.

"Dr. Hayden." He looked at me when I spoke. "I am interested in researching your collections here at Hayden's Ridge. You have no website, no contact information, so—"

"So you thought you would come to my home—my private home—in hopes of pushing your way in."

My lips parted. A streak of rage slithered up my spine because

7

he was rude, because I had not expected this, and because, yes, okay, he was right. "I sent you letters," I rejoined. "I assume you received them?" There was no response.

He flushed slightly and looked away. "Our collections are not public. Thank you for your interest. You will find a nice list of peer-reviewed books on the Virginia history website."

No. Just no. I was not leaving. "I...have come a long way," I said, trying not to sound desperate. "I do not intend to just...walk away."

His brows drew together. "I own the house. By the terms of my father's will. I have a copy if you would like to see it."

I gritted my teeth. This was a project I had been wanting to see through since college in New Hampshire. And this was going to save my career, confound it. "I have something to *say* about this property. I can feel it; it's like it is calling to me. There is a story to be told here," I said firmly. "And you are preventing that by not making your collections public."

He was stoically silent. Then finally he said, "My family has made the decision to keep our archives private. That is our right. You are not the first to show interest, and you certainly won't be the last—"

"But you are committing a crime against humanity, or at least against history! Can't you see that?" I exclaimed with passion.

A slight pause. He lifted his chin. "Name one good reason I should let you see anything. Given the fact that there have been hundreds before you, mind you."

I breathed in through my nose. I was angry, but I also sensed a sort of last chance. "Because I have come five-hundred and seventy-two miles. Because you're sitting on a treasure. Because I am the best damned historian in the field—"

Lifting a brow, he started to walk away. I stopped him.

"—and because you owe me that much, Samuel."

HE STOPPED, going stock still. He looked at me for I don't know how long—time seemed to warp—and then I could see something shift in his eyes. He lowered his gaze, taking a step back, and opened the door.

And looked at me like he was waiting for me to move. Too stupid to realize my victory, I only just refrained from jumping and hurried to precede him into the house.

I don't know why I didn't think to look around. I was being given access that precious few had ever received. Instead, I found myself saying tartly, "A shotgun? Really?"

"I let you in the door; I did not invite commentary." He shut the door, nudged the dog away from a stand with other guns, and put the shotgun down. Thankfully.

"I heard your wife left you."

"I heard you got *canned*," he retorted.

I bit my tongue. Crossed my arms. "You heard about that?"

"I think everyone in the free world has heard about that," he said, inclining his head after a considering moment.

I wanted to brain him with the iron fire poker I glimpsed nearby. I shook my head. My violent inclinations were neither here nor there. If word of my ignominious downfall had spread *here*, two leagues from civilization, I'm not sure what that even said. That my career was more thoroughly finished than I thought?

I refocused. Looked at the man across from me, who was looking at me, to be honest, as if I were a ghost. I felt suddenly self-conscious. I used my purse as a shield, for what that was worth.

"I'm not going to shoot you," he said.

I looked up and met his eyes. Moss green, in case you were wondering. "Huh?"

"The shotgun," he said. "I was going out to look to see if the coyote had been caught."

"Coyote?" I asked, trying to comprehend.

9

"It's been bothering the sheep."

"The sheep?"

"Indeed. The sheep." He was starting to sound sarcastic again.

I crossed my arms, trying not to hesitate as I asked, "You are going to give me access to your archives?"

There was a long, drawn-out silence. His mouth was closed; he seemed to be running his tongue across his teeth, like you did when you were thinking. Reconsidering, that was. "Limited access," he said.

Which meant, none of the good stuff. Oh, you could make something of almost anything. But "limited access" wouldn't salvage my career.

"That was not what I was hoping in coming here." I gave him a direct look.

Calling in my favor, again. That old score to settle.

He gave a long sigh. "Maddie—" He broke off, clenching his jaw. "Dr. Apkarian... My father just died two months ago. I'm trying to get everything sorted out, to mourn him, and...it hasn't been easy." I started to speak, to express my sympathy, but he marched on. "He requested that I not make certain things public. To be honest, I don't even know which things he is—was—talking about. I'm trying to catalogue everything, and I *do* want to make as much as possible public. Of course I do. But I have to respect his wishes, so it's...complicated."

I studied him. Considered what he had said. "Well... Why don't you let me meet you halfway?" I possessed a certain scrappiness. I could adjust, adapt, overcome.

"What do you mean?" he asked, again with a note of suspicion. Whatever this family's secrets, they did not want them known.

"I mean you could let me help you organize and catalogue," I said. "Do you think you could find someone more suited *to* help you with such an overwhelming task? *You* let me use primary documents—only the ones you approve me to use," I said, holding up a finger as he started to speak, "—and in exchange you would have *my* help with my promise of keeping private anything I've seen. I love the history too much to be indiscreet."

He sighed, almost in exasperation. Made a little turn, ran his hand through his brown hair... Clearly he had not thought I would assault all of his bulwarks. Or that I would make him an offer that would be tough to refuse.

I pictured a mountain of work waiting, one that would still be here when his hiatus was finished, I imagined. Because something like that was simply too much for one person. And he was dealing with coyotes, to boot.

"Where would you stay?" he asked in a forbidding tone.

"I don't know. You tell me. Given that we seem to be at the back of beyond, I imagine I will have to stay here."

He did the tongue across teeth thing again.

"Obviously, you don't have the room," I said, matching his earlier sarcasm, as my voice echoed in the cavernous hall. "We would be *very* cramped."

He gave me a level look. "Fine," he said. He looked defiant. Like a bull.

"Okay." I bit my tongue. "I'll get my suitcase." I turned and departed out the door. He looked scary, like the aforementioned bull, and I had no intention of waiting out his wrath.

Now would be as good a time as any to mention that I was acquainted with Samuel Hayden. We had gone to college together in New Hampshire. We had known each other, had even worked together pretty closely, and things had not ended well.

Water under the bridge. Not really. Whatever. It had been eleven years. Time had to march on, didn't it? Grievances had to be brushed under the rug. Maybe they had an expiration date? That remained to be seen.

I had not gotten what I had wanted here, but I had gotten all I was going to get through bargaining, and I was determined to count that as a victory. I needed a victory. I had to salvage my career. There was no way I would be here, imposing on that old connection, otherwise.

What to say about Samuel Hayden? He was Anglo-Saxon-handsome. High cheekbones, firm jaw, noble brow, a fine nose... Tall. I had forgotten that I had to crane my head up to see him, even though I was of average height for a woman. Time had been good to him. He was still fit, toned but tending toward slender-ness. He seemed to have very few gray hairs. (I was plucking them wildly after my recent life's debacle.) He had always been an intriguing mix of polished and rugged. His face was currently a little scruffy, like a five o'clock shadow plus about two days.

It was sexy, if I were honest. But I was very rarely honest. At least with myself.

He was brilliant. He had been my best competition in college. His area of study was primarily the Civil War, and he lectured at UVA in Charlottesville now. His professor rating was good online, and he had the chili pepper by his name, if that meant anything (it didn't).

He was now climbing a set of back stairs with none-too-gentle steps. He *was* carrying my suitcase because it was huge. I could roll it, but no more. He had already made several disparaging remarks against Mavis (that was its name), and he clearly thought I was a *princess*. Well, he was the one who had inherited a freaking colonial castle.

I kept these thoughts to myself. It couldn't be easy to lug a slightly-over-fifty-pound bag up a spiral staircase that seemed to reach to heaven.

He set the suitcase down at the top of the stairs, extended the handle, and turned it over to me. He refrained from tossing me an ugly look, but I imagine he wouldn't have if he had been a few years younger. Our deal having been struck, he was quiet now.

We seemed to be in a wing off the back of the house where, I imagine, the family had lived over the years.

We passed two bedrooms, and then he stopped in front of another one.

"You can stay here."

I nodded. "Thank you." I looked around. "The bathroom...?"

He inclined his head toward another door.

"My own?" I asked hopefully.

He looked around at the historic setting meaningfully. "What do *you* think?"

So that was a *no*. I nodded.

A silence descended. He swallowed.

"Well I've got to—" He said it at the exact same time that I said, "Well, I'll settle in."

He nodded, sidestepping Mavis and taking off down the spiral staircase.

Samuel

HE STOPPED, staring into the distance, which was actually just the wall in front of him. He had shut himself into his room and was taking a turn on the carpet. He could hear her in her room, unpacking, adjusting things...

Madeleine Apkarian was *two doors down*.

He paced for another turn, drawing his hand through his hair. And again.

TWO

"The art of life is the art of avoiding pain."
-Thomas Jefferson

I had finished my Chex Mix. All of it. There was nothing left in my suitcase, and my stomach was rumbling fiercely. I had unpacked, laying my belongings in neat piles and stacks and tucking my suitcase into a tiny closet. My phone *pinged* about halfway through this, and I looked down to see a text from my former co-worker, Judy.

Did you make it?

I exhaled. I hadn't expected her to check on me because she wasn't precisely a motherly type. She was, however, one of the two people speaking to me in Boston. I typed out a reply.

Yes. Safe and sound. Thanks.

I smelled something cooking. I lifted my head, considering. He could feed me. On the other hand, I was loathe to take anything from Samuel Hayden.

I nibbled the inside of my cheek about a minute before I gave in. I was no hunger martyr. At least not when I suspected spaghetti might be on the menu.

I followed the scent through a narrow, dark, musty hall until I saw swinging doors that seemed to lead toward a kitchen. The sizzling of a pan steadily grew louder.

His dog immediately attacked me upon entrance. In a friendly way (some might say overly-friendly), he sniffed me, licked me, and looked up at me with expectant brown eyes. His owner looked over his shoulder. "Chester, down."

Chester (I think) continued to stare at me. I melted. Kneeling, I rubbed his ears. "Good boy. Yes, such a good boy," I cooed. "What did you call him?"

Samuel focused on his cooking. He said wryly, "He is Chester Arthur Hayden."

"I'm assuming there's a story."

There was a slight pause. "A stupid inside joke with..." He broke off, so I would assume he had been about to say "Jenna."

I remembered Jenna. Sorority type. Pretty. Beautiful, even. Smart. Rich. She hadn't had to work for things like I had to work for things. Not her fault; not my fault. Life was such a bitch.

"You're lucky to have him," I said in the same sweet-talking voice as I held Chester's large, loving eyes.

"I hope so. It cost me a new SUV to keep him," he said sarcastically, plating a dish. One dish.

Who took an SUV in exchange for a dog in a divorce? But there were more pressing matters to consider. I rose to my feet. Eyeing his plate, I said, "So, about food... I am happy to contribute. But for tonight...?" I winced.

He eyed me for a minute before (reluctantly) handing me a plate. I smiled brightly and turned to the stove to fill it. Looking around, I eyed a jug. "Can I have some tea?"

He motioned toward it broadly. "Be my guest."

I was afraid I *would* brain him before this sojourn was over.

We ate in silence. Only the clock made noise, along with Chester Arthur Hayden's panting. I swallowed. *Tick, tick, tick. Pant, pant, pant.*

I drew a breath, taking another bite. Once I had chewed slowly, I said, "I wanted to apologize for...earlier. I shouldn't have said what I did about your...divorce. I was lashing out because my temper is thin these days."

"Stands to reason," he said shortly. "You're a social pariah."

I breathed in deeply through my nose. Tried for calm. Remembered my therapist's admonitions. *Your rage is directed at your employers, your persecutors, and Bradley. Not at the ketchup bottle you dropped.* Or at this man sitting next to me at the island, whom I hadn't seen in eleven years. Even if he did happen to be just as impossible as he had been then. Everything came crashing back, seeing him.

Trying for empathy, I said gently, since it was all out in the open, "What happened?"

He looked at me, seemed to realize I was talking about the divorce, and then settled into silence. He took a swig of his sweet tea. "She said she needed to find herself."

I lifted my brows. "Original."

A thoughtful pause. "In fairness, she kind of did," he said. I almost choked. I had forgotten the *deep* sarcasm of which he was capable.

"Well, I...hope she does," I offered.

There was a pause. I thought he would leave the subject. But we were like forty miles from civilization, and I was all there was, so I imagine he was willing to say things he wouldn't otherwise be. "She is currently in Thailand, practicing some sort of...interesting iteration of mysticism. A fake one," he added more bluntly.

"But she's a Spanish professor!" I exclaimed, before I could think.

He shrugged. "It's all peace and harmony and inner truth—none of to which I have any objection. Just to paying someone a thousand dollars to give you a mantra," he said bitterly. He took another bite. After a moment, he added, "And if I can't support her in her new path, maybe I am a quench to her spirit, or some

16

bullshit, and it is time for our spirits to part paths. Direct damn quote."

I winced. Bit my lip. "I'm so sorry, Samuel," I said quietly.

He looked up quickly, flushed, and looked away. I'm not sure he had been talking to *me*. Just talking to someone. He was like Mr. Rochester holed up here, going crazy, or at least turning inward and reclusive. One trusted he didn't have a spare wife in the attic, however.

He pressed his hands to his temples. "Geez, I think I'm spiraling. I hardly know you anymore. I'm sorry."

I didn't admit that I was spiraling, too. But I *totally* related to the feeling.

Something licked my foot. I jumped. We both looked down, and I laughed, bending to pat Chester's head. "Hey, you were able to keep this guy," I said with gentle positivity.

Chester put his paws on Samuel's thigh, and he smiled for the first time I had seen. In the baby-talk voice I had used earlier, he said, "Twenty-five thousand dollars' worth. Yes. For such an enlightened zen, your mommy wanted all of the money, didn't she? Yes, she did." Chester panted merrily.

I laughed. He looked at me, smiling a bit (he had always been stingy with his smiles), but then he remembered that I had invaded his lair, and his expression leveled out.

His eyes flicked over my face. I wondered what he would *see*. Well, I knew. Long hair that was some indiscriminate dark sandy color usually caught up haphazardly in a messy bun (although it was rather straight and pretty when loose). In some lights, it even edged toward a true brunette. Deep brown eyes, a straight nose, thin lips, thin cheeks. And I was rail-thin after my recent psychological breakdown. We would, however, choose to go with the term *willowy*. I wondered what he would *think*. Would he think I had aged? Or that I had more laugh lines? Or maybe I looked just the same.

"So you were fired," he said.

I looked at him, mouth hanging open before I had the good sense to close it. I was outraged, as any red-blooded woman would be. "I was given the option to resign," I responded icily.

He lifted a brow.

How did he do that...lift only one like a character in a Regency romance? However it was, I wanted to slap him as much as the heroines always did.

"*And* my boyfriend and I broke up," I retorted tartly, sardonically.

"Yeah, I heard about that, too."

I gritted my teeth. But I channeled Marla (my therapist), pasted on a smile, and said tightly, "Oh?"

He gave a fleeting smile. "Academia. Things tend to spread quickly."

"Glad to provide you all with material," I said.

"It was a font," he agreed.

Waves of anger in varying degrees swept across my chest. "You kept us pretty well-supplied, yourself," I remarked, smirking. I seemed to remember a tidbit about a royal row at their house in Charlottesville. Something about a couch being thrown from a window.

His eyes narrowed. He was reminded again of my invasion; that was plainly obvious. He stood, picking up his plate. "We begin early in the morning."

My brows drew together. "How early?"

He cut a look at me. "Six a.m."

———

I WOKE UP. There was an owl or something screeching.

Where was I? Hayden's Ridge.

That was so odd. I was sleeping in a house I had always wanted to see. And I had seen almost none of it. Was I really in Virginia? Out in the middle of nowhere?

The panic came crashing in as my circumstances returned to me. I had been fired; I was a non-person. It only ever took a few seconds after regaining consciousness. I wondered vaguely if Samuel Hayden felt the same way. *My marriage is over; my ex-wife is in Thailand.*

Wave upon wave of anxiety hit me. It really wasn't rational. There was nothing threatening me out here. It was all over now. I couldn't do anything to change what had been done. But when such a truck of problems had hit me, I swear I had gotten chemically imbalanced or something. Channels weren't flowing correctly. Anxiety feeding anxiety. My therapist hadn't recommended medication yet. Somehow that relieved me, the thought that I had the toolbox to claw out of this. Or at least that she was going to give me the toolbox.

I tried the breathing exercises. Usually they helped; in the irrationality of waking up from sleep, they did not. Best just to comfort myself, then. That was the next step. *I am safe, I am loved, I am valuable.* It was a good thing I was a Christian, because I was pretty sure there was no way I could believe I was loved otherwise. Because I wasn't. Not by humans. I had been in such an all-fired hurry to get validation and acclaim in my career. Well, academia giveth. And academia had taken away.

A tear tracked down my cheek. I tried to think of an example of unconditional love I had seen. Not my mom. Not my dad. My grandma had loved me to the ends of the earth, but she wasn't the reassuring type. Didn't make sure I knew my value, didn't make sure worth and love seeped into my bones. She was the tough love type. Not that I was complaining. I was smiling, just thinking about her. I missed her.

But I had trouble even thinking of what God felt toward me because I hadn't seen it. I couldn't picture what that steadfast, reassuring, all-consuming, never-ending love looked like.

Jessie. A smile formed. My best friend from Alabama. To this day, which was a miracle. She was convinced I was great. Wouldn't let me say otherwise. Wouldn't hear of it. Oh, she'd tell me quicker than anybody when I was out of line, but... I don't know. I had never had to question that she understood there was something of value within me. Maybe that was a picture of God.

I sat up quickly. Enough deep thinking. I needed to go to the bathroom anyway, and sometimes getting up helped. Picking up my phone, I used it as a flashlight to guide me down the hall. The floors creaked and moaned, and I was convinced at every turn that I was about to be attacked by an intruder. This would take some getting used to.

When I touched the bathroom door, it squawked wildly, so I decided to leave it open. Not a creature was stirring, and I wanted to keep it that way. I had a feeling Dr. Hayden would not take kindly to being awakened. I pictured him like a dragon exiting his lair and almost smiled.

Lowering my pajama pants, I did my thing—and was just about to straighten when someone came in and closed the door.

I shrieked.

"God!" I heard. My flashlight had caught Samuel Hayden shielding his eyes, whether from the piercing light of my phone, fear of attack, or my state of undress I was uncertain. I could only hope the light didn't similarly illuminate me.

"Are you naked?" he exclaimed. He turned his back to me.

I shimmied my pants up. "Why in the hell would I be naked?" I exclaimed.

"Because you're in a *bathroom*," he said wrathfully. "For God's sake, close the door next time!" And then he slammed out.

I pressed my lips together, stood in the darkness, collected myself, and feared my pride was in a shambles unlikely to recover. I turned on the light. Washed my hands. Stared at myself in the mirror for a minute and, finally, exited.

Samuel was standing in the hall. Great. I shined my light on him, hoping I blinded him.

To my surprise, he looked sheepish. Sorry, even. "I'm sorry," he said. "I didn't know you were in there. I wouldn't…"

I flushed up to the roots of my hair, though, please God, he couldn't see. "It's fine," I answered, thrown off my balance a bit. He obviously felt like I thought he was a creepy male, and that was probably the best thing we could have landed on here.

"I mean, I usually knock, but that would require a door to be closed," he said.

"I didn't want to wake you."

A pause. "Thanks."

I nodded sharply. Side-stepped him. Went to my room. Closed the door. And replayed the horror in my mind for a good hour.

THREE

"I find friendship to be like wine, raw when new, ripened with
age, the true old man's milk and restorative cordial."
  -Thomas Jefferson

He put me to work in a cellar. A *separate* cellar, just to highlight
the point that I was *not* to get in his hair. It smelled. I
decided I did *not* actually love must. He had like seven dehumidifiers going, obviously necessary to preserve the old stuff, but it
sounded like I imagined an air base might. I had been instructed to
wear gloves, as if I were a freshman intern who didn't have a clue.
And I highly suspected that I had been put with the absolute most
boring, uninteresting, and uncontroversial stuff possible.

   Ledgers. Accounts. Bank notes. He had actually gotten further
than I would have thought in organizing everything. It seemed to
be in chronological order, and the box I started in was about 1880,
which was more than a hundred years past where I wanted to be.
Cognizant of my promises and responsibilities, however, I worked
diligently in sorting and preserving.

   At noon, my stomach started grumbling. Samuel, without

speaking, came in and emptied the dehumidifiers, which were full of water, and left. Okay, then, no lunch. And apparently no talkie. If I were an actual intern, I might have starved, but I was thirty-three. You took less at thirty-three. You were bolder. And so I climbed the stairs.

Going straight into the kitchen, I opened the fridge. There was some sandwich meat, and, looking at the counter, I saw some bread and a tomato. It would do.

I ate clandestinely.

There was a call I needed to make, so I put on my coat and walked out into the sunshine of the front lawn. I dialed Jessie.

When she picked up, I heard the roar of machinery. "Just a second, hon, let me cut off the combine," she said.

I waited.

The noise continued, she shouted at a few people, and finally, she cut the engine, leading to blessed silence. "Well, hello, Yankee Doodle," she said.

"Why are you using the combine?" I asked.

"I'm a farmer, hon."

"It's January."

"I have my purposes," she answered cryptically.

All right, then. Far be it from me to question farm secrets.

"I put flowers on Grandma Andrews's grave with the money you sent," she said. Grandma Andrews was not her grandma, but Jessie called her that to let me know she thought of her like family. I did the same with her grandma. "Your daddy, too, because I had a little left over."

My throat burned. "Thank you. How are you, Jess?"

"A lot better than you, I'd bet. Still barricaded in Boston?"

I paced on the lawn. "Actually...I'm researching."

She *whooped*. "I *knew* you wouldn't stay down long. You never do. Now we just have to find you a husband."

"Let's find *you* a husband," I quipped dryly.

"It's a lot easier for you. I'm not feminine, I'm what you would call plus size, and I'm half wildcat. You're more marketable."

"You think I'm not half wildcat?" I asked.

"Girl, don't I just know you are. Where are you?"

"In Virginia."

"Plantation, or city?"

I hesitated. "Plantation," I said casually.

"By yourself, or what?" she asked, obviously using a toothpick.

"It's not open to the public. The homeowner lives here, so I'm not alone."

"What if it's some creep?" she demanded. "I'm coming up there."

"He's not. It's...Samuel Hayden," I said, not sure she would even remember.

There was a pause. A very long pause. "Are you still on birth control?" she asked seriously.

"Jessie!" I exclaimed.

"Well, Grandma Andrews would want me to tell you not to have sex before marriage, but that horse has done busted straight out of the gate," she said, "so I'm just being practical here."

I pinched the bridge of my nose. "I'm going to kill you. And then myself."

"Hon, I'm just saying—"

"Jessie, if you continue this, I am going to han—"

"Okay, okay!" I pictured her holding her hands up in surrender. "Moving on then. How are you doing?"

Such a simple question. But so few asked it. And the sympathy in her voice... I don't know, it just about undid me.

"Are you crying?"

I swiped a tear. "What's wrong with me, Jess?"

"Not a thing," she said. "You're just about the smartest chick I've met, you're classy as all get out, you dress to kill, you're brave as the day is long, and you've got a whole lot of kindness. I wouldn't say there's a *darn* thing wrong with you."

"Jess..." I said, overwhelmed. I brushed away tears fiercely.

"Now, buck up, Missy," she said lovingly. "You've still got a whole lot of living left in you. A whole lot to offer the world, too. So best just be getting on with your living now."

GIVEN THAT IT WAS JANUARY, I was freezing to death down in the cellar, so I grabbed a sweater before returning to my hole.

I repeated this process for five days. Work, steal lunch, work, battle anxiety, retire to my room with my laptop, lose my battle with anxiety, finally drop dead in exhaustion. I saw Dr. Hayden only when he dumped the dehumidifiers. Usually he left the pots on the stove long enough for me to grab dinner, but we didn't eat together, and I was pretty sure he had receded into himself. To a world where I was not allowed. I was a nuisance, like a fly that got caught in the house.

I started to develop a chest cold on the sixth day. The dampness of the cellar, mixed with what had always been a weak upper respiratory system, and I found myself driving to the nearest town (a *long* way away) to buy some antihistamines. While there, I also restocked our grocery supply.

I returned with these in my rental BMW that was scheduled to be picked up on Sunday. Then I would be well and truly stranded out here, but Samuel had at least two vehicles, and he *would* let me use one of them, I determined, if needed.

Going back to the kitchen, I reflected that this room had been redone rather successfully. It wasn't fussy, but the historic charm had been kept, while there was also a welcome modernity to it. I was reaching to put milk in the fridge, while also fighting off a round of deep, rumbling coughs, when I heard something.

Looking over my shoulder, I saw Samuel. "Hi," I said, when I was finished coughing.

"Hey," he said, looking at me. "I didn't know you were sick."

"Not contagious," I said, removing butter from a bag. "I have my own little respiratory thing going. Always."

But he had already been walking toward me, not away, so I would have to assume that wasn't his concern. He reached for the sandwich meat I had bought to restock and handed it to me, along with a few other items. His hand accidentally grazed mine, and I looked at him. He was looking at me. I looked away.

"If you need a doctor—"

"I don't. This is a wonder," I said, shaking the pill bottle I had bought. "The cellar is bothering me."

He handed me the eggs. Then he stored the new loaf of bread under the old. "Why don't you take tomorrow off. Explore the house."

I looked up quickly. This was an invitation the likes of which I wasn't likely to see again any time soon, if ever. As casually as I could, I said, "All right."

He nodded once. "I know the cellars aren't the best place for the documents. I'm working on a grant to build a climate-controlled archival storage building."

I thought this was great, and interesting, and I was prepared to discuss it. However, he departed almost immediately.

Alrighty, then.

⸻

IT WAS the arched doorways which got me. No, it was the wood paneling. No, the fireplaces. Every way I turned was a wonder. Some of the rooms could obviously use some upkeep and preservation, but by and large, everything was in great condition. And with the family continuity here, there were original pieces remaining that you usually didn't have.

The dining room was paneled and crowned and shod with thick and intricate molding work, even over the wide doorway, the fireplace, and the ceiling. A colonial-era dining table graced the center of a large rug, and you might be forgiven for thinking George Washington was about to pop over for lunch.

The lofty foyer boasted a dark wood floating staircase, along with portraits of colonial relatives hanging from ribbons. When you walked in the front door, the first thing that greeted you was a long hall running perpendicular to the door, although this was alleviated by the opening for the foyer. Given that the house was long rather than deep, the front hall was used to access most of the rooms which ran side by side along the back of the house.

There was a ballroom reminiscent of the Governor's Palace in Williamsburg, with original wood floors and gray painted panel work going up about ten feet before giving way to white walls that set off an elaborate chandelier. The library was more masculine, the trim work painted a dark green while the room was painted a deep gray.

The bedrooms (not where we were staying, but the original ones) were simpler, but charmingly so. The ceilings were still lofty in this area, but there wasn't any ornamentation except excellent, thick trim. And the beds were amazing. Probably they had been shipped along the James River from England or Philadelphia. I didn't know if they were original, but I would love to.

All of this was breath-taking, and I had never dreamed it could be so beautiful. But inevitably, I found myself in the attic. I could now confirm Samuel Hayden had no spare wife kept there, and that was reassuring.

However, I wanted to know more about the enslaved people of long ago. That had always been my greatest interest. Following my instincts, I went to the areas where I imagined the house servants would have lived.

But it was hard to make anything of the space. There was so much in storage. In fairness, I imagined a family could collect a lot of crap over the course of 250 years. My grandma had certainly collected a lot in seventy-five. I walked through, careful of the floors because you couldn't be sure they were perfect.

However, they seemed pretty sound, and they would have to be to hold the weight of everything up here. There were small windows, so light was not plentiful but *was* present. Dust motes floated through the air, prompting me to cover my face with my shirt. You didn't get pneumonia three times before the age of thirty without learning to be careful.

My greatest wish was to find a painting of an enslaved person. They were few and far between, and I knew it was an almost hopeless wish, but *that* would be a find, and if I could put a name to a face, and a story to a name... Unfortunately, I saw nothing.

There were pieces of furniture stowed here and there, some of it junk, but some of it antiques. In particular, a tall secretary desk caught my eye. I had been (before my mighty descent) on the board of a historic house museum in Boston, and they had one that was similar. Identical, really. I walked over to it, smoothing my hands over it and wondering if the two pieces had the same craftsman. Going to the back, I saw the same markings. I smiled. That was so cool.

I saw a catch on it, and the memory triggered in my mind of the Boston director showing me a detachable back. Just a neat design feature, but I remembered saying to her: *You could hide something back here*. She had laughingly agreed.

I smoothed my hand over the latch, debating. It would probably be as empty as the Boston piece. And Samuel almost certainly wouldn't want me to try it. It was very old, after all.

I carefully lifted the latch.

As gently as holding a newborn baby, I pressed my hands on the back to keep it solid as I gently swung open its effectual door. Something *thunked* with the force and volume of a bomb. I froze. Maybe it hadn't been bomb-level, but I was so jumpy my heart pounded. Releasing the door, I walked around to the other side of it. And saw that what appeared to be a portrait had fallen flat on its face.

I winced. Big time. Almost certainly this was something that had been stowed away, perhaps for hundreds of years, and there was a chance I had just broken it. And that the homeowner would murder me.

The frame was large and gold, and very old. I could tell that, even from behind. With careful fingers, I lifted the massive, heavy thing, carrying it to the nearest wall, against which I leaned it. It wasn't broken. I saw that first. And then I breathed and looked at it.

I smiled. It was a lady—beautiful, and obviously from the upper classes. Her dress was very fine, and I would date it about 1770. She looked intelligent. Life radiated from her hazel eyes, dignity and strength from the tilt of her head, despite the fact she appeared to be in her early twenties only. Almost delicate, she was of average height but petite. Her hair was lush, a soft auburn that almost went fair occasionally. Her figure was small, but shapely. Even today, with much-altered beauty standards, she was striking.

"What are you *doing*?" I only just refrained from jumping. Looking over my shoulder, I saw Samuel in his coat and gloves. "I had just come back in, and I suddenly thought the roof was going to fall down on my head," he said, looking none-too-pleasant.

"You couldn't have possibly heard that from the foyer," I argued. "There is a whole floor in between!"

"What did you drop?"

I hesitated. Looked at the secretary, then back at the portrait. He followed my gaze. "I found something," I said.

He looked between the two items again. "In the desk?"

I nodded. "There's a false back. It's a door, really."

He walked forward. I heard his knees crack as he knelt in front of it. Removing his farm gloves, he handed them to me. I took them, and he touched the frame, and then the canvas. "I thought it must be a reproduction," he said. "But it's not."

"No," I agreed. "It's not."

He looked at me, as the weight of that statement settled over the room.

"Who is she?" I asked.

He shook his head. "I have no idea."

"Not an ancestor?"

"I... No. I don't think so. From this era..." He considered. "The lady of the house was Jane Hayden. She had dark hair, almost black—I mean, when it wasn't powdered."

"Who married her son?" I asked, stepping forward to look into the portrait. I noticed now in the background, in addition to a draping blue curtain, there was a piano, or what would have been known then as a harpsichord piano forte. You almost didn't notice it, however, so lovely were the lady's eyes.

"Julia Hayden. Another brunette."

"And her son?"

"Etta Hayden." He thought for a second. "Maiden name Wayles. She was different. Reddish hair, yes, but..." He studied it for a moment. "No, it's not her."

"Maybe she's a Hayden, then. A sister of one of your many-greats grandfathers?"

"Maybe," he agreed. But I could see he wasn't sold on the theory. His wheels were spinning.

I walked forward, tilting the portrait away from the wall and looking at the back. Its bindings were fragile and almost falling apart. Samuel lifted it, turning it around so that the back faced us.

A little card was wedged in the bottom right corner. Removing my gloves from my pocket, I retrieved it. Turning the paper over, I saw something written in French.

Ce monument de son amour.

"I get *monument* and *love*," I said. I looked at him for further elucidation. You weren't married to a Spanish professor for nearly a decade without also picking up a bit of French. Usually they taught both. It was a pretty safe bet.

And I was right.

"'This monument of his love,'" he read. He stared at it, his eyes freezing for a second, and then going faraway, but active, as he thought.

"Is it a reference to something?" I asked. "Do you know it? I don't."

"Something...I don't know. Something triggered in my mind, but I lost it. Google it," he said.

Pulling out my phone, I did so, figuring that it would be a literary reference easily found. It was not. I only found several monuments around the world built in honor of love, or of a person's love for another. No literary references at all.

We looked at each other for a long moment, both thinking. And then I coughed, a long, hacking miserable eruption.

"All right, let's get you both downstairs," he said, picking up the portrait and motioning for me to lead the way.

Still hacking, I was happy to oblige.

THAT NIGHT, he invited me into his lair. That sounds more hospitable than it actually was. I happened to be passing by an old room that was made up like an office (although not with any of the *really* antique furniture that we could damage), and he called out. Spread out on his desk was an oversized family tree with copies of mini-portraits next to each person's name where available. It turned out that he wanted help perusing the massive compilation and looking for answers.

An hour later, he said, "She isn't a Hayden. I didn't think she was. She doesn't *look* like a Hayden. We all have the same chin."

They kind of did.

"And I don't think she married a Hayden, either. We have portraits of all the women in my direct line from this era."

"Unless she married your great-great-great-great-great uncle, Willy," I said, tapping his portrait. The flames from the fireplace cast shadows on the paper, illuminating and receding from the visage of an eighteenth-century man of whose wife I hadn't yet seen a portrait.

Samuel was already shaking his head. "We have a description of his wife as a brunette in a letter."

"A neighbor, then," I said, settling on the only option that now seemed possible to me. "Picture this: it's 1930, and some neighbors are having to sell out after the stock market crashed. Your great-grandfather attends the auction and buys it, thinking it will be nice to add to his collection. It's era-appropriate, and a neighbor, to boot."

His eyes narrowed on my face as he considered the theory. "Why's it in the attic?"

"Your great-grandmother decided it didn't fit with her décor."

"So you stick a drop-cloth over it and lean it against the attic wall. You don't ram it into a piece of furniture with a hidden door so that it's literally never seen again. Someone didn't want it to be found."

My eyes held his in the standoff. Darn it. He was right.

I sighed, going to sit down next to his box of tissues. I took one gratefully and blew my nose. "And what about the note?" I asked. "Do you have any great love stories in your family?"

He had come to sit on the arm of the sofa. He shrugged. "Not to my knowledge. Pretty much run-of-the-mill arranged stuff right down the line."

I smiled. Leave it to Samuel Hayden to be realistic even about his own existence. "Well, I think there was a man who loved her. Very much. And I think he lost her."

His eyes studied my face as he tried to make sense of that. He was less rigid for the moment, softer. "A monument usually being something that comes after death?" he guessed.

I nodded. "It sounds like something a man would do. Not knowing how to express his unspeakable loss or to convey his existential experience of profound love, which obviously shouldn't die with the person. *That* would seem to be against the laws of nature. And so he conveyed that love in the words of a monument, which is used to mark something or notate it throughout history."

"Probably a mistress, then," he said, without missing a beat.

I pressed my lips together, shaking my head menacingly. If I could just slap him *once*. "Why on earth would you say that?"

"If you love her that much, why else would you stuff her in a piece of furniture? And besides, the note doesn't make a lot of sense to tuck into the back of a portrait, you know." He said this despite knowing it would be a disappointment to my romantic-tragic theory.

I looked at him. "But it may be a reference to something. You said it sparked something for you?"

He shook his head. "I lost whatever it was. And it won't come back. My memory is not very good right now."

I met his eyes. Grief did steal your memory. I was struggling with that, too. How shocking that it could do that. And how surprising that he admitted that it had.

"I'm sorry about your dad, Samuel," I said gently.

He was not the type who liked condolences, dragon that he was. He stood. In a clipped voice, he said, "Yeah, well... I should be getting to bed. Goodnight."

I LAY IN BED. The moon beamed onto my blankets through the crack in my curtain, keeping me awake. At least, that was what I told myself. I was in a sort of haze of remembrance.

It was our senior capstone. That was where things had gone off the rails. We had the semester to finish our final project for our major, and each student had been assigned a partner. Samuel Hayden was mine.

I was attracted to him. That was never in question. I buried it because I knew he had been dating another girl since freshman year. I was acquainted with her from a couple of classes. Sometimes I wondered if he was attracted to me, too. But I never explored it, of course. Frankly, I didn't like his girlfriend, but I had a line, and I wasn't going to cross it. I went on with my life.

And so we worked together all semester long, meeting in the library or at cafes, and sometimes, when deadlines closed in, at one or the other's dorm. He never crossed a line either. I never worried about that with him. He was steady. He had a girlfriend, and that was that.

He was ornery. Even then. Sometimes he made me want to scream. We argued so loudly intermittently that the librarians reprimanded us. One time they even kicked us out in the rain. But overall, we worked well together. We were well-matched in intelligence. Disagreements eventually worked into a compromise, one that strengthened the project.

Because of my interest in colonial studies, he told me about his family home. That led him to talk about his dad. He became animated talking about either. That tugged at my heartstrings, but I buried it. Deep down.

But I *was* interested in his house. We had learned about it, of course. I asked if someday his father would be willing to give me a tour. He agreed to that. It wasn't easy to get Samuel Hayden to agree to anything, so I felt a special sort of victory. Later on, of course, I would learn more about the house's massive significance and untapped resources, and that fueled my drive to see it.

Would I say we became friends? Maybe. Sort of. That was hard to say. *Sometimes* I enjoyed his company. We did argue a lot. And there was that—let's be honest—sexual tension. But his commitment to Jenna never seemed to waiver. They were talking about studying abroad together in Europe during the summer before they went to grad school.

Then the week before the project was due, Samuel and I stayed in the library late one night. We were arguing over whether to insert the word *and* or *or* in our thesis, and it had gotten ugly. That was usual. It did not concern me.

Then I had reached to hand him the notecard on which I had written my preferred method. And his hand brushed mine. And lingered. Or at least, I thought it did. Frankly, I have replayed it so many times I could not say now. I looked up. His gaze was riveted on my face.

Or I thought it was. My grandma always said that sometimes we imagined things to be true when we wanted them to be true. Time seemed to stop; outside sounds could not be heard. That was what I always went back to. You couldn't manufacture a moment. You couldn't have a *moment* by yourself. But I had to have been mistaken.

The following morning, I received an email from him. He and Jenna had decided to leave early. They were going to skip walking at graduation. And I was left to finish the project and submit it on my own. Without an explanation or apology.

I was flaming mad. I could have killed him with my bare hands. And I never saw him again.

Until last week.

FOUR

"This institution [University of Virginia] will be based on the illimitable freedom of the human mind. For here we are not afraid to follow truth wherever it may lead, nor to tolerate any error so long as reason is left free to combat it."
-Thomas Jefferson

I descended into the cellar. There was no need to be replaying things that were eleven years out of date. Time marched on.

Speaking of moving on...I needed to call Bradley. That wasn't to say I wouldn't rather take a beating, which was probably why I waited until lunchtime to do it—why I had waited this long to do it at all.

I went outside, where I dialed him as I walked over the dead winter grass in the yard in front of Hayden's Ridge. Some part of me wondered if Bradley was wanting me back. That was probably arrogance speaking. But surely if he had been in half the pain I was, he would be less than sure of his precipitous, emotional decision.

"Madeleine."

"Hi," I said. There was a pause. I didn't know how to do this, how to talk to him, even, anymore. We had been together for a long time. But he had deserted me. And from his end, I had very nearly destroyed his life. So... That made for some long silences. For some reason, rage started to bubble up inside of me. I couldn't fully explain it, but I could name it. I fought to curb it and decided just to get down to the facts.

"Bradley, I need you to call the bank to see what needs to be done about taking you off as a co-owner on my bank account."

There wasn't even a pause. "Got it. Done."

I didn't know what to say. "I'll do the same."

"Thank you. Was that all?"

I blinked. His tone was clipped. And, like before, so thoroughly *finished* with me. "That is all," I said, somewhat ironically.

"All right. Goodbye."

He hung up before I could say the same.

REJECTION IS A CRUEL BEAST. My grandma always said that we thought we were separated from God, and so we looked for affirmation of our goodness every which way but up (a direct quote, you understand). She had a way of cutting to the heart of the matter, Grandma Andrews.

It wasn't that I wanted Bradley back. Frankly, I wouldn't have him.

But that didn't mean I wasn't surprised with how *thoroughly* he was finished with me. He hated me. He, who used to hold me in his arms, who used to make supper for me, who called to check on me at work once a day for two weeks after my grandma died, *hated* me. There wasn't an ember left in his heart.

There would be no validation of my emotions. He would never apologize. He would never, ever see things from my perspective. He would *always* leave me hanging where he had left me: on the expressed belief that I was crazy and selfish. That he was right, universally, across the board, in this apparently oh-so-clear-cut question of morality. And he would leave me to wonder, in the darkest hours of night, if maybe he were correct.

I pocketed my phone and walked.

I had no idea which direction I was going, but I ended up behind the house. My eyes met the beautiful James River. It really was one of the most visually pleasing rivers I had ever seen. Wide and clean, bracketed by thick, tall woods, and curving like a snake. Whatever *Pocahontas* had gotten wrong historically, the images of scenery had been spot-on. I could almost see sparkling, magical leaves dancing across the landscape even today.

I sat down on a rock on the bank. Therapy helped. I learned not to suppress my emotions. *Let them up*, Marla said. I learned that I could self-affirm. Which reminded me... I had been neglecting my journal over the past few days, which was probably one of the reasons Bradley's cold tone had hit me like a punch in the gut.

I swiped a tear away. It was too cold to be crying.

Why did, every time I thought I was out of the dark swirl, something bring me back, making me realize just how fully I was not healed? I had gotten over *so much* in the past. Was I really going to let this break me? Was my gritty determination going to fail me now?

I heard a limb snap and looked over my shoulder.

A man (carrying a shotgun for the coyote, of course) and a dog were walking toward the river. Well, Chester was running, tongue lolling merrily, and he got to me first. I looked up, met Samuel's eyes, didn't attempt to hide my tears... I was too exhausted for that.

He didn't ask me what was wrong. Didn't ask if I was okay. He knew what was wrong, and he knew I wasn't okay. He sat next to me. In silence.

The river rippled slightly. Occasionally a bird swooped down. Chester settled on the other side of Samuel. How long we sat

there, I couldn't have said. We looked out at the almost impercep-
tibly moving river. My mind reflected as I sat there with a man
content with the silence: *still waters run deep*.

At length, he looked at me. "I remembered where I had seen
'*This monument of his love*,'" he said softly.

I turned my head to him quickly. "You did? Where?"

He hesitated. "Are you up for a road trip?"

"Absolutely," I said with enthusiasm. That sounded like just
what I needed.

He stood and, to my great surprise, extended his hand to help
me up.

BY THE TIME we had been traveling for close to an hour, I was
pretty sure Samuel had kidnapped me. He planned to leave me
out in the woods somewhere to get me out of his house.

In keeping with his split personality, he had a hybrid Volvo
SUV, presumably from his life in Charlottesville, and a pickup,
presumably for his life on the farm. He had looked between them
and opted for the Volvo for this journey. So we were probably
going a good little distance, but not in rough terrain, I
established.

"Are you going to murder me?"

"Not today."

I sat back. *Well, then.*

"Are we going to Charlottesville?"

"Yes."

"To get something at your house?"

"No."

And that was about the sum of the road trip conversation.

At length, we were in Thomas Jefferson's hometown. The
author of the Declaration of Independence had founded the
University of Virginia. He had even had a view of it from his little

mountain. It was a neat town, and Samuel navigated its streets easily, like the long-time resident he was.

Pretty soon, we were going out of the city and curving up a mountain.

My eyes scanned the vista. "Monticello," I said.

He didn't correct me, so I assumed I was right. Opening his console, he pulled out a lanyard with some sort of pass on it and put it around his neck. If he had restricted access, there were some things I would very much like to see. But I didn't want to push it.

We parked and rode the buses up the hill with the other tourists. With the massive yearly foot traffic, the employees were experienced and operated like a well-oiled machine. There was something about the house which rose in the distance. Something compelling. It was a World Heritage Site now. I would imagine that was because of Jefferson himself and because of the enormous volume of knowledge to be gleaned from the enslaved lives here.

Hayden's Ridge could give us as much or more. I gazed bitterly in accusation at my travel companion. But he was looking out the window, in his own world.

I thought we would head up to the house. To my great surprise, he took me instead to the Monticello Graveyard. This was where Jefferson was buried. I could see the President's tombstone from a distance, looking like a miniature Washington monument, if you will.

There was a light dusting of snow from the night before, settling on the stones peacefully. No one was out here. There were other, more interesting things to see, of course. The sidewalk was icy. To my still greater surprise, Samuel took my hand in a business-like fashion as we navigated it. That may have been because he walked really fast with his long stride and didn't want to wait for me.

Just outside the heavy iron gate, we stopped and looked at the monument to Jefferson, who had wished to be remembered for three things: *Author of the Declaration of American Independence, Of the Statute of Virginia for Religious Freedom, and Father of the University of Virginia.*

Samuel went instead to the side that read, *Martha Jefferson, Daughter of John Wayles.*

Jefferson's wife.

I read the inscription in full. After the date of her birth, it read:

> *Intermarried with*
> *Thomas Jefferson*
> *January 1st, 1772;*
> *Torn from him by death*
> *September 6th, 1782:*
> *This monument of his love is inscribed.*

"'This monument of his love,'" I said softly, slightly in wonder. "There you go."

I looked at Samuel. He had a faraway look, the one he got when he was thinking deeply. And he appeared both perplexed and a little uneasy.

"There are no portraits of Martha Wayles Jefferson," he said, almost as if to reassure himself.

"No *known* portraits," I responded quietly.

He looked at me, breathing in through his nose. "Why would we have a portrait of Jefferson's wife?" he whispered, looking around to make sure no one was listening. Yes, that would be an object of interest to Monticello, indeed. And we didn't want some sort of media storm over a found portrait for what would likely end up being just a distant relative of the Haydens. Or, yes, a mistress of one of them.

I took out my phone and looked at the picture I had taken (with the flash off) of the portrait. "Samuel, the clothes are just the right era." I felt him standing like a brick wall beside me. I looked up at the stone for her date of birth. "She's just the right age."

"How many girls were born in Virginia during the decade Martha Wayles was born?" he questioned. "That proves nothing."

"She could have been about twenty-three here. If she married Jefferson in 1772, this would be about the right timing for a bridal portrait."

"She was in mourning for her young son from her first marriage, then," he said. "And yet, her dress is blue and purple and yellow—rich with color."

"You wouldn't have worn mourning for a wedding portrait," I said. "At least, it would have been unusual to have done so." I smirked. "My romantic-tragic story would have been spot on, if it *is* her. She died when she was just thirty-four. And we do have accounts of theirs being a love match, even to the extent of Jefferson not coping well upon her death. Samuel, this could be huge."

"Why would she be stuffed in the back of a piece of furniture a hundred miles away?" he asked, intense eyes on my face. "I don't believe it's her."

"I don't know," I admitted. That was the biggest thing cutting against the theory. "The family was very private, for various reasons. Most of her writings were destroyed by them. We don't know much about her as a person. We don't even know what she *looked* like," I said, my excitement growing at the thought that we *might*.

"Exactly," said Dr. Buzzkill. "Which is why we could never verify it to be her just by looking at the portrait. The only connection we have is the note on the back, and that is a very tenuous connection. So we are *not* going to alert Monticello, and we are *not* going to tell the world that we *think* we may have found something."

I gritted my teeth. "Is this because you don't want a media

storm descending on Hayden's Ridge? What *is* it with your outlandish security measures? What is your family hiding? What could *possibly* be worse than the fact that the Haydens enslaved thousands of people over course of three centuries?"

His wrath had been kindling until I said the last sentence. Then the fire seemed to die out of him. "Very little," he said. He stared at me in a brooding, bullish fashion. I refrained from saying, *Well then? What is there to hide?* He turned and started walking away from the graveyard.

I followed him. I kept off the sidewalk this time, since no help was forthcoming. My boots got a little wet, but that didn't concern me. They were made to turn water. The cold made me cough a little, but not very badly. We caught the next bus back down to the parking lot.

When we were in the Volvo, he didn't immediately start the engine. We sat quietly. Into the silence, I said at last, "What is it, Samuel? If we're going to work together, we need to be honest."

He looked at me. After a long silence, he said, "Let's get some lunch. You're hacking again. Take your medicine."

I REMEMBERED Samuel as a younger man. In looks, he was the same. Maybe a little more handsome. In some ways, he was completely different. In others, precisely as I recalled. It had been eleven years, of course. But for some reason, when I thought of college, a night at the theater always returned to my memory with vivid clarity.

As part of the senior seminar class we were in, the professor required us to attend at least one cultural event on campus. It was strongly suggested that we attend with our capstone partner, to foster a working relationship. He had preferred a classical concert in the music building. I had preferred a Roman-era comedy titled *A Funny Thing Happened on the Way to the Forum.*

I had won.

We had argued about our introductory paragraph for the full thirteen minutes we were in our seats in the playhouse waiting for the play to begin. My heart was pounding, my blood pumping. Samuel's forehead was in his hand. He was miffed.

I smelled victory. He knew I was right about not beginning with a quote.

And then the curtain rose, the lights dimmed, and...it was *bawdy*. Not long into the first Act, Samuel looked at me, eyes wide, as if to say, "*You chose this?*" I held his eyes for a second before letting a silent laugh escape. Eyes twinkling, Samuel refocused on the stage. The actors tore it up, keeping us in constant laughter, gasps, and delight.

By the time it was finished, Samuel was more mellow. I hugged a couple of friends who had sat in front of us, told them I would see them soon, and followed the queue out with him.

It was dark out. It hadn't been when we went in, but it was autumn, and the days were shorter. Campus was beautiful at night, with old-style gas streetlamps and landscape lights shining on the brick buildings. There were crisp fall leaves on the trees, a golden sheen blanketing everything after the light rain which had fallen while we were inside.

Despite the beauty, I wasn't crazy about the thought of getting back to my room alone in the dark. There were some areas that weren't as well-lit as this, and there had been some campus incidents this year. Professors didn't think of things like that when issuing decrees from their podiums to attend things at night.

I wouldn't do that when I was a professor. I would develop cohorts to attend events together, including carpooling and group walking, so that no one would feel unsafe. And to ensure they functioned as they should, I would attend the cohorts *myself*. I wouldn't go home and just wait for the reaction papers to be turned in. I was going to be a great professor.

"I'll walk you home."

I looked up. He was looking down at me. A simple statement. Yet it had all of the tension draining out of me in a second. "Are you sure?"

A pause. Another pause. "Yeah." We set out toward my dorm, his shadow lengthier than mine. Oh, to be a man over six feet tall, to have all of that male lean muscle mass and rarely anything beyond a wallet that anyone would want anyway.

Our breath fogged in front of us. It grew chilly fast after sundown in New Hampshire. It had been an adjustment for both of us. Today had started unseasonably warmly, so I hadn't brought an appropriate coat with me. I could hear my grandmother back home. *Check the weather every morning, Maddie.*

We walked on, past building after building. I could tell what he was thinking. The fact that I was cold was driving him crazy. But he wasn't going to offer me his coat. I also knew that. Nothing was spoken, of course, but it would be inappropriate.

And he never did anything inappropriate.

To break the silence, I said, "Was that a *cowbell* in that man's pants?"

"Toga," he corrected. Voice quivering, he added, "And yes."

A choked laugh escaped me. "Honestly."

"*You* picked the play. *I* would have chosen a peaceful night of Mozart," he pointed out.

I cut my eyes at him.

"I think it's your Alabama showing through," he said.

"I resent that!" I protested hotly. "How dare you?"

I could see him smiling, despite the darkness. He stopped, pocketing his hands. I hadn't noticed we had come to my dorm, but we had. He studied my face in the glow of the streetlamp. He was peaceful now. "You're right about the quote," he said.

I studied the planes of his face. "What?"

"For the capstone." Oh. Right. "You can remove it," he said, granting me my victory. "We need something stronger."

I smiled, feeling triumph seize me. It was amazing how unsatisfying it was.

"Do you feel safe once you get inside?" he asked. He glanced up at the building. "In the stairwells, and stuff?"

He probably walked Jenna all the way up to her dorm. Probably went *into* her dorm with her, in violation of university rules, I might add. He was in a committed relationship. He had shown no indication of wishing to change that status. And *I* had a date next Saturday. I was pretty sure that one wasn't going anywhere, but still... There was absolutely no reason I should be feeling like the rug was jerked out from beneath me. I had met this guy a month ago.

"Yes," I said. "It's safe inside. Goodnight."

───────────

MICHIE TAVERN WAS NOT VERY FAR AWAY from Monticello. It had servers dressed in colonial garb and original buildings, and let's just say I was in heaven. I could barely taste my food due to the sinus infection, but in theory, it looked delicious.

I wasn't sure why I had gone down memory lane in the car. Sometimes the way he turned his head or a flash of something in his eyes brought it back.

We sat at one of the benches alone, and after our drinks were brought in tin cups, Samuel looked at me. At last, he said, "There is a family legend, almost more of a rumor, that we have an African American ancestor."

I considered this revelation as I took a drink of my sweet tea. "There is nothing unusual in there being African American family members at most plantations, defining family as we now do. Sons, daughters, nieces, nephews, concubines..." I said, motioning in the obvious direction of Monticello.

Martha Jefferson herself had brought her father's concubine to live with her at her husband's home (as a slave, of course) after her father's death. Elizabeth Hemings had brought with her a young daughter of that union, Sarah.

Or Sally.

And after Martha's death, Jefferson and Sally would go on to have at least seven children together, four of whom would survive to adulthood, all of whom were raised at Monticello.

"No," Samuel said, shaking his head. "I mean we were thought to have an *ancestor*. In the direct male line—down to me. The thought is that a Hayden wife was unfaithful."

I lifted my brows. Now, this was interesting, indeed.

"A long time ago?"

He nodded. "Late eighteenth or early nineteenth century."

My wheels started spinning, imagining scenarios that could even make that possible. However it had come to be, this, if known, would have been an absolute taboo. It would have caused hysteria among the neighbors in either of those centuries. It might have put the child's *life* in danger even. And yet, legally, it would have been the child of the husband, if I remembered the laws correctly. Talk about turning the social order on its head, long before the world was ready for it. Even in succeeding generations, the social stigma to the Hayden family would have been something to have avoided at all costs. The world had not been a free place, nor had it been accepting. Now, however...

"Why privacy now? Oh, you said it mattered to your father," I said, answering myself.

"Not in the way you might think. He was a different generation, but...not like that." He paused, collecting his thoughts. "Do you know how many peer-reviewed books have been written about my family, Maddie? Seven. All unauthorized. All of them, for all of the acclaim they received, slightly missing the mark. My father knew the interest in the place, but he didn't want us to be some oddity for historians to come pick over and prod at. And moralize over endlessly. Who would want that for their family?"

Despite my instincts, I did understand his reluctance to share the family oral history. It *would* create a lot of buzz in academic circles, in the way that the Jefferson-Sally Hemmings story had done. Families tended to become *things,* not people, once they took on historical significance. I could understand the elder Mr. Hayden's desire to protect his son from that, especially given that the son himself wanted a career in history. That being said, a lot of families had oral histories. The very best that they could be used for was anecdotal evidence. "This is just word-of-mouth evidence," I said.

There was a slight silence. "There is a bit more than that," he said. But didn't offer any more. Instead, he said, "The Haydens are important historically. I get that. And if it were just up to me, I would probably hand over all of it. But my father asked me not to invite anyone to bring the family to the forefront of historical imagination. And I feel like I have to honor his wishes. He wanted us to recede from memory, to keep our heads down. And if I have no more proof than we have now that that's Martha Jefferson, I'm not inclined to break his request."

CHAPTER

FIVE

"There is not a truth existing which I fear...
or would wish unknown to the whole world."
-Thomas Jefferson

I sat in the slightly newer part of the house at a desk I had co-opted, parsing all of this new information out—even if it had nothing to do with the portrait. From my twenty-first century perspective, this would be an interesting find. If I had understood Samuel correctly at lunch, one of his ancestresses had a baby with an enslaved man. And that baby went on to continue the male line at Hayden's Ridge. Which would, interestingly enough, mean that Samuel was not actually a Hayden.

But that was neither here nor there, and I didn't get the impression that Samuel really cared one way or the other. The thing was, I couldn't fault the family for hiding it in the past. *Loving v. Virginia*, making interracial marriage legal in Virginia, didn't even take place until 1967. So yeah, any time before that, it would have been suppressed at all costs for legal, inheritance, and social reasons. The implications, if known, would have been profound and chilling.

You didn't hear of that very often—of a plantation mistress having a relationship with an enslaved man. The other way—a white man with an enslaved woman—yes, often. All the time, and in varying circumstances. But for a white woman... The taboo would have been unspeakable once upon a time. The social punishments would have been drastic for both parties. I had only heard of it exceedingly rarely. At a plantation of this level—never.

That was why I wondered... Could it not be possible that the enslaved ancestor had instead been a *woman*, and the father a Hayden, who had perhaps convinced his wife to pass his illegitimate child off as her own?

I stood quickly. Drawing on my sweater closed against the chill, I went up to my room. I was thankful I had recovered from my cold because the stairs had killed me while I was struggling to breathe. I snatched a kit from my bag, hurried back down the stairs, and marched into Samuel's office.

"I need your DNA," I said, extending a tube to him. "Spit."

He scowled at me. "Who carries a DNA kit in their suitcase?"

"I had planned to use it for myself," I said with dignity, "but never got around to it. Given that my career was destroyed, my relationship ended, and my dog died. Spit."

He studied me for a moment. "I've already done this," he said.

I lifted my brows, lowering the container. "Have you?"

He nodded, motioning me around to the back of his desk, where he pulled up a browser. He glanced at my tube. "You better go ahead and spit since you've already released the stabilizer."

Turning away, I did so, capping off the lid. Alrighty, then. We would be mailing that off tomorrow.

He pulled up the ancestry website and clicked the link to his results. "I'm *very* English," he said.

I glanced at the map. Yep. Ninety-eight percent. "You're more English than the royal family," I said.

His lips twitched. Briefly.

"What is the other two percent?" I asked.

"German. That's from my mom."

"Hmm."

"I don't know what to make of the family stories," he said. "I know how family rumors get wild pretty quickly. At various points I've heard that I am descended from Catherine the Great, Thomas Jefferson, and Napoleon Bonaparte."

Now *my* lips twitched.

"It seems pretty conclusive, doesn't it?" he asked, indicating the genetic map. "I mean, shouldn't I have at least one or two percent Senegal or Gambia, or something, if the story were true?"

I considered. "It's been a long time," I answered. "A really long time. *We* have a family story of having a distant Native American ancestor. But my grandma took a test years ago, and not a single indicator of that ancestry showed up."

He was shaking his head. "You're Armenian. The surname."

My eyes twinkled. "I *know*. This would have been on my dad's side that I'm talking about. And we didn't have just a random family story. We had names, a family tree... What I'm saying is: it had been too long and just didn't show up."

He stared at me, his wheels spinning.

"What other evidence do you have?" I asked. I remembered what he had said in the tavern. There was something other than just oral legend that was backing this rumor up.

"A letter," he answered. He pulled something else up on the computer. He got up so that I could have the chair.

Sinking into it, I saw a scanned-in photograph of a letter. I focused on the beautiful, but almost illegible writing. Ah. It was in French. *Les bénédictions de dieu sur votre beau bébé, ma chère.*

I glanced up at Samuel expectantly.

"'God's blessings on your beautiful baby,'" he read.

I smiled. Very sweet.

Personne ne le saura jamais.

I looked at him again.

"'No one will ever know.'"

My eyebrows lifted. "I see."

"Yep."

My eyes scanned over the script. "It *could* mean other things, but..." I looked up at him. "How do you know this person is writing to a woman? The letter is not addressed. It's not even dated."

"She uses a feminine endearment," he said, pointing.

"Samuel...this is the same handwriting from the portrait note," I said, suddenly aghast.

"You're just saying that because it's both in French," he retorted.

Really, he was so immovable. "No, I am not. The writer has a unique way with R's." I pulled up the picture of the portrait inscription on my phone and showed him the similarity. "Do you see this very irregular loop here?"

A long pause. "Yes," he admitted, with all the enthusiasm of a child agreeing to eat his vegetables.

I looked at him, smugly victorious. My heart pounded with excitement. "This person, distinctively writing in French...has likely been in this house. And he or she tucked away a portrait upstairs."

"Or not," Samuel said, pricking my bubble. "If, say, your theory about the stock market crash auction and my great-grandfather is correct, the portrait would have been brought into the house long after someone ever stuck the card in it."

"The *Martha Jefferson epitaph* card, whose handwriting matches a letter in your collection," I reminded him, just for good measure.

"The card could have nothing to do with the grave. I just noted a similarity in wording."

"It is the exact same wording," I argued. "And very odd wording, it is. *This* monument to his love? It's straight off an actual stone marker, so clearly it is a reference to the actual stone. If you were going to treat a portrait as a monument to love, wouldn't you say, '*A* monument to his love?'"

"You would," he agreed, looking like he was about to snap a vein in his temple. He always had hated it when I outsmarted him.

"And if you have a letter with the same handwriting on it in the Hayden's Ridge collection, then wouldn't it stand to reason that the portrait has been in the house for a very long time?"

Samuel stared at me levelly.

I sat back, pleased. "This person...whoever brought the portrait of the auburn-haired lady in... He or she knew about the baby swap, or whatever type of shenanigans went on. The two are connected. And if we find who this person is, maybe we'll know the answer to both."

I DIDN'T SEE Samuel Hayden for three days. Literally. Did. Not. See. Him.

He seemed to care about this whole mystery very little. But it consumed me. I imagined him off in his cellar finding exquisite historical tidbits about the Civil War that were going to win him a Pulitzer Prize, a thousand accolades, and probably a huge salary increase. That was simply the trajectory of his career thus far. Meanwhile, I was *persona non grata*, and I was hanging by a shred onto my career. If my university could have stripped me of my doctorate, they probably would have.

Bitterness aside, I *had* enjoyed having my mind occupied by something else. When Samuel's DNA seemed to be a dead end, I sat with the portrait for a while. Got on Monticello's website, read everything I could find about Martha Jefferson... Mild and ladylike. Intelligent and talented. Attractive and good-natured.

Ah. A man named Henry Randall had quoted Mrs. Jefferson's

granddaughters as to her looks. *Large expressive eyes of the richest shade of hazel—her luxuriant hair of the finest tinge of auburn...*

I texted this furiously to Samuel.

He texted back: *Thomas Jefferson's granddaughters never met their grandmother. A highly unreliable source.*

I pictured him immediately going back to his research, swatting this metaphorical gnat out of his mind. Okay, then. He wanted to lecture me on sources, I would find some more reliable ones. (I was perfectly aware this was not a good come-back.)

I texted one of the two people in Boston who were still speaking to me, my friend John Granger, who was a Conservative historian and Founding Fathers scholar, to ask him where to start on Martha Jefferson. He texted back references to several works on the Hemings family. *There are great details out there about the Wayles family,* he wrote. *Sally H. and Martha J. had the same father, so the ancestry exploration from that side would be the same. You'll also find in these a more comprehensive analysis of J's wife than you will usually find from his own scholars.*

I sent him a high-five emoji.

AND THEN THERE was the harpsichord.

I rediscovered this item the next day as I had my lunchtime stare session with the portrait. I took a picture, circled the harpsichord piano forte on my phone, and sent it to Samuel. I said: *You will notice the instrument. Jefferson's wife was famous for her talent on the piano forte. Typically, if an item was included in a portrait, it meant something to the person depicted. It also could be the reason for the 'monument' reference. Jefferson and his wife played music together often, he on the violin, she on the other. It was one of the things they reportedly fell in love over.*

He texted back: *Leave me alone.*

I made a sour face at the phone. Pocketing it, I sighed, stared at the auburn-haired, hazel-eyed woman, and went back to my filing system in my cellar. Ledgers were a bit of a let-down after the prospect of finding a portrait *no one knew existed* of a *very important person.* I'm not sure why I blamed Samuel for my inability to say definitively whether we had just found the world's first known portrait of Martha Wayles Jefferson. But I did. If he would just be a little bit of *help.*

That night, I ran him to ground in the living room. He looked none-too-pleased.

"I'm doing some research," I said. "I believe I might find something in the more modern library. I know about the historic one, but...I was wondering if I could peruse your more recent books."

"Oh, sure," he said, surprising me by standing. Chester Arthur also stood. "My dad's library has everything."

We did not talk as we walked down the hall. This portion of the house was truly separate living quarters. It was still historic, but it was almost as if the family had carved out apartments back here that were their space, separate and apart from the too-old-to-touch other part of the house.

He flipped on a light in his father's library, and we walked in.

There was his and Jenna's wedding portrait, a rather large one, hanging directly in our vision. "God," he said, removing it from the wall and turning it around backwards on the ground. He looked over at his dad's desk. "*Gah,*" he exclaimed again, flipping another picture of him and Jenna downwards.

I refrained from comment, although I did bite my lip to prevent smiling as he looked around, as if for other unknown missiles. "Think you got them all," I said.

"Yep," he answered shortly. "Make yourself at home," he said.

"You know I will."

He left, but Chester stayed with me. "Who's a good boy, huh?" I asked sweetly. Chester looked up at me, panting as if to affirm that *he* was. I rubbed his ears and walked around the wall-to-wall bookshelves. Right behind the desk, in the place of honor, were all of Samuel's published books.

I touched the spine of one. *Embattled Legacy*. The subtext read: *How the Confederacy's Natural Heirship and Political Appropriation of the Legacy of the American Revolution Presented an Ideological Battle for Lincoln's Administration*. The next: *The Last Two Years: Slavery in the Old Dominion After the Emancipation Proclamation*. I pulled that one out. Tables and charts and line graphs—all very Samuel. *Well done*, I thought, giving him a mental toast.

I looked at Samuel's father's pictures. One with Samuel when he was about five, another at one of his graduations later. I picked up the one that had been turned down. It was Samuel and Jenna with his father, probably a couple of years ago. Mr. Hayden had been a very handsome man, but he was clearly unwell in it—very thin. I suspected cancer, although I had not heard Samuel say. Jenna was kissing her father-in-law's cheek, and Samuel had his arm around his dad, his head against his.

My heart tugged. Samuel had lost his entire family. I knew something about that. And it sucked. It sucked big time.

I swallowed. Anyway... Mr. Hayden had possessed a very robust collection of colonial books, naturally, and I found just the ones I needed.

I DIDN'T EMERGE from my commandeered office for about three days. When I did, it was because I heard the door slam—the main door—and high heels tapping down the hardwood floors.

"Darling," I heard a woman say as Samuel entered another direction.

I could tell she was a little older, and, indeed, when I caught a glimpse of her, I guessed her to be in her early sixties. She was beautifully tailored in a luxurious cream pantsuit. Her blonde hair was fading to white in an elegant way, and she wore expensive jewelry.

"Aunt Enid," Samuel said, sounding surprised. He crossed to her and kissed her cheek.

"There you are," she said, returning the kiss. "You're looking well. Or well-ish."

"Thank you," he said, in his customarily dry tone.

"Darling, your mother wants to see you."

"Then she shouldn't have left me when I was seven," he returned with sarcastic niceness, completely merciless.

"Of course she shouldn't have. You were adorable, and your father was very good in bed. She told me."

"My God." Samuel sounded horrified.

His aunt, unaware, sniffed the air. "There is a woman staying here. Chanel No. 5. It is my very own scent. I *sense* it."

I stepped out of the shadows, walking into the grand foyer. "Hi," I said, giving my professional-professor smile.

Aunt Enid looked me up and down, her brows lifting, a smile hovering, mischief entering her expression. She looked at her nephew. "Well, well, well, what have we here?" she asked suggestively.

"Dr. Apkarian is here researching," Samuel answered coldly.

"*Researching*," she said with delight. "Is that what they call it these days?" She walked toward me, extending a hand, while Samuel looked at his aunt's back like he could murder her. "Enid Landry, my dear," she said. "And you are...?"

"Madeleine Apkarian. And I really am *just* researching."

Completely unruffled by my equal directness, the woman said, looking back at Samuel, "*Why* on earth?"

He appeared to be on the brink of blowing a fuse, regarding his aunt with an intensity as if to convey something telepathically. Even as a very faint flush stole into his cheekbones.

She didn't heed him. She turned back to me and made a long

study of my face. Recognition flickered. "Oh, yes. You were cancelled," she said to me.

Great. Even random people knew.

The woman went to sit on a bench in the foyer. Samuel lifted a hand, as if to indicate that it was too old for sitting. But sit she did, and he pocketed his hands, clenching his teeth.

"Now," she said, "we were discussing the fact that the two of you have not slept together?" she said.

"No," Samuel said with finality. "We were not."

"Very well, then, if you prefer to talk about your mother, we'll talk about your mother."

"I don't want to talk about my mother."

"Well, then what will we talk about? I have a very good heart, and I love my sister and my nephew, but my reservoir is rather dry, my dear, if you don't wish to talk about either your mother or sex." She looked at him like this was a perfectly reasonable problem.

I adored her immediately. I don't know what it was, but I had to use the utmost self-control to prevent bursting out in laughter.

"Ah!" she said, hitting on something. "We will talk about Jenna."

"No. We will not."

"Jenna Brenning. *Dr. Jenna Brenning.* I find that a very odd sort of name to give a girl. Jenn, Brenn... Why, it rhymes!" she said, looking at me for commiseration at this oddity.

"Mmm," I said noncommittally, noting that Samuel Hayden was drawing ever nearer to an apoplexy.

"Not that I have any particular sort of opposition to a rhyming name," she added conscientiously.

"Of course not, ma'am," I responded.

Samuel tossed me an ugly look.

"Well, the thing about it is, it would stand to reason that she would prove to be a disappointment, doesn't it? I mean, she doesn't like macadamia."

My mouth worked; nothing came out. Finally, I managed, "Doesn't she?"

"Despises it. I think that says something, don't you?" She threaded her hands on her crossed knee, atop her elegant pants., "I think, in her soul, she is a lesbian."

"What the hell...?"

She looked up at her nephew calmly. "My dear, I have a *sense* about all things sexual. *You*, like your father before you, have a great deal of sex appeal. I can tell, just by looking at you, that you are a *prime* lover—" [Somewhere, Samuel had begun to give a choked moan, rather in the manner of a person who believes he is dying.] "It is one of my life's greatest regrets that I never slept with your father. Celia wouldn't have minded. What was I thinking?" She looked at me, again in the way of one seeking agreement on something simple like *I really wish the subway weren't so crowded.*

And it was too much; I let a ripple of laughter escape. She didn't appear offended. she merely smiled at me serenely. "What I am trying to say is, if Samuel was not satisfying her, then likely her soul craved a very different—"

"Aunt Enid, I don't know how much one person can really be expected to take—"

"—Experience. And, in her journey to discovery, I believe she will find this." Enid glowed triumphantly, her theory having been artfully bared.

"Are you finished?" Samuel demanded.

"I am, yes."

"Then shall I suggest we retire to the living room? And henceforth restrict our remarks to the weather," he added savagely.

THE DOOR CLOSED at last on Enid Landry, and Samuel turned to me in the foyer. "Sorry," he said, drawing his hand through his hair.

"It's okay." I smiled. "She's an original."

"That woman," he said, "is sex-obsessed. I have said it before, and I will say it again!" Coming down from these wrathful heights, he said, softer, "I...wouldn't want her to have embarrassed you." His eyes lifted to my face, searching. "I'm sorry if she did." His cheeks were flaming now, and this caused something warm to spread in me.

"She didn't embarrass me," I said in the same soft tone.

He scratched the back of his head slowly, awkwardly not saying anything for a few moments. "I'm...going to go feed the sheep," he said, turning, picking up his shotgun, and leaving, closing the door behind him.

CHAPTER
SIX

"I was bold in the pursuit of knowledge, never fearing
to follow truth and reason to whatever results they led."
-Thomas Jefferson

I sat in front of Samuel's iMac, logged into his ancestry website
account. I had an idea, and, leveraging his aunt's sexual
harassment, I had somehow managed to make him sit with me.
Like an evil genius, I had browsers open everywhere, and I clicked
and tapped. He leaned on the desk, watching me. I was coughing
intermittently again. And blowing my nose. And feeling drainage
down the back of my throat. I highly suspected that working in
the cellar was killing me slowly. I wasn't about to say so, however.
That would provide an all-too-convenient excuse for Samuel to
kick me out during one of his ornery fits.

At length, I looked up and said, "You have a match."

"You put me on a dating website?" he asked, sounding horrified, as if only just realizing the full horror of *me*.

"A DNA match," I said drily. "With this random Hayden guy
out in Wyoming."

His brows lifted. "We don't have any family in Wyoming."

61

"Exactly. You're matched as *really* distant cousins."

Samuel looked at the screen as I turned it toward him. "He's not very attractive," he said.

"He's like seventy," I responded, levelling a look at him. "Here's the thing: this particular website does what is called an autosomal DNA test. You and..." I narrowed my eyes on the screen. "Buckeye Hayden—"

"My God."

"—Buckeye Hayden both spit in a tube, and they test autosomal chromosomes, which everyone has, male or female. When there's a kinship match, they issue out a list of all your relationships. Look," I said, pointing at the screen. "Here's Enid, looking *fine*, and she matches as your aunt. Boom."

His eyes twinkled, looking at Enid's perky picture she had apparently sent in for her profile.

I turned away from him to cough. "But there's something called a Y DNA test that only males can take. The Y chromosome replicates itself virtually unchanged from father to son. This website doesn't do that type of test. But there are other places that do."

He regarded me in deep suspicion. "And the point would be?"

"Y chromosome tests show the ancestry of the true, or direct, male line, right back to Adam, if you will. They can be very revealing, historically speaking. For instance, in a study conducted in the American South, more than a third of African American males had European haplogroups in Y chromosome tests, meaning that there had been a white father at some point in their male line. Said father passed the unique Y chromosome to his son, which he passed to his son, and so on."

I picked up the book John Granger had recommended to me: *Thomas Jefferson & Sally Hemings, An American Controversy*, handing it to him. "Annette Gordon-Reed, a historian, proved pretty soundly the theory that Jefferson fathered Sally Hemings's children with historical evidence, even before the DNA tests scientifically proved it. Despite everyone's claims that Sally Hemmings's children were fathered by everyone *but* Jefferson, there was a long-neglected interview by Sally's son, named Madison, who pretty much laid the truth out.

"Then a retired pathology professor, Dr. Eugene Foster, decided to conduct a Y chromosome test. There were three universities involved. He tested male descendants of Eston Hemings, another of Sally's sons, and male line descendants of Jefferson's paternal uncle, who would have all had the same Y chromosome as Jefferson if the theory were correct. They couldn't test any male line descendants of Jefferson and his *wife* because there weren't any. Only daughters of theirs survived to adulthood. Foster also tested male line descendants of other men who supposedly fathered Sally Heming's children. I think they may have also conducted tests on a control group of men descended from the first families of Virginia to ensure there were no random false positives." Something flickered in his eyes, and I stopped, lifting my brows in encouragement.

"Yes. My father participated in it. I was a child, but I remember. They sent his blood sample to a lab in England, with a code for anonymity—"

"Yes!" I said excitedly. "Ah! So your father and his test group showed there was no odd distortion of the old Virginia families' DNA based on all of the...um..."

"Inbreeding?"

I glanced away. "Mm hmm." Samuel met my eyes levelly, almost teasingly.

"There were no matches of Eston Hemings's male descendants to *any* of the men tested—including the ones that historians had always posited were the theoretical fathers—except to the Jeffersons. They matched perfectly."

Seeing my delight, something twitched in his lower lip, and (I think) he almost smiled.

"Between them, Gordon-Reed and Foster had proven

hundreds of years' worth of deniers wrong. The work revealed a lot about the way black Americans' stories and accounts have been disregarded and swept aside by historians through the centuries. But I veer off track."

He considered, looking into the distance. "It *is* remarkable. Historians said for years that Jefferson couldn't have fathered the children of Hemings, and then...there is a perfect Y chromosome match in the 90's with some Hemings men, what—in the Midwest?—and some Jefferson men in Virginia."

"Exactly. And if your family similarly violated social taboos, it has been covered over quite as thoroughly, I should think. But all of this is to say: if you send in a blood sample, your Y chromosome will come back, likely, with either British or African markers. We possibly could either confirm or eliminate the theory that the African American parent in your family line was male. And if this other Hayden man out in Wyoming is a distant *enough* cousin from a split on the family tree way back before we suspect the line fell outside of the legal marriages...and he is *still* a Y chromosome match to you, it would show that the African ancestor theory, if true, would include instead an African American *woman*. This will be easiest to prove if you and he are descended from different sons of *George Richard* Hayden, the original Hayden in Virginia. I'm doing the math in my head based on your kinship, and it is possible." I clicked a button. "I'm going to ask him to share his family tree."

"I'm lost."

I coughed again, and sneezed, and he offered me a tissue. I took one. "If you are both descended from the original Hayden who came to America and have no succeeding ancestors in common—and you *still* have matching Y chromosomes, there would have been no chance for male line illegitimacy. And we would really be on the wrong track altogether. The ancestor would have to be female instead."

He looked at me suspiciously. "Why do I get the impression

that you are about to produce a needle and ask me to present my arm?"

I laughed. "Of course not. You'll have to go through an accredited lab."

"Of course," he scoffed. "How stupid."

My lips twitched.

Bloom. The computer's noise signaling a message sounded, and immediately, a message from Buckeye Hayden popped up, with his family tree attached. Apparently he was some sort of genealogy, um, nut...and was thrilled.

I opened the family tree. He had traced it to England and beyond, but *boom.* He was descended from George Richard, and George Richard's son Thomas. Samuel's family line was descended from George Richard's son Arthur, the eldest. I could feel excitement pounding through my veins. It was highly unlikely that they would even be a DNA match on the website if there had been any male-line illegitimacy, in that case. But there was only one way to prove it.

I angled the keyboard toward Samuel. "Ask him for a sample to be sent to this lab," I said, pulling up another browser with the lab's information and requirements.

Samuel looked annoyed. He also looked slightly intrigued. And I knew he was going to do it. Inside, I did a happy dance. "What should I say?" he asked wrathfully. "*Can I have a Y chromosome, please?*"

I rolled my eyes. "*Explain* it to him. I think he would be willing to help."

He sighed long-sufferingly, paused, and then began to type out a message.

Bloom. Almost immediately, Buckeye Hayden emailed in the affirmative.

"Haha!" I exclaimed, clapping. "We are in business!"

Samuel huffed. "I *hate* having my blood drawn."

SEVEN

"I agree with you that it is the duty of every good citizen to use all the opportunities, which occur to him, for preserving documents relating to the history of our country."
-*Thomas Jefferson*

I went downstairs the next morning, my soft sweater topped by a thick cardigan, and a box of tissues in my hand that would only add to the redness of my nose. I was pretty sure my throat had tried to close over at least three times last night, and the pressure in my sinus cavities was intense. Deciding to skip break-fast, I slipped out into the main historical part of the house and found my way to the passageway down to the dungeon. Probably, today would be the day I died for history down there.

I halted. The foyer was different. About ten card tables with protective booties sat against the original wooden floors. Resting on them were about thirty bankers boxes of what appeared to be primary documents.

I heard a noise and turned to see Samuel ascending from the stairs below, another box in his arms. He stopped. "Good morning."

"Good morning," I said, eyeing his box, then looking out at the organized chaos in the massive foyer.

"You can't be down there anymore," he said simply. He placed the last box on a table. "There."

I blinked. I looked around, surveying what looked to me like the best sort of amusement park. "Thank—"

But he was already gone, departing down the steps to his own private lair, not to be seen again for the rest of the day.

I walked toward one of the tables. Opening a box, I removed one of the files. A stack of letters from 1771. My breath caught. Turning, I reached behind me into another box. More letters. No crappy ledgers. No inventory lists. He had brought me colonial and early American primary sources. I was not going to die of pneumonia.

And, peering around the room, I saw my future spread out before me.

I TOOK myself back to the library in a haze. I needed desperately to figure out who all of these historical actors were if I had any hope of piecing anything together. And Samuel had left the family tree, complete with picture portraits, in there for me.

The first thing that I had found was a series of correspondence between an Alexander Hayden and a man named William Wayles, beginning in 1823. But they were really letters from Wayles's sister, Etta (or sometimes Ettie) to the Hayden man. The men did the proper thing to protect her reputation, but it was clear that this formality concealed a courtship. Very Jane Austen. It might not be of huge relevance historically, but it interested me.

I spread out the family tree on the desk. Ah, yes. Samuel had mentioned Etta/Ettie as the future granddaughter-in-law of the house during the era of the lady in our portrait. Etta was the only one who had given him pause because she, too, seemed to have a reddish tinge to her hair. I studied her closer. But he was right. Etta Hayden wasn't the same person as the mysterious portrait lady.

She was of interest to me, however. Wayles was not a terribly common surname in Virginia, or anywhere in the country, for that matter. And it had been Jefferson's wife's maiden name. Maybe if Martha Wayles Jefferson had been related to Etta Wayles Hayden, it would explain the Monticello tombstone reference on the portrait.

From my recent historical reading, I had Martha Jefferson's family tree in my head. Her father had come to the colony as a servant and had climbed his way to being a wealthy man. He outlived three wives, but he had only daughters from those unions. With Sally Hemings's mother, *Elizabeth* (the daughter of an African woman and the English Captain Hemings), he had three sons: Robert, James, and Peter. But they had been born enslaved, of course, and they had carried the surname Hemings rather than Wayles and would not have passed the latter name on to children.

So where had my in-love Etta Wayles Hayden come from? I ultimately decided it was probably just a coincidence, and that there must have been another Wayles who had immigrated to Virginia during the colonial era. Surely there could be no relation to Martha Wayles Jefferson that was unknown to the Haydens. They would have passed that down in their oral history, certainly.

I saw, in folding the family tree up and returning it to the desk drawer, a photo album. Smiling, I lifted it. Samuel's father seemed to have been a sentimental man. Photos were simply everywhere. Especially of Samuel.

There were even some in the early years with Samuel's mother, indicating that perhaps Mr. Hayden and his ex-wife may have come to terms, even if his son had never done the same with his mother.

I felt for Samuel on that score. At least I didn't have abandonment by choice in my record. My mom had abandoned me by death, my father by addiction.

I turned the page. My eyes lingered. Samuel and Jenna in our college's pullover sweatshirts, appearing to be at a football game. He looked very young. I suspected him of being a freshman or sophomore, which would have been before our infamous senior project. They looked totally giddy and googly-eyed for each other.

Things had seemed different by the time I had known him, but of course, who was to say what they were like when alone? I had to smile at some of the youthful antics in the pictures, many of them obviously at parties and concerts and Halloween parties. Somewhere along the way (probably upon seeing a very steamy photo in which he and Jenna were kissing), it struck me: this must be Samuel's album, not his father's.

I shut it quickly, feeling intrusive. And sad. And ruffled. And guilty.

**William Wayles to Alexander Hayden,
documented and preserved by Madeleine Apkarian,
Ph.D., M.A., B.A.**

June 1823
Washington City
Dear Mr. Hayden,

I am enclosing your requested tickets of admission for our lecture in the city. I enjoyed meeting with you and look forward to partnering with you on future ventures of a scientific nature. Please know you are always welcome in my home.

Sincerely,
Wm Wayles

Postscript:
Dear Mr. Hayden,

Of all of my brother's serious scientific friends, I believe you must be the most amusing. I very much enjoyed making your acquaintance and appreciate your invitation to add my thoughts to your letters from my brother.

I do hope you enjoyed your visit to Washington City. We have lived here a year and a half now, and I believe I will never tire of its charms. I believe you, too, will enjoy yourself once you have settled into your bachelor's lodgings.

I enjoyed discussing all matters political with you. It is a great trust indeed, for you to have been chosen by the gentlemen of your district to represent them. I have a suspicion that you shall not fail them. Until next time, I bid you adieu.

Yours Very Truly,
Etta Wayles

I WORKED ALMOST without cease for the next few days, enjoying myself tremendously and beginning to feel alive again. I saw very little of *Dr. Hayden* for the next few days, as he seemed to be on some obsessive academic binge of his own.

However, he did drop in to ask me if there was anything I needed on the day he was to drive to Richmond to have his blood drawn. He appeared to be preserving his equanimity, so I assumed he wasn't too mad at me. *Something I don't have to cook for myself?* I had joked.

At lunchtime, the house to myself and quiet, I slipped up to my sunny little bedroom, where I laid on the bed and dialed Jessie. She answered, this time without the background noise of farm animals or machinery.

"Well, if it isn't the most infamous woman in academia!" I heard her voice filling the line with the tones of home.

I smiled. My chest squeezed. "And how are you?"

"Well, I just ate a big bate of catfish, so I'm feeling good, but kind of like I could throw up. What about you? Are you eating, hon?"

I didn't answer her.

"Maddie!"

"What does it matter?"

"You're going to dry up and blow away like a dust ball!" she warned.

"Sometimes I think the spirit of my grandmother inhabits you," I said.

"It does, and we'll both haunt you if you're not careful. How's your man?"

"I don't have a man."

"The man you're living with."

I pinched the bridge of my nose. "I have told you that there is nothing going on."

"Nothing at all," she said skeptically.

"Jessie! Why do you keep bringing this up?" I demanded, trying to practice mindfulness. I could feel the soft mattress beneath my back, the quilt beneath my feet, the annoying-ness of my friend ringing in my ears...

"Hon, you know he was the one who got away."

I froze. Silence filled the line between us. "I never had him," I said, voice scraping a bit.

"But you *wanted* him, if you know what I mean. That was why we decided it was unfair for you to hate that girl he was with back then. You can't be objective about a woman who's with a man you want to bang—"

"Jessie, I am going to hang u—"

"Well, nobody could!" she said reassuringly. "We all have burning passions. Dale Tilton, now, he really does it for me. I told him that, so we'll see where it goes." She sighed. "Hon, I wouldn't be surprised if you didn't subconsciously go down there because there was unfinished business between the two of you."

"I will have you know that he has been nowhere near me," I said coldly.

"Really? He hasn't seen you naked?" she said skeptically.

"There was," I said with dignity, "an unfortunate toilet incident. Other than that, *no*."

"Huh," she said, sounding surprised.

I drew my fingers through my hair and pulled. Why had I called her again? That was the Southern family for you. Deep love, followed by agonizing homesickness, followed by supreme annoyance in proximity.

Jessie spoke again. "What I meant by unfinished business, really, before you took it straight to funny business, was of the emotional kind. You two had a connection, Maddie."

I swallowed. "If there was a connection, it was one-sided," I said, my voice weak.

What was *wrong* with me? All I had felt was anger about the project. I had convinced myself it was all in my head.

"Big feelings are strange," said the Sage of Alabama (I do not say that facetiously). "They turn you inside out, but if you're not allowed to have them, you can completely deny they exist. Push them down. Convince yourself only the spoken things were real."

I wasn't ready to admit that much. But I will say that my friend was very wise.

"Now, are you interested in him?" she demanded.

"Of course not!" I hissed, outraged, crossing from love for her back to supreme annoyance.

"Not even a teensy bit?"

"I am hanging up the phone."

"But *are* you still on birth control?" she demanded hurriedly. *Click.*

"*WHO IS DALE TILTON?*" I texted Jessie about an hour later.

She responded at a leisurely pace. Apparently, he was another local farmer, wore the right brand of coveralls, and was a nice guy. I took a deep breath. Okay, then. As long as she wasn't flirting with disaster.

As for me, I profoundly was not.

It was ancient history. I would do my research, and then I would leave.

Suddenly, I heard the back door open, and Chester Arthur, who had been reposing with his head in my lap, jumped up and totally abandoned me, running hell-for-leather toward the back door. I stood and followed him more sedately.

I came face to face with Samuel. He looked at me, and I looked at him. I was suddenly tongue-tied. I *hated* Jessie.

"Hey," Samuel said cautiously. I'm pretty sure he thought I had broken something. He was a little on his guard.

"Hey," I managed. My gaze shifted. He had brought home Chipotle. I looked up at him. "Samuel! I was joking."

"I don't think either of us is going to get any if Chester has his way. Down!" he said. Chester obeyed, his tail wagging furiously. Samuel cracked a smile. "I do have new dog food in the car," he promised. Chester shot outside toward the vehicles.

Samuel handed me the bags and went back out to get the rest of his purchases.

Going into the kitchen, I got us drinks and started emptying the food bag. The restaurant employee had written *Samuel* on one box and *Maddie* on another. In a few moments, I heard dry pebbles *ping* into Chester's bowl, to the pooch's approving yips of excitement.

Samuel entered and went to wash his hands. "You will be glad to know," he said sarcastically, "that I have given so much blood that I developed a migraine on the way home."

"No, you did not," I returned, opening the bag of chips he had brought.

"Well, it was enough that I *should* have."

"If you had been less tough," I suggested.

"Exactly," he responded savagely.

I strove to keep from smiling as I crunched a chip. He had ordered my bowl exactly how I would have, and I didn't even want to know how he had done that.

He said, apparently not finished, "You roll up without warning—"

"Because *you* owed me a favor!"

"Because *you* were sacked!"

I eyed him. "You're lucky I came when I did. You were spiraling."

"I was not."

"You said so yourself."

"I did not."

"You did!" I exclaimed, eyes shooting wrathful darts at him. "You had been deserted, you were living here like some half-crazed Heathcliff, and you had thrown the couch out the window of your house in Charlottesville!"

He had been regarding me balefully, but his expression shifted slightly when I mentioned the couch. "That," he said, and I could have sworn I caught a tremor of laughter in his voice, "was an exaggerated rumor."

"Oh? You *didn't* shove a sofa out of a second story window?"

"She did," he said, crunching a chip, I thought, in an attempt to hide his twitching lips. "But it was an accident."

"How—?"

He pinched the bridge of his nose. "It's a long story," he said. I'm pretty sure his hand was hiding a smile. It was fleeting, however.

Resuming his scowl, he looked back at me and recommenced: "As I was *saying*, you roll up and then here I am a few weeks later, giving a gallon of blood in Richmond for some hairbrained DNA project that *I don't care about*."

I had known the blood extraction would set him off, to be honest. So I made a sympathetic noise, declining further incivilities.

"And I am *finished*. I warn you, I will participate in no more crazy ancestral schemes."

"Of course," I answered placatingly.

I crunched another chip. We would see about that.

EIGHT

"But as it is, we have the wolf by the ear, and we can neither hold him, nor safely let him go. Justice is in one scale, and self-preservation in the other."
-Thomas Jefferson

The courtship progressed.

Alexander Hayden, apparently a young representative in the House of Representatives, was quite smitten with his scientific colleague's sister. I tried to determine the nature of his and William Wayles's scientific experiments. They spoke of them, of course, as two people deep into a conversation would, without providing context for me. Yet, at some point, given references to sailing in the same sentences with flying, I was fairly certain they were early balloonists.

Given his scientific abstraction, I thought it was sweet that William Wayles had made that statement: *Please know you are always welcome in my home*. He wanted his sister to be happy. He wanted her to marry Alexander Hayden.

So much so that he was willing to humor a correspondence

that grew to be ever less about the mechanics of hot air balloons and ever more about romance by the week. And apparently, as trust grew, he was content even to allow his sister and Hayden to correspond without the chaperonage of his own words penned to paper.

The day was warmish, so I took a notebook outside, where I flipped through the copies I had made of letters. I sat on a stone wall in an old carriage drive, where people would have exited and gone into the house.

I could see the river from here, and breathing deeply, I absorbed peace. Released stress. Breathed in hope. Breathed out fear. I listened to the trickling sounds of the water and to the birds. My heart rate, continually escalated, seemed to slow to a normal pace. Marla was a wonder.

Taking out my phone, I snapped a picture to send to Jessie—and brought my arms back down to almost collide with Samuel, who had a dead coyote over his shoulder.

"*Good grief*, Samuel!" I exclaimed, scooting back so as not to touch even an inch of *that*.

"Got him," he said shortly, passing on.

Alexander Hayden to Etta Wayles,
documented and preserved by Madeleine Apkarian,
Ph.D., M.A., B.A.

October 1824
Hayden's Ridge, Virginia

Dear Miss Wayles,

I dash this note off to you just before I return to the city from

Hayden's Ridge. I wish to see you as soon as may be possible. In truth, I pine. I have never felt so lonely, nor so lost as I have the whole of my time away from you. I was bereft of my friend, my champion, and my dearest dream.

How to say this to you? I had not <u>meant</u> to do such an ungentle-manly thing, nor to discuss it with you without first speaking with your brother. I mean you no disrespect, but I cannot wait a second longer. Will you be my wife?

I will call upon you the minute I enter the city. I wait with bated breath for your answer but wish you to feel yourself under no constraint to answer yes or to answer me immediately.

Please know that my love is profound, and lasting.

Yours Very Truly,
A. Hayden

THE PRESCRIBED two weeks passed after Samuel's DNA test, and he, standing in the foyer, told me he had gotten an email with the results.

"Ah!" I exclaimed, rising up from my dive into a cluttered box. "What does it say?"

He shrugged, taking a drink from his tumbler. "I was busy yesterday."

Yesterday. Enflamed, I demanded, "You got it yesterday?" I walked around my table toward him rapidly, but he did not appear to be alarmed.

"I got it yesterday," he confirmed. "And I did not tell you until now because I knew you would demand that we drop everything."

"You are correct," I replied, metaphorical tail twitching. Imag-

78

ining my eyes were narrowed to slits, I headed toward his office. Once there, I sat at his desk at once and slid a notepad and pen toward him. "Your username and password for the lab site, please."

I felt his eyes boring holes through me. There was a delay. Then he reached for the pad and dashed it off. Satisfied, I tapped the keyboard, bringing it to life before typing in the information and navigating through the disclaimers.

I made a squeak.

"What?" he demanded.

I looked at him, smiling. "You and Buckeye Hayden have substantially similar Y chromosomes. So you *are* a Hayden in the direct male line."

He stared at me. "I don't know how many times I have to tell you that I don't care."

I rolled my eyes. "You are being crabby on purpose. You have to admit the process is fascinating." I narrowed my eyes in thought. "And what a testament to the fidelity of women! Every single woman married to Hayden men in both yours *and* Buckeye Hayden's line has been faithful for hundreds of years."

"That is a low bar, Maddie," he intoned sarcastically, "not something to celebrate."

Appropriately chastened, I ducked my head, laughing inside but choosing not to provoke him further. I noticed, however, that he stuck around.

I read through the results, saying excitedly at some point, "This means that if you do have an ancestor with roots originally in Africa, it would have been a woman." I didn't remind him that this had always been the most likely theory to me.

"How do we trace that?" he asked.

I shook my head, trying to remember the things Bradley would drone on about—I mean, that we would *discuss*—at the dinner table. In a way, I was grateful to him now, strangely. Ancestral history involving DNA had been one of the few subjects in my field which truly interested his scientific brain. "Well, women don't have Y chromosomes. So your possible ancestress wouldn't have passed anything like that down." I tapped a bit on the computer, scanning the screen after my searches. "There is something called an mtDNA test. Mitochondrial DNA. It tests the matrilineal line. Men *and* women can take these because we all have mitochondria. But mitochondria is only *passed on* to the next generation by women, so the test will show only female ancestors. No male."

"In which case, my DNA would be profoundly useless. It would start tracking us through my mother, to my maternal grandmother, and so on," he said. "Thank God."

I sighed. "I *think* so." Feeling frustration, I said, "I don't think there *is* any way to track up through your Hayden family tree for the women ancestors. Because they are *not* Haydens—"

"Except for a few cases of measured inbreeding."

"—and each have their own family trees entirely."

"There is no way to trace it, except through the simple autosomal DNA test that the ancestry website conducts. That I had *already taken*," he said, just as a reminder.

"Autosomal DNA will show blood relationships from the modern day," I said. "And from there, you can carefully trace back up through family trees from documentation and shared DNA with relatives from that tree. But if you had a mistaken person listed somewhere way back—for instance, a wife of a Hayden male line ancestor when it should instead have been another woman, possibly an enslaved woman—it wouldn't show that." I paused. "So the best you could hope for in the way of DNA tracing would be finding a legitimate Hayden half-sibling of the child mothered by the woman of African descent, so that you could show ancestry branching off for their children with different mothers. But that far back, it would be nearly impossible."

His sigh was complete with notes of his suffering. "I went to grad school for history so I wouldn't have to do science, Maddie."

"You'll survive." I tapped my fingers on the desk as I thought. "The best we can hope for is to find documentary evidence. And I will, of course, map an extensive family tree for you on the ancestry website, similar to the one you have in the library. It would really be best if you had a near Hayden relative who would take a regular test to anchor my findings. I could balance those against your Aunt Enid's test so I would know what came from your mom."

"I am quickly losing patience—"

"Do you have any near Hayden relatives?"

He shook his head.

My eyes widened, thinking about the noble, long family line of the Hayden dynasty—the type of unbroken male line nobility in England or Japan could only dream about. "Is this the fall of the house of Usher, then?"

He gave me a scathing look. "If you're talking about blood relations, there is only my aunt. My great-aunt, actually. Millicent Hayden James."

WE DROVE toward a ritzy assisted living facility in Richmond three days later. How I had convinced him, I would never be sure. His grandfather's sister, according to Samuel's account, was a handful at eighty. She had shouted him down on the phone for even *suggesting* she do something so ignominious as spitting in a tube. And later, she had agreed.

"Why will your Aunt Enid be there?" I asked.

"They're close," he said. Later he added, "Because of me."

I turned my head, studying him in profile as he drove us. I didn't say anything. He said reluctantly, "My father didn't want me to become a misogynist—"

81

"Were you a baby misogynist?" I asked.

"No. But I hated my mother." His lovely, veined hand twitched on the console. "He didn't want me to hate all women, so he asked them for help with my raising." He was silent a second. "I can't say the influences were ideal, but..." He smiled for a second. "They could have been worse."

I was glad for him for that, at least. I said, "I'm sorry, Samuel."

We parked outside his aunt's facility, which, as I glanced up at the imposing structure, looked like a hot take on Kensington Palace. He said, "Water under the bridge." He was ready to go in. He did *not* want to talk about it. Just like he didn't want to talk about anything. Opening his door, he said, "If we're late, she'll castrate me."

I lifted my brows. "The fall of the house of Hayden, indeed."

He shot me a look, closing his door.

I put my hands in my coat pockets, following him through the entrance. He held the door for me, and I entered the palace. I had expected to navigate to a single room. However, we appeared to be approaching a formal parlor. From out of its cased opening floated an old Virginia accent demanding, "Who is she? What's her name? Does *she* want children?"

"I gather they are not actually dating," Enid's languid voice drawled. "Both assured me that they are not sleeping together."

Samuel's eyes widened. He glanced at me with me a look of horror that said: *Sorry could never be enough*.

I covered a smile, despite myself.

"A good thing," the older woman spat out. "Sex is a mortal sin."

"Dear me. I suppose I shall go to purgatory."

"Enid, you are going straight to hell."

My eyes grew huge. I fully expected an altercation. However, both women burst out laughing. Into this fray, we entered cautiously.

"Darling," Enid said, standing and taking Samuel's hands.

"You're looking well, for someone whose wife deserted him." She turned to me. "Hello, dear, *cancelled* Dr. Apkarian." While Samuel kissed his Aunt Millicent's cheek, Enid Landry turned to me. "Still haven't jammed the clam?" I lifted my eyebrows, not catching her meaning. "Buttered the biscuit? Passed the gravy?" Seeing my failure to catch on, she persisted, "A bit of the old in and out?"

My God. That one I got. "No. Thank you for asking."

Millicent Hayden James queried over the din, "Enid, what are you saying? The girl's as white as a sheet."

"She was saying *nothing*," Samuel said, giving his Aunt Enid the stink eye. "She was leaving Dr. Apkarian alone. As promised."

"Darling, I promised nothing," Enid said, smiling like a cat. That was to say, scary. "Sit, sit, you two. Come now, don't you want *my* DNA?"

"We have yours already," Samuel said, looking relieved, for once, to talk about DNA. "We found you on the site."

"You're not a Hayden, you loon," Millicent said. Then she fixed her eyes on me. They were clear blue, her nose and entire demeanor rather hawkish, at odds with her collared blazer, pearls, and pinned white hair. "I assumed you were courting my great-nephew, but Enid says not."

I flushed. Good heavens, they were a pair.

"It may interest you both to know," Samuel said stridently, "that women can have interests other than partnering up!"

They both attacked him.

"Watch your tone, young man!"

"I won't hear a lecture from *you*, a *man*, about what women want or need."

"Whippersnapper!"

I produced the tube. "Here, Mrs. James," I said. "Thank you for graciously agreeing to help us."

She studied my face. Seemed to draw a picture of it in her mind's eye. Seemed to see right through me, actually. She glanced at Samuel. Her expression softened. She reached and pressed my hand before releasing it. "Well, turn around!" she screamed at all of us suddenly. "I won't have you watching me!"

Samuel refused, she bellowed at him (I was beginning to see from where he got his recalcitrant nature), and finally he complied. The ignominious spitting finished, we talked for a while, and then Enid departed with us to get lunch.

"OH, yes, I imagine Thomas Jefferson to have been a very good lover," Aunt Enid said, biting the end a strawberry. "Of all the Founding Fathers, he is the one I imagine to be the most...succulent," she said, finishing off the strawberry. She sat next to me at the bar of a snazzy little lunch place, where we dined on overpriced sandwiches and salads.

Samuel, despite the fact that she annoyed the devil out of him, seemed to trust her implicitly. Even with his concerns for privacy, he had told her of my "outlandish" hypothesis on the portrait we had found. He seemed to have no concern that she would blab and send off a firestorm of historical analysis.

How we had gotten from the possibility of the portrait being Martha Jefferson to sex, I am unsure, and always will be.

I regarded Aunt Enid in awe. "You think so?" I asked.

"Mmm," she said, not choosing to expand further. "Do you think this will jumpstart your career, my dear, if you make some big finding?"

"I don't know," I admitted. "My career is in the toilet."

She said, "Let's talk about that."

"She doesn't want to talk about that," Samuel rejoined.

"Yes, she does." She swiveled her bar stool elegantly toward me. "Where do we *go* from here?" she asked. "I think you were right not to apologize. It never does any good. But do you have any hobbies which we could make into another career?"

"She doesn't need another career," Samuel said icily. "She's a historian."

"Very well, but...*money*. I had to make money after my father went completely bankrupt, which was why I got that cushy job at the portrait gallery. Unless..." She looked at me, eyes kindling with excitement. "Are you independently wealthy? Like your fellow Armenians, the Kardashians, did you, too, have a celebrity lawyer for a father?"

"No," I answered, trying not to let a bubble of laughter escape.

"Well, you are certainly beautiful, like them. *Ripe* for the picking. I have several elderly friends who would be happy to rescue you from your current financial situation, if you get my drift...?"

Oh, I did. I definitely did. "Aunt *Enid*," Samuel said.

"Well, darling, I started with other career options. When that didn't pan out for her, I turned to the only other option there is. It's just *practicality*, my dear."

"Practicality? I call it prostitution!"

"Well, yes, but don't be such a *stick*, Samuel. There's nothing wrong in prostitution."

"Isn't there?"

"I," Enid announced, "am thinking of marrying a younger man. For sex, you understand. Not for money."

Samuel groaned. "Not another wedding, I beg you."

She popped another strawberry in her mouth. "My dear, weddings are lovely and holy."

"What I meant was: not another *divorce*."

"Well, aren't you a big one to talk!"

"I've had *one* divorce. *You* are pushing the legal limit in Virginia. And *I* don't call you at two o'clock in the morning panicked about frozen bank accounts and property divisions and the IRS!"

"It is your duty to help your aunt," she responded, nose in the air.

Things continued for an hour or so, with her talking scandalously, enjoying every minute, and Samuel protesting in varying degrees of exacerbation.

We rose to go. Samuel hugged her, and she hugged me, too. She sent me off with a wink and a recommendation to *make the beast with two backs,* and went off toward her expensive, shiny SUV.

I had ceased to be horrified.

MY HEAD AGAINST THE HEADREST, I watched the Virginia landscape roll by in the waning light. "Are you sure you don't want me to drive?" I asked, thinking he might be tired.

"Yeah."

More fields passed in the window, the silence soothing but also somehow charged.

"What did Aunt Enid say to you as we left?" Samuel asked out of nowhere.

"Oh... I don't remember."

He was silent for a moment, obviously not buying it.

"I'm sorry she compared you to the Kardashians," he said, face stoic. I could tell he was experiencing that special type of irritation one feels when one's older relative has said something offbeat.

I tried not to smile. "That's okay."

Appearing to be grimly checking off a list, he added, "And I'm sorry she brought up your career."

"That it's in the toilet?"

He scratched his head. "Yeah."

"It's just the truth."

He sighed. "Enid could understand that sort of thing, you know," he said quietly after a moment. "She was a...vocal advocate...during the sexual revolution. She let herself be a test case for the ACLU one time. She had a feeling her boss at a government agency would fire her if she told him she was living with a man. He did, and that's how we have *Landry v. Rucker*. It wasn't easy for her. No woman enjoys being called the things she was called. But she stuck to her guns."

I thought about it. Enid had quickly identified with me, or at least grasped the situation in its entirety. Maybe that was why I liked her, no matter how shocking and offensive she was.

"Wow. That's...amazing. I didn't know that. But it sounds like she's a legend; I'll never have that sort of impact."

He glanced at me, that skeptical look on his face, mixed with annoyance.

"What?"

"I don't know if this is false modesty, or—"

I breathed in through my nose, incensed. "Of course it isn't!" I said.

"Well, then you're in denial. You have an impact. You had one before you ever took a stand."

Truly bewildered, I demanded, "*I?*"

He looked at me for a moment. "I teach your thesis, Maddie. We all do. It's required reading."

I flushed. Looked away. Tucked my hair behind my ear. I was feeling whatever the sophisticated version of *"Aw, shucks"* was. I cleared my throat. I was silent for a time.

Later, I asked, "Are you sure you don't want me to drive?"

"No," he said. "You've asked like six times. You are not driving."

I turned my head. "I'm a perfectly adequate driver."

"And I am a *good* driver," Samuel retorted.

"Just because," I said, flame kindling, "you happened to be with me the one time when I was running late for class, and you could never understand that I simply did not *see* the campus squirrel—"

"And almost killed me, *and* a guy on his bike."

"You are being dramatic, as you were dramatic then," I retorted, voice slightly raised.

"*You* suck at driving, as you sucked then."

"*You* suck at empathy, as you always shall."

We lapsed into silence, both apparently satisfied with our moral ground.

NINE

"What a stupendous, what an incomprehensible machine is man!
Who can endure toil, famine, stripes, imprisonment & death
itself in vindication of his own liberty, and the next moment . . .
inflict on his fellow men a bondage, one hour of which is fraught
with more misery than ages of that which
he rose in rebellion to oppose."
-Thomas Jefferson

I carefully made copies of every document I found. The originals would have to be preserved. Some were so delicate they almost crumbled when I gently took them into my gloved hands. But the copies would be scanned in and would be part of what I *hoped* would become an online database someday. The world needed the Hayden's Ridge collection. Of that, I became more and more certain.

It was easy enough to track the Haydens who had lived here, more difficult to learn about the enslaved. I was keeping a notebook. Every time I found mention of a slave in a letter, I jotted down the information. I then compared it to slave rolls, which Samuel had already grouped, preserved, and copied. In this way, I was tracking the silent historical actors, uncovering *people* whose lives had been lost to history. For each individual, it felt like a victory. In the aggregate, I felt certain they would tell us weighty and insightful things about Hayden's Ridge, the slavery system, and the country at the time in which they had lived.

My skin tingled when I saw a *Lucy* mentioned again and again. The hair on my arms stood when I learned that she had a taste for lemons, that she was strong-willed and *talked back*, that she was a talented seamstress... Here was a *person*. She had *lived*. History had not forgotten her. That never failed to take my breath away.

Coincidentally, it was why I had been loved as a professor. I had brought that realness of the past to life for my students. Even the ones who didn't like history.

I was tracing a *Jack* now. He seemed to have been purchased at the auction on Thomas Jefferson's estate after the former President's death. One of the books I was reading at night, *The Hemingses of Monticello*, had described the tragedy that had taken place there once Jefferson was no longer alive to keep his creditors at bay.

His and Sally's children had all gotten away from slavery. Jefferson had promised Sally that they would be given their freedom when they reached twenty-one. The eldest son, Beverley, had attained that age in 1819. Interestingly, he had seemed to linger at Monticello until he was twenty-four years old. That would tend to indicate there was a family agreement that he would wait until he could accompany his sister upon her twenty-first birthday three years later. Both Beverley and Harriet had "run away" in 1822.

Legally speaking in those days, they were white under Virginia law, given that they were seven-eighths European. Likely, there were discussions. A decision to free them legally would necessarily "out" them as having been enslaved at birth, leaving a legal record that could be found. Such a thing had happened when the younger two children, Madison and Eston, were freed under

Jefferson's will (mentioned casually as if they were merely some apprentices of his favorite plantation craftsman). At the time of their father's death, Madison had only just turned twenty-one, and Eston was eighteen. They were freed, and they moved into a house in Charlottesville with their mother.

Not so for many other slaves at Monticello, including some of Sally Hemings's family members. Children were sold away from parents, families torn apart, horrible scenes, unthinkable things... Some families were still trying to patch themselves together, with free members purchasing or searching out enslaved members, decades later.

I considered young *Jack*. Why had Alexander Hayden purchased him? I didn't think it was unusual that the Haydens had attended the Monticello auction. Likely nearly every planter in Virginia had done so. Jefferson was famous at an almost unimaginable level; the chance of purchasing one of his items would have been tantalizing, especially given his role in the American Revolution. But a young slave?

I had studied slave auctions enough to know that prime purchases were considered to have been young men, followed by young women. With a child, purchasers were taking a risk that they wouldn't make it to adulthood. And I had determined Jack was about eight years old. Why go all the way from near Petersburg to Charlottesville to purchase a child?

I wondered, suddenly, if the boy was a Hemings. One of Sally's nephews, perhaps, or a cousin? If so, that might explain it. The Hemings family was well-known as being skilled, and were privileged if such a thing can be said to exist in slavery. Lucia Stanton, a historian at the Thomas Jefferson Foundation, had written a compilation of documentation on the enslaved at Monticello. I knew my next task would be looking for Jack there.

I FOUND *Jack* three days later. By then, I was ready to become an advocate *against* cursive writing in schools. Who cared if it was pretty, if it was going to make a historian insane a couple of hundred years from now?

Anyway... Before her relationship with Martha Jefferson's father, Elizabeth Hemings (Sally's mother) had another relationship, likely with a man of African descent. They had four children. I think Jack was descended through *this* line of children and would, therefore, have been a Hemings of Monticello.

I tried to think of the implications of his purchase by the Haydens. I could think of many and none. There may have been a reason, but it was lost to history. Sometimes you just hit a wall.

I hadn't eaten in like two days. I did that when I got down a historical rabbit hole. Suddenly ravenous, I went to the kitchen, where I tracked down the peanut butter and jelly and made a sandwich, packing a lunch bag. I threw in some Chex Mix for good measure.

It was unseasonably warm, one of those bright February days that God gifts with the promise of spring. There was an old stone wall overlooking the James River out behind the house. I decided to take my lunch there.

As I approached, I saw Samuel. He was doing the same thing.

Smiling, I gave a little wave and sat at a distance, but not too far.

He almost smiled. A movement of the lips. I felt it down to my toes.

We didn't talk. By lunchtime, you needed a mental break, and we usually gave that to each other. When I was finished, I packed my leftovers and discards, waved, and headed back to work.

Alexander Hayden to William Wayles, documented and preserved by Madeleine Apkarian, Ph.D., M.A., B.A.

February 1827
Hayden's Ridge, Virginia
My Dear Sir,

I hope this letter finds you and your wife well. My own is quite well in health, you will be happy to know. I confess that I have felt some degree of anxiety for her in these past few months. My mother tells me that there is nothing to concern me, that ladies in such a condition very often are not quite themselves in spirit, especially after a disappointment such as ours last year.

I believe she feels the loss of your own mother keenly. Such a near female relative would surely be a comfort to her, I believe, in this her time of great anxiety. Poor Ettie jumps at loud noises, sits far too long by herself in her chamber, and stares at herself in the looking glass. She can only be comforted when I am with her, and I regret very much that my political duties carry me so often away from her to Washington City.

I was hoping to have seen you at the auction of the great Jefferson Estate. Most every family in Virginia was represented, I believe. I know that your science keeps you much-occupied, however. It was a sad day. It would have been sadder still for you, I imagine, in dwelling on your own burned family home in the Piedmont. That was a sad misfortune for your family, but one I shall never personally regret, as it brought your sister to Washington City, and into my life.

Nothing would do her but that I purchase one of the slaves of the near-famous Hemings family. She was quite emotional and adamant, as I believe anything from the Piedmont is a reminder of the home and parents she has lost, and the brother she misses. Naturally, I wished to humor her, all the more because that slave family are renowned as great craftsmen. Alas, I was only able to afford a boy! A mere child, but I must say, I have him training as a carpenter at Hayden's Ridge, and he shows promise.

Ettie dotes on him, and it frankly breaks my heart, William, to see what is so obviously a longing for our own son, who entered the world too soon and was never to be. What a sad business is motherhood. But I run on and risk embarrassing you with dwellings of grief.

We hope to see you and your new bride at Hayden's Ridge as soon as may be practicable. My greatest felicitations upon your recent ballooning successes.

Yours, etc.,
A. H.

CHAPTER

TEN

"...Our liberty depends on the freedom of the press,
and that cannot be limited without being lost."
-Thomas Jefferson

I ran into the lone other occupant of the house two days later at breakfast. I was having granola and a yogurt. He glanced at my choices before seeming to decide they were a good idea. He pulled the same from the pantry and fridge and sat two bar stools down.

"Good morning," I said.

"Good morning," he answered. Nothing further.

Conversation was so easy around here.

He glanced at me furtively. After a moment, he said, "I saw another professor at your university was sacked this morning." He watched for my reaction.

I lifted my brows. "Was it something similar?"

He nodded. "They're going to cancel themselves before it's over."

I glanced at him. "Does it ever worry you? That you'll say the 'wrong' thing while you're teaching?"

"Yes. Like every day. But I'm less revolutionary than you," he said. "I imagine I could talk myself out of ruffled feathers if I had to."

"I'm not revolutionary," I retorted with dignity.

He tossed me a look. "Come on, Maddie. You were taking a stand. You may have felt persecuted, and I'm certain you were, but you weren't backing down either, were you?"

"No," I admitted rather pensively. I swallowed, thinking of another person going through what I was. I just hoped it didn't hit them as hard.

He studied me for a second and then said, "Why don't we spend some time looking into the, um, portrait? It's time we take a day off from cataloging."

His face was handsome. Particularly when he wasn't scowling. When he was being kind, his eyes were the deepest shade of green, his lips generous, as if designed for kissing. You could always admire just how masculinely elegant his cheekbones and jawline were, but kindness took beauty to heights unknown. I hoped he could see in my expression that I was grateful. I think he could. "Well, I do have an idea..." I said.

"Of course you do," he responded dryly.

"I DO NOT HAVE the training for this!" Samuel griped.

"You have a Ph.D.," I said, kneeling on the other side of the portrait. "How much more training do you want?"

We were in a little alcove upstairs, the sun shining brightly through one of the dormers, even though there was only a small window. He ran his gloved hands over the back of the portrait, looking for a way to take the backing off.

"I can write a strong thesis," he said. "I can teach a class. That doesn't mean I know how to take this thing apart without destroying it."

"That's why I asked you to do it," I rejoined. "It's your personal property, so I can't take on the liability of ruining it."

He looked up at me, meeting my eyes with a sort of annoyance, leavened by amusement, or at least recognition of a fencing hit.

Going back to it, he worked for another twenty minutes, at which point he glanced up at me for a second. Shaking his head, he said, "I'm not going to do it."

I nodded, understanding. "If you can't break in without hurting it, I agree."

He sat up, standing the portrait against the wall. Pushing back his hair (which he needed to have cut), he looked at the portrait for a long moment. "I'm sorry."

"It was an unlikely chance there would be something between the painting and the frame anyway," I said.

He was silent for a long moment, considering. "It's not even *signed*."

I sighed in commiseration.

He glanced over at me. Moving our supplies, he dusted off the floor to make room for me, patting the ground once beside him. I sat.

"Do you know much about paintings?" he asked.

"A little." I was an art history buff once upon a time. "It's oil on canvas."

He shifted, his hand on the floor. "Does that track with the time period?"

"Oh, yes."

We heard clicking. I turned my head. Chester, having maneuvered his way into the attic, strolled amiably toward us, for all the world as if he were supposed to be here.

"Chester!"

"Hi, boy!" I said. Chester nuzzled me with his wet nose on the way by.

He went and sat next to Samuel, despite the scolding, and

looked at the portrait for a few moments in a scholarly fashion before laying his head in his person's lap. Samuel drew his hand in strokes across the Lab's head.

"Any idea as to the artist?"

I shook my head. "Only that if the subject is American, it most likely would have been painted in America. Very few ladies travelled abroad."

His forehead wrinkled in thought. "Who did that portrait of Jefferson? The one in his early forties?"

I lifted my brows. Entertaining the idea that it could be Martha Jefferson now, were we? He ignored my look.

I answered, "Mather Brown. He was an American, but he operated out of England, mostly. It was painted while Jefferson was visiting London in 1786. Martha Jefferson was already deceased by then."

"Never mind, then." We both studied her for another long moment.

"What we *need* is fresh eyes," I said. "Someone who could give us first impressions. With a bit of an outsider's insight—"

"What you would like, is for me to take it to Williamsburg, or Monticello—"

I held up my hands. "I deserve no such accusations! I had someone particular in mind."

He regarded me suspiciously.

"Enid."

"No."

I levelled a look at him. "That was a very quick response."

"I don't know why it would be anything else," he replied, standing, which displeased Chester, who had just been settling in for a nap. He dusted off his hands in quick motions. "When she is not propounding speculation of my inability to satisfy my ex-wife, she is reflecting on her regret that she never railed my father! Why on earth would I willingly invite her here?"

I gave a valiant effort not to laugh, but I was unsuccessful.

He sent me a look.

"Well, she is going to come anyway," I said. "Wasn't she trying to get you to do her taxes?" She had been texting him on the subject recently. And often.

His forehead was in his hand, and he didn't answer.

"She is the only person you seem willing to allow in on the secret of the portrait. She has not been staring at it for weeks on end. *And* she worked in a portrait gallery."

He lifted his head, leveling a stare at me. I knew I had him. My logic was often unimpeachable. And when I presented it thus, how could he say *no*? He looked like he was deliberating it, however. In fairness, she did tread on territory no aunt should tread. On the other hand, there was never a dull moment in her presence.

"Just remember you asked for this," he said gruffly.

And I smelled victory.

ELEVEN

"When angry, count ten before you speak;
if very angry, an hundred."
-*Thomas Jefferson*

"I imagine her as a woman who was very satisfied with her coital experience."

Enid stood in front of the portrait, which she had insisted we mount on an easel in the large, grand foyer. In her hand was a requisite glass of wine. Beside her was her nephew, already growing annoyed.

"That was not the question."

She looked at Samuel innocently. "Oh, I'm sorry, dear, what *was* the question?"

"Dr. Apkarian asked you," he said, jaw rigid, "what you thought of her."

She lifted her brows. "That was my answer."

Since Samuel appeared to be on the verge of exploding, I rushed into the breach. "Do you think I have her placed right? Around 1772?"

Enid stepped forward, examining the frame and canvas closely.

"Oh, yes." She studied it some more. "American, obviously."

I glanced at Samuel. We had that right, then. He did not see me. He appeared to be exercising all the powers of forbearance within his personal toolbox.

"The fact of the matter is, she *could* be Martha Jefferson," Enid said finally. "There's nothing indicating to me that she *couldn't*. But of course, my dear," she added, looking at me, "I could stare at it for days on end and never know."

I sighed. "I know." But at least I had the opinion—of someone who knew—that I wasn't completely off the rails. I would probably go to my grave believing it was Martha Jefferson. But she was right: there was no way to verify that.

I TOOK Enid back to the living room, where we sat and enjoyed a comfortable chat while Samuel annoyedly did her taxes. She had brought in four three-ring binders, which appeared to be in a mess with papers stuffed here and there, falling out, and tucked sporadically.

She told me about her current younger boyfriend, and about their plans to visit France in the summer. I told her about my trip there with Bradley three years ago. It had been a working trip for him, in which he had visited a lab and met with some boards in Paris. I probably shouldn't have gone. I was stuck with the husband of one of his colleagues, who was more interested in sampling every variety of wine known to man than in a historical tour of one of the *most historic places in the world*.

This made her laugh. "He sounds very unromantic, your Bradley," she said. "Imagine going to France, only to tour a lab."

"In fairness, it was his job," I answered.

She flicked her wrist. "My dear, I understand *your* frustration, given your profession, but I won't be touring much history myself. I intend to sunbathe topless, visit the lavender fields of Provence, drink goat's milk right from the udder, and tour the wine country: Bordeaux, Burgundy, Champagne..."

I smiled. "That sounds lovely."

"It is finished." We both looked behind us at the desk where Samuel sat, pressing his palms to his eyes. "I am blind, I have a headache, and I have no perspective left on life, but we have saved you from tax evasion from another year."

"My dear, don't be so dramatic. It has never come to that."

He tossed her a look.

"Two or three tiny audits..." She stood, touching my cheek. Her pretty eyes met mine. "Goodbye, Maddie. Don't quit. You are a fighter. You'll discover who the lady is."

Samuel

HE WALKED her toward the door.

"Thank you," his aunt said. "Truly."

"You're welcome." He almost smiled.

Turning, Enid looked at him, tilting her head. "My dear, your mother wants very much to see you. If not that, then to speak with you."

His jaw tightened. "I've told you how I feel about this."

Her eyes settled upon his in a vaguely disconcerting way. "You don't get to choose your mother, Samuel."

"That's for damn sure."

Her gaze never wavered. "You were connected to her before you were born. You will be connected to her as long as she lives, and, I imagine, hereafter, too. It's not something from which you can continue to run. She will *always* be your mother."

If he maintained his silence, maybe she would cease trying. Because it was a conversation that was going nowhere. Of that she could be certain.

"Just speak to her."

In growing frustration, he asked, "Why does she want to talk to me?"

"She wants to explain why she left. She has her story, her justifications—not an excuse, but an explanation."

"If she wishes to tell me some fabrication about mistreatment from my father, I won't believe her and never will."

"Of course not. That is not her story."

"Then why does she want to talk to me?"

"She fears that her leaving will have been connected in your mind with Jenna running off to Thailand."

"You think?" he asked sarcastically.

She sighed. "Yes."

He looked away. He knew, despite every wish to the contrary, that she was about to go there.

"Well, if you won't talk to her, you'll talk to me... I believe in a once in a lifetime kind of love, Samuel. I don't mean that you can't fall in love more than once over your lifetime—of course not, that would be silly. But there is a difference. I've experienced it. I lost him, and it was my fault." To his surprise, her mask slipped for just a moment. "I watched you and Jenna over the course of...goodness, how long? Fourteen years? I am your aunt. Of course I did. The point is, dear, that I never thought *that* was what you and she shared. I give you credit for making a marriage work a long time, which is something I never could accomplish. But..." She studied his face. "I know you feel as though all of the romance has been drained out of you. And you married young, so you feel like you are very old now and your time has passed, but... that is nonsense. My dear, you are thirty-three years old. Your life has only just begun. I can promise you, there will be new adventures. Life. Love. And yes...*sex*." She smiled, reaching up to touch his face. "There is nothing about Jenna leaving that has anything to do with your mother leaving. She wanted me to say that. And you are going to need to remember that."

CHAPTER

TWELVE

> "Pleasure is always before us; but misfortune is at our side:
> while running after that, this arrests us."
> — *Thomas Jefferson*

There was a new article about me.

I woke up to this. My professor friend, Dr. Carroll, an old-style Liberal professor, had texted me to let me know. Judy, as I knew her, was a second-wave feminist who refused to wear a bra and whom I suspected to have supported slightly more drastic forms of social protests back in the 70's than she now discussed openly. She was loyal and brutally honest. And she had defended me like an unmovable fortress.

"They say you want people to die, or something," she said.

I got out of bed and went down to the library. I sat in front of the fireplace, an untouched cup of hot chocolate before me and a chocolate Lab at my side. Bracing myself, I brought my iPad to life. I tapped the link to the newspaper article she had sent me. Just the thought of something like that being said made my stomach churn. I loved people. All people. I blinked through the tears which were forming to read the headline. *"The Violence of Her Words: Dr. Apkarian and the Class She Represents."*

I read: *"Dr. Madeline Apkarian seems to be entirely ignorant of the fact that one person's words can do enormous damage to another. She refused to apologize even in the face of the universal outrage and emotional pain caused to students campus-wide at her university. She holds the banner of free speech as one might a sword, to ward off progress, and buries her head in the sand in the face of the very real truth that some people and their violent, detrimental philosophies* must *be silenced. This classes her among those who are beneficiaries of such privilege that they will never see the needs of others. This breeds violence. And violence must never be tolerated. This is what they mean when they say: 'Down with the patriarchy.'"*

I stared into the distance, running my hand over Chester's head absently, travelling back through time...

People marching on statues. A student body president asking that the statues on campus be left alone. A lone voice in defense of his right to say what he thought. A firestorm erupting... A Maoist struggle session... A conversation that rapidly declined into a mob...

Ambushed in my office by the school journalists, I was asked, as a historian, whether I agreed. I stated that while statues were complicated, I believed the president of the student body had a right to his opinions and to speak precisely as he wished. I said that nothing should be undertaken in haste or illegally. I then advocated in detail a plan for forums on campus to discuss the concerns of all, which no one ever quoted. I refused to budge from those positions; I was punished. And here we were.

"How can removing one of the few female history faculty bring down the patriarchy?" Judy demanded sardonically through rapid-fire texts. Before I could respond, she texted again, *"And wasn't your mother's ethnic group the victim of a GENOCIDE barely a hundred years ago? How can they say you are privileged?"*

She was then gone on a rant. I let her anger run its course

while I read the article. It was brutal. It seemed only to get worse after the opening salvo.

I didn't know what to say. There was nothing about the situation that Judy didn't know. She knew I was misquoted, half-quoted, excoriated, and lampooned six ways from Sunday. I still couldn't quite grasp what had happened, how it had gotten so out of control, and how it could lead to death threats and the destruction of my entire life.

I typed: "*I will never understand, Judy.*" I pressed "send," and the text whooshed away.

I sat for a moment. I heard a noise and looked over my shoulder. Samuel had stopped in the doorway and was looking at me.

I was pretty sure I looked haggard. He must think I was a basket case. I waited for a biting comment. It did not come. He held my eyes, looking like he didn't know what to say or do, his expression a bit helpless.

Which was even more embarrassing. He knew.

I cleared my throat and attempted to smile wryly. "Guess I'll get back to work."

I looked away, and felt him watch me for a moment.

Finally, he departed.

* * *

Samuel

HE SAT at his desk in the darkened room, the iMac's light glowing. After glancing once at the door, he pulled up articles from a few months ago about Maddie.

They were less-than-favorable. *Brutal*.

There were pictures of her and Bradley McCarthy (also employed by the university as a research scientist) going into their apartment amidst camera flashes and film rolling. They were in coats—this would have been in November. In the first ones, the boyfriend looked protective and angry. Later, stressed. And at last, numb.

And Maddie...like a shell of a human, with hollow eyes.

———

MY MIND WANDERED that night as I lay trying to go to sleep. It wasn't a terror-ridden drama cycle, but more of a recapitulation.

The ostracism still chafed. Why did it hit me so hard?

I had just wanted security. A safe place. A place to be useful. To use my mind. Being human, I had wanted love, I suppose, though you never thought of that until you profoundly didn't have it. And wanting to be loved, to belong, was universal. To be excommunicated surely was one of the most difficult things with which the soul ever could wrestle.

I knew, too, that it hit me hard for personal reasons. My depression was situational. I was at greater risk for it, Marla said, because I had suffered from depression as a child. That meant I had to stay proactive at prevention. It also meant that when life became a shitstorm, sometimes I just would not be well.

The thing is, I am very strong. Most people with depression are, I think. You'd have to be. It's a dark hole. It's unfounded panic that feels so real. It's unhappiness. It's unworthiness. It's feeling like your stomach is about to fall out of your butt, and I know that is inelegant, but I don't know how else to describe it. You feel like you're rotten. Messed up. Like you mess everyone else up. You feel fragile. Susceptible. Dark. Physically sick. Like you're spiraling, and you're scared.

I suffer.

But I get through it.

As I laid in my bed, afraid to try to go to sleep, I acknowledged that I was not through it yet. And I told myself that was okay. You always had to tell yourself your life would be better. *No* part of your brain believed that during depression, but you grasped it existentially. Like the tenderest thread tethering you to something solid, preventing you from being lost in outer space.

And you finally drifted off to sleep, eyes swollen from tears, and rested for two hours. Until you had a dream that came from the tortured pits of hell. Someone you loved was dying. Or you were going to be buried alive. Or someone in Boston was going to prove, somehow, inarguably, that you were unworthy to breathe the same air as the moral people.

And then you went back to sleep, woke up with a stuffy nose, sinus pressure, weighted limbs, and exhaustion. At least, I did today.

Most every day, no one knew I was dying inside. I literally could perform as well as your average circus monkey. High functioning. But just occasionally, I couldn't even get out of bed.

It all started the moment you woke up: the chest pounding, the remembrances of everything that you're homed in on to feed your anxiety, and the *fear*. You might think, having lost everything, the fear would have receded. I literally—thank you, Franklin Delano—had nothing to fear but fear itself.

But fear itself was a terrible thing.

I comforted myself, wrapped my arms around myself like someone was hugging me and reminded myself that I was profoundly loved.

By lunchtime, I was able to move. Small victories? My therapist would say so, but I highly suspected Marla wasn't quite the over-achiever that I was. In fairness, few people were.

I rose and put on my clothes, pulled on my sweater... My skin was tender. I tried to be gentle. I tried not to make sudden movements because I felt like I might, you know, physically implode. Which would, of course, be considerably more embarrassing than being caught naked in the bathroom with the door open.

I smiled. There was always something to smile about. Always

humor. If that didn't prove there was a God... And then, for whatever reason, I couldn't stop smiling. There was joy even in depression. I pictured that scene, and I couldn't help but laugh. Even though I teared up moments later, and it receded...God had shown me a glimmer of light. That was how you kept the faith. How you knew you would, somehow, feel alive again.

I WENT GINGERLY DOWNSTAIRS.

I ambled to the kitchen because I knew I needed to eat something, not because I wanted to. I was queasy, actually, but that would pass. It always did.

Going through the door, I saw Samuel standing near the counter. I said, not making eye contact, "Hey."

"Hey," he said gently. Incredibly gently.

I looked up. His eyes met mine, held, then his lips parted as though to speak, but he didn't, and finally he just said again, "Hey."

Then I figured he must be wondering why I hadn't done anything all day. "Sorry I didn't work this morning," I said.

"That's okay," he answered, and I could feel his eyes on my back as I retrieved the oatmeal.

"I was...feeling a little bad. A migraine." That was always a good excuse. I *had* had a migraine.

A pause. I glanced at him. Found his eyes on me. He was too smart to buy it. I looked away, putting the pot on to boil. "Is it lunchtime already?" I asked.

"Yeah, um...in an hour or so."

I glanced around. The kitchen was spotless. It certainly hadn't been last night. I looked at Samuel. Invariably, within an hour of being at work in the cellars, his sleeves were rolled up or shoved up forcefully. Not today.

I met his eyes. Was he... Had he been worried about me? Had he stayed up here all morning? I studied him.

He looked away, turning to pick up a rag and wipe a nearby portion of counter. "Kitchen was a wreck," he said.

"Yeah, we've just kind of been slinging stuff," I said. "Sorry about that."

"No, that's fine," he said quickly. "Not your fault."

I almost smiled. My oatmeal finished, I sat on one of the barstools. He sat next to me.

I ate, glancing at him out of the corner of my eye, unsure of what to make of this unprecedented behavior. The silence was thick, but this was Samuel: he wasn't going to say anything.

I started to speak just as he did. He gestured, "Go ahead."

Then I couldn't remember what I was going to say. The air grew ever more awkward. "Um, how are the sheep?"

A pause. His brows rose infinitesimally. "They are well."

"Have you always raised sheep?"

"No."

Ah. That topic was finished, it would seem.

My skin was starting to feel less tender, very slowly. I had burned my tongue from lack of sensation there, if that didn't seem wholly unfair. Ah, well. Who needed taste buds?

I looked at Samuel, who was looking at me with concern. I couldn't believe it. It was genuine, and suddenly, I felt sensation in my *feet*, as well as my tongue and other places. *Whoa, Nelly*.

I felt warm. I swallowed. I could feel him still looking at me.

My oatmeal had long since proven uninteresting, so I looked up. I cleared my throat.

"Would you like to help me with the sheep while the soup cooks?" Samuel asked.

I smiled. I have no idea why that made me blush. "Yes. Of course."

I knew he valued peace and quiet, aloneness, and privacy. But he wanted me within his sight. As we walked outside in the waning sunshine, it felt good to be outside. Spring was just about upon us, with a chill still lingering but the first bold spring flowers making an appearance.

Samuel did that thing again when we were crossing over a rough patch of land, where he took my hand without fuss or ceremony, just efficiency. We walked across the pasture. For that brief moment that I felt the pressure of human touch, I let myself imagine what it would be like to have support. Of the romantic, relational kind. That was something I didn't let myself imagine much, if ever, since Bradley.

I had become completely self-dependent. Internally corrective and restorative. I knew other humans could be a support, and that God designed us to help each other along. But for whatever reason, He had taken that away from me along with everything else. Someday I would know why. Or maybe I wouldn't. And that would have to be okay.

We walked on. Once we were through the ankle-turning territory of holes and limbs and Samuel had helped me through the fence, he seemed ready to give me back possession of my hand. I crossed my arms against the chill.

As I looked up, I saw sheep.

They dotted the land before me as elegantly as any English pastoral scene. I smiled. They were adorable.

Samuel told me about them—their breed, that the lambs were arriving now that it was late February, and how his eccentric dad had introduced them to the property to give it an English country estate feel. And because the kids loved them when they hosted schools on the grounds. There was a local man, apparently, who looked after them when Samuel had to be away in Charlottesville.

"I imagine they're a lot of work," I said, smiling at one which had come near and extended its sweet face up toward me. "Oh, my goodness," I said, outspreading my gloved hands to its wool.

I saw genuine pleasure in his eyes as Samuel likewise patted the friendly sheep.

"I'll let you and her commune while I feed," he said. "I warn you, she'll probably desert you the minute she gets a whiff of the feed."

"I'll help," I said, rising to my full height and dusting off my gloves.

"The bags are kind of heavy," he warned.

"That's fine. Show me what to do."

I followed him into the barn, where he opened an area that was padlocked against hungry sheep (and possibly coyotes). Side-stepping the tractor, he dragged out the feed. I picked up a bag—and geez, he wasn't kidding about the weight. Feigning indifference, I helped him fill the troughs. We also checked their water and refilled the bins. He gave shots to a couple of ewes who appeared to be feeling a bit under the weather, and while he accomplished this, I soaked up more sheep sociability.

Somewhere along the way, I became aware of the fact that I hadn't had a suggestion of anxiety while I was out here. I felt relaxed. A sheep butted Samuel with its head, and I laughed. He turned to look at me, smiling.

"She's a little mean," he said.

"I think she was just putting you in your place," I replied, as he looked my way.

A smile played about his lips.

THE SOUP from lunch heated up nicely for supper. I ladled it into bowls from the stove. Then I placed the ceramic dishes on the counter, sliding them in front of the stools. I glanced at Samuel, who was sitting down.

I joined him, and then, cutting my eyes over to him, I said, "I...um...have situational depression." I added moderately, "Not often, but...every now and then. And when it comes, it's for an extended period, but it always passes."

"I know." In the face of my surprise, he added, "I remember."

My lips parted. I had totally forgotten that I had told him. Must have stuffed that away in the File of Great Regrets. I hadn't even told Jessie until two years ago, when my grandma had died. I had *never* told my grandmother. Or Bradley.

Why had I done that? *Because we were talking, and it was easy like breathing, and it had felt like telling yourself.* Okay, then. Marla told me not to undermine my decisions based on *succeeding* emotions and facts, so we were just going to tuck that away and move on.

"The thing about what you've been through..." he said. "It was a situation." He looked grim. "There was a cause. And it leads to things."

I studied him in profile. "Like sabbaticals?" I asked, very gently.

He looked over at me, green eyes meeting mine. "I didn't necessarily handle things well," he admitted.

"None of us can, not all the time," I replied softly.

He nodded.

I took a breath. And I asked him something I had been wanting to ask him. "Level with me, Samuel. Do you think what I did was completely crazy?"

There was a long silence. I cringed. The thing about asking Samuel was: you had better be ready for the answer.

"Do you want to know what I think, Maddie?" he asked, sounding like he had a fire in him. "I think you're brave. You stood up for that kid and defended his right to say whatever he wanted to say, and more power to you, because the last time I checked, freedom of speech is a *right*. Without it, you have nothing. Not that that's something those close-minded witch hunters who wanted to bury you could ever envision. And you stuck to your guns in the face of overwhelming cruelty. Do you know how few people would do that?"

I blinked. Swallowed. Thought I might cry.

"I hadn't known where you stood," I said, throat a bit constricted. I tried not to show it. I had thought there was probably a little judgment; or maybe that he was too caught up in his own troubles to care. Apparently not.

"I'm...ornery, but I know what's right."

It could be his epitaph. Which is why I had always wondered... What had made him do exactly the *wrong* thing all those years ago? What had compelled him? What could make this man, whom I had known even then to have a finely tuned moral compass, leave me stranded with no help? And why the heck did it still nag me like a rock in my shoe?

I sat for a long time. Then I nodded once silently.

SOMETIMES WHEN I WOKE UP, I thought I was still in Boston. I felt the coolness of the breeze even off the closed window, making the curtain brush aside, and I could imagine I was in my historic apartment. Old brick buildings. Cobblestone streets. American flags hanging ideally beside freshly painted doors. Picturesque sidewalks where I had walked my dog.

A long way from Alabama.

Boston represented a lot. Grown-up girl's dreams breathed into life by a little girl. Having arrived. Security forever.

I was wondering occasionally here lately why that had been so important to me. The picture was pretty. Pretty girl in pretty clothes. Austere office and expansive lecture halls. Published articles and fine awards. The best dog leash. The right brand of wellies and coat.

It had been a paper tiger, a false illusion, a gold-flaked figurine. A castle in the sky which had been brought down by an argument over campus statues. Or by my insistence on the right to have the argument itself.

I felt another gust of wind.

By now I knew I was in Virginia.

I could hear birds in the distance. Not the charming kind. The howling, screeching, rural kind. A far cry from Boston.

And yet...

And yet.

THIRTEEN

"I had rather be shut up in a very modest cottage with my books, my family and a few old friends, dining on simple bacon, and letting the world roll on as it liked, than to occupy the most splendid post, which any human power can give."
— *Thomas Jefferson*

I drew on my cardigan, tucking it against the drafts in the house. The old floor creaked as I searched for Samuel. I hadn't found him in any of his usual haunts, and I was down to the really old part of the house. I ran him to ground in the massive, soaring old library, which was kept in pristine condition. He was obviously doing some maintenance on some of the trim work, and he looked up as I stood in the doorway.

"I'm going to take a few days off," I said.

He didn't say anything, just looked at me, not precisely expressionlessly.

I tucked a strand of hair that had fallen loose from my messy bun behind my ear. "I'm going to Alabama."

He rose to his full height, eyes searching my face. "You're leaving?"

"My friend Jessie called, and we were talking... I'm fine financially, but if I'm going to be out of work for much longer, I would be more comfortable if I could replenish my nest egg." I cleared my throat. "She's been trying for years to get me to go down and put my grandma's house on the market." I shrugged, not mentioning that I had avoided that. Avoided going through the memories, some of them difficult, some precious. Avoided *going back* at all. I said simply, "It seems like now is the best time."

He looked, for once, like he didn't know what to say. He studied me. At last, he nodded slowly.

"I'll be gone a few days, but I'll get back to work as soon as I return," I said.

He swiped some dust from a nearby windowsill. "When are you heading out?"

"Tomorrow morning."

He looked up. "Do you need a ride to the airport?"

"Oh, I..." I hesitated. "I have a cab coming." I hadn't considered that option. As he held my eyes, I don't know... I wondered if maybe I should have.

He nodded, going back to his work. "Safe travels."

———

I TOUCHED down in Montgomery at eight in the morning. Most of the airport shops were opening up, and, following a heavenly scent, I may have had a Cinnabon before stepping outside and collecting my rental car. And I may have enjoyed it. I walked along to the car rentals and spoke with the representative. Once the registration was finished, I took a deep breath.

Okay.

I drove south for about thirty minutes before everything began looking rural—wide, open fields, some of them sown with green winter wheat, some instead laying barren and awaiting the spring. There was the occasional house here, cattle and horses sprinkled in fields, and sometimes just thick woods. Exiting off the Interstate, I drove for thirty more minutes on a highway through more sprawling, vacant farmland.

Not so different from Virginia. Except the Tidewater region tended to be swampy, and this didn't. I came upon a small town I knew well and passed through the few traffic lights until I was outside the city limits.

I drove by memory toward Mulberry Lane. Passing several house trailers and broken-down bungalows, I felt numb. I had wanted to be alone, unsure of what my reaction would be once I saw my grandmother's small farm again.

I went on for a mile down the lane until I saw the white cottage of my childhood. My father's mobile home had been removed at some point. Parking, I stared for a minute before getting out and shutting my door.

Dried up leaves crunched beneath my riding boots, and a cool breeze brushed my face. I took stock. The porch was sagging, but the roof and actual structure looked sound. I had paid one of my grandma's neighbors to keep the yard semi-tidy and his wife to check on the house and keep things functional. But I hadn't been back since my grandma's funeral.

I remembered coming here long ago, that first day, to live. The woman had scared the living daylights out of me. But not for long. She didn't say all of the right things, didn't make me feel welcome, but I soon learned that her bark was worse than her bite. She was there, she took care of me, and no one else was or did. She knew I was smart and pushed me hard in school. I swiped a tear and went to the door, carefully navigating the porch and placing my key in the lock.

The handle was cool beneath my hand. I remembered the door so well. Old fall leaves rustled and scattered on the porch in the wind. I was frozen. Suddenly, I stepped back, glancing back up at the house for a long minute. Then I turned away and walked back toward my car.

Not today. Tomorrow was another day.

I PULLED up at Jessie's perfectly kept farmhouse. The gravel was new, the white house freshly painted, the porch swept bare for winter, and the fences tidy. It was a breath of fresh air. I stood and got Mavis out of the back, placing her on the ground and extending the suitcase handle.

"Oh, my gosh, it's Yankee Doodle!" Jessie exclaimed from the porch, the door flapping shut behind her.

Grinning, I said, "Don't call me that!"

"Well, get on up here!" she exclaimed.

She was wiping her eyes as I went up the steps, and she embraced me in a crushing hug. We held each other for a long moment. Jessie was just like I had remembered her; she hadn't changed a bit. She was in overalls, her blonde hair springing wildly. Joy and confidence still radiated from her. "You look skinny," she said. "*Skin* and *bone*. What would your grandma say? Never mind, come on in! I'll fatten you up." Then she dragged me into the house, hefting my bag and then slamming it down on her hardwood.

I looked around. Everything smelled like Pine-Sol and vinegar.

"I've been cleaning for your arrival," she said. "Everything around here had just about gone to the dogs."

"Jessie, this is beautiful," I said, looking at her old staircase, whitewashed walls, and cozy furnishings. The kitchen was huge and nice, albeit decorated with every farm animal known to man. Cows were everywhere.

I smiled. Jessie had done well for herself, and I was proud of her.

Before long, we were sitting on her big sofa with hot chocolate and cozy blankets, catching up, talking a mile a minute. We steered away from the university drama, focusing on my trip to Virginia, my current accommodations, and my flight here.

I told her eventually that I had gone to my grandma's house but hadn't gone in. I dragged my fingers through my hair. "I don't know what I'm going to do. She had so much stuff."

"Here's what we're going to do," Jessie said with a can-do attitude. "We'll go get out everything you want to keep and put it in storage in my barn. And we'll sell the rest of it at the auction."

I nodded, sighing with relief. "Yeah. Okay. I've got to get a realtor."

"You'll go with Dan Bailey. He'll take care of you."

My father's friend. I looked up at her, lifting my eyebrows. "Isn't he big-time now? Do you think he'll even have time to fit me in?"

"He'd do anything for you," she answered.

The next morning, Jessie made me a huge Southern breakfast, of which I could only eat roughly a quarter, and then we climbed into her truck and drove into town. It was a bit like an out-of-body experience, being back. The town square hadn't altered a lot, except a few of the businesses had changed hands, while others with the same owners had been renovated.

Bailey Realty and Auction was one of the latter, the brick store front freshly painted a charming dark gray, while the sides were left in the original brick. The awnings were crisp. As we opened the door, a bell rang, and a friendly secretary led us back to a nice office.

Standing, Mr. Bailey beamed. He hugged me and then put his hands on my shoulders. "You look like your father. Your mother, too, but I see him. He'd be so proud of you." I wondered if he knew the whole recent, sordid story of my downfall, but I thanked him. He had been there for me in a lot of ways after my father had died.

I knew my dad must have been a good friend once upon a time to have inspired such loyalty, hard as it was to picture.

Somehow I was able to envision, looking around me at what Mr. Bailey had built for himself, a different route for my dad, a life he would never have. And that was incredibly...difficult.

"Your grandma's old place? Oh, sure!" he was saying. "We'll get everything set up. You were her only heir, weren't you?"

"I was," I answered. "Mr. Robertson was the attorney; he should have all of the documents. Thanks, Mr. Bailey."

"Well, of course, hon," he answered, just about making me tear up.

Leaving there, we walked down the street to a coffee shop. This was one of the new businesses, and I admired its chic interior design as we stepped through the tinkling door. We ordered and then sat at a little round table.

I looked across from myself at Jessie. "Tell me about Dale," I said.

"I think this one's finally going to stick," she responded inelegantly, but with such a smile that I knew it must be one of those relationships that was different. The kind in which you knew from the very beginning.

"I want to meet him," I said.

She said that it could be arranged, mentioning having him over for supper.

"Jessie! Maddie!" the barista called out, sliding our cups across the granite counter. I leaned behind me and collected them, taking the top off mine to allow it to cool a bit. It was a frosty day outside, so I put my hands around the cup to warm them.

"Is there anything better than when a relationship just *fits*?" Jessie mused.

"No," I answered. "There isn't."

She studied me. "Do you ever talk to Bradley?"

"I don't."

"Hmm," she said.

After we had sipped all of our coffee, we drove back out to my grandma's cottage. Jessie steamed through the necessities like a freight train, leaving me no time for memories or sadness or nostalgia. Thank goodness.

"Don't forget the drawers!" she called from a different room. "Got to make sure there's nothing special tucked away."

"Okay!" I responded, dreading to think what could be in the drawers. Probably a mouse nest.

"And the closets! There could be stuff in the closets."

"Got it!" I called, smiling a bit.

In the end, we retrieved a few pieces of small furniture and a couple of tubs of stuff, which Jessie hefted up into her truck without waiting for my help. She said she would keep the items until I figured out where I was going next, when I could combine it with my belongings from my storage unit in Boston. The rest—whatever we left—would be prepared by Dan Bailey's employees for the auction. I just needed to leave the key for him, he had said.

I don't know why it felt like I was losing the last thing I had, the last connection to home and to a family. I hadn't needed the house or any of the stuff in it during my adult life. Still, it was something to have roots.

But not everything in life could be retained forever.

Locking up, we headed back to Jessie's farm.

Samuel

THE MORNING LIGHT slanted through the old windows of the kitchen. He ate cereal, staring into the distance.

The house was quiet. He could hear a few winter birds singing outside. The refrigerator cut on, humming as it warmed to life. Somewhere behind him, one of the clocks *tick-tocked*, giving a low chime every fifteen minutes. In the distance, the dehumidifiers turned on and off.

Nails clicked on the brick flooring, and he turned his head to see Chester entering the kitchen from the laundry room, a beige house shoe in his mouth.

Getting up, he went to the dog, kneeling beside him and saying, "That's Maddie's." He patted Chester, who looked a bit forlorn, and he eased the slipper from his jaw.

He rubbed the dog's ears, tilting his head as he looked at him. "Let's go for a walk."

"He's divorced now, isn't he?"

I looked up from my perch on Jessie's couch, where I was surrounded by throw pillows, wrapped in a blanket, and reading a slightly-more-than-steamy romance that Jessie had left on my nightstand.

I blinked. "Samuel Hayden? Yeah."

"Interesting." She was sitting there in fuzzy pink pajamas and slippers, typing away. "When is his birthday?"

I frowned at her. "December 17th." I wasn't sure how I knew that. Gosh, surely not from college?

"Of what year?"

"Same as us."

"Hmm. So how's the research going?" She continued typing away.

I sighed. "Frustrating." I told her about the portrait, knowing its owner wouldn't mind me saying the simple fact that we had found one. I also told her about how we couldn't find who she was.

"That *sounds* frustrating!" she commiserated, letting me talk on.

"It's just so odd for there to be a portrait of that quality shut away in an attic, nameless, with seemingly no tie to the house, you know?"

"Uh huh, uh huh. Do you happen to know his social?"

My eyes widened. "Jessie! Are you doing a *background check* on him?" I sat up.

"Don't worry about it," she said calmly. "Keep talking."

"Jessie!"

"Never mind, I've found him." Her eyes scanned the screen. "He's clean," she said, looking up with a satisfied smile.

"I could have told you that!" I exclaimed. "What on earth...?"

"Well, you are living with the man—"

"Not in that way; I've *told* you that!"

She returned to her laptop. "I'm on his Facebook now."

I whipped her laptop off her, snapping it shut and retaining possession of it.

Giving me a placating look, she said, "All right. Fine."

I held her eyes. She must have sensed the level of *I-don't-want-to-talk-about-it* that I was feeling.

After a moment, she said, "Well, it's as plain as anything that there's something you aren't telling me about this portrait, so spill it!"

I held her eyes for a moment. Then I sighed. "All right. You have to promise not to tell anyone."

"You think anybody I see cares about some ancient portrait up in Virginia? You think I'm going to blab to a bunch of academics?"

"No," I agreed. I paused. I studied her. "We think it may be Thomas Jefferson's wife."

Her eyes widened. "No kidding! Tell me!"

I briefly explained my theory, and she listened closely. "Well, how do you prove it?" she asked.

"Well, I'm not going to find a document stating: 'that portrait in the attic at Hayden's Ridge is Martha Jefferson.' So we'll have to look at context clues. Let's say she was Martha Jefferson. Does she look like any of the portraits of Jefferson's eldest daughter?" I pulled up a picture of Patsy Jefferson Randolph on my phone and showed Jessie. "No. She was a female clone of her father. Patsy did have red hair, like the lady in our portrait, but then, so did Jefferson. It would stand to reason she would be more likely to have had red hair if both of her parents did, but that isn't conclusive evidence to say this woman was her mother."

"I see your problem. Any other family members we could compare her to?"

"Her daughter, Maria, was often said to favor her more. But I can't find a portrait of her. She died in her early twenties." I looked at the portrait of the auburn-haired beauty again. If she *was* Jefferson's wife, she was Sally Hemings's half-sister. I could try to trace a likeness between them, but we don't have any portraits of Sally either.

"I always forget that they were sisters. How do you think *that* worked?"

"Well, in succession. Sally was a just child when her sister died."

Apparently growing deeply immersed in the fascination that was history, Jessie asked, "What do you think about all of that? I mean, he owned her." It was a question that I got from my students all the time, so I wasn't unprepared for it.

"Well, most posit that there was no way for an enslaved woman to have had a consensual relationship with a white man, especially an owner, because of the power deferential. Quite literally, under the law, she could not say *no*. Of course, there are problems with the theory. Enslaved women were grown women with mental agency. To say there were no differences between situations in which enslaved women were violently forced into relationships and those in which they made a decision to enter them is to put enslaved women in the position of people without capacity. Or that's a competing opinion in the scholarship, at least."

"Well, did she? Make the decision to enter the relationship?"

"In Hemings's case, she was in Paris with Jefferson when she first became pregnant by him. Under French law, slavery was illegal, and anyone who applied for freedom there received it. Sally knew this and toyed with the option of taking her freedom and remaining in France. According to their middle son, Madison, Jefferson made her promises regarding their future children's freedom. In the end, she decided to return to Virginia with him."

"Well, there you go, I guess."

"Well..." I tilted my head. "After that, of course, she couldn't have left if she had wanted to. Not if *he* didn't want her to. We don't know whether she did or did not."

"What do *you* think?" Jessie asked, lifting her brows.

"I think all women, but especially enslaved women, were treated abominably under the law. I think she didn't have a wide array of options."

"Well, that's true." She took a deep sigh after the heaviness of the topic. Then she said, "All of this is kind of depressing, hon. You sure you want to live knee deep in history every day?"

"Very sure."

She looked across at me with a wistful smile. "Will you teach again?" she asked.

"I honestly don't know if that will be an option."

She nodded. "Well. I've worked up an appetite. Lasagna."

I MET Dale when he arrived for dinner that night. I watched him closely as he interacted with Jessie, my guard up. Maybe I had become leery of men. *Check it back a notch, Maddie*, I instructed myself. I smiled, extending my hand.

He was nervous, red-faced, whipping his hat off, and speaking a bit jumbly. I took that as a good sign. He wanted to please the people who loved Jessie.

"Yes, *Dale*, she's pretty," Jessie said, increasing his embarrassment tenfold.

His eyes widened.

"Jessie! Don't put words into his mouth, for heaven's sake," I exclaimed.

"So you're from Massachusetts?" he asked, swallowing.

"No, she's from here," Jessie responded, eyes wide with exasperation. He flushed again.

"I am most recently from Massachusetts," I cut in, flashing Jessie another look. I caught a gleam in her eyes that told me she was being a devil on purpose.

Jessie shepherded him into the living room while we finished up the meal. "He told me he doesn't know what to say to a professor," Jessie said while I sliced an onion.

I shook my head, unsure of what to say to that. "It would help a lot if you would stop tormenting him!" I hissed.

We settled to eat and, as she did indeed cease to torment Dale, conversation progressed into a smooth rhythm. I enjoyed watching them together, the fun, the love, and the respect. It was heartening.

While they were off on an argument of their own, I heard my phone *ping*. Since they were engrossed, I figured it wouldn't be rude to glance at it. The message badge on my phone read: *Samuel*. I reached for it quickly and slid my thumb to open and read it.

Where is the milk?

I narrowed my eyes, pressing my lips together.

Glancing up at the lovebirds, who were still squabbling, I typed out: *I may have left it in the small fridge with the drinks*.

So typical.

Ten minutes later, another *ping*. I looked down quickly.

And the bread? I can't find anything.

If he had said it aloud, it would have been in the same tone he had used when he told me there was no way I could stay at his house. Annoyance.

I relished typing out: *There is no bread.*

Okay.

"But I do think that hitch will work, hon," I heard Jessie say in the background.

"Well, but the last time there was a coupler misalignment," her love responded.

As I was watching my phone, I saw the three bubbles that indicated typing appear and linger for several minutes. I glanced at it every few seconds. Just when I thought another text would appear, the bubbles went away.

"There was nothing in the world wrong with that hitch. Maddie, what are you doing?"

I looked up guiltily, clicking my phone off. "Nothing at all." I smiled.

"Cobbler?" she asked, getting up.

"I'll help," I answered, rising also.

I HUGGED JESSIE.

"Well, the ball is in motion, and you are set to make a couple hundred thousand," she said. "Dan Bailey will see to it soon."

I studied her. "Am I doing the right thing, Jess?" I asked softly.

"Selling your grandma's house?"

I nodded.

"Time marches on, hon," she said. "She's not there anymore. You carry your past right there in your heart, and nowhere else."

I nodded and hugged her again before climbing into my rental. I couldn't weep now, even if my throat felt tight and my eyes burned. Mavis was safely stowed into the back of the car, and I had a plane to catch.

"Thanks for everything," I said.

"Hon, I've had a blast. Be careful, now. And you call me when you get to Richmond!"

I SHUT the door on my cab, the pebbles crunching beneath my boots.

The day was moody and gray, the temperature chilly. Standing, I surveyed Hayden's Ridge with fresh eyes. What an absolute treasure to still be standing. And what a tragedy that it shouldn't be open to the public.

Turning, I extended the handle on my suitcase just before catching the *yip* of an excited dog. I looked back around to see Chester Arthur bounding out the door and running straight for me.

I knelt and let him lick my face. Laughing, I rubbed his head with gratefulness. Quite the welcome! I lifted my eyes to see his owner standing in the doorway, smiling a bit.

CHAPTER

FOURTEEN

"I am a woman. And society says, 'Thus far and no further [shall]
thou come'—Why then has nature given me a mind
so active and enquiring?"
— *Margaret Bayard Smith*

"How was your trip?"
I looked up from my stool in the kitchen. *Well, knock me down with a feather*. Was Samuel Hayden making small talk? I lifted my eyebrows. "Very nice." I watched him, waiting for him to elaborate.

He didn't. Rather like those three bubbles on text.

He went to get the stuff for a sandwich instead. He sighed. "There is still no bread."

I held up my hands. "I arrived yesterday."

He glanced at me, lips pressed together. But he did go into town later. I stayed and catalogued, Dr. Hayden's canine companion staying close. Whatever academia thought, Chester Arthur Hayden, at least, thought I was fantastic. Granted, he was a little annoying as he assisted me, but what he lacked in social graces, he made up for in genial warmth. At some point, I gathered a box and took it into the library so he could lie on the rug in front of the fireplace.

Perhaps chronologizing letters was something for which I was a bit overtrained, but someone had to do it, Samuel had deemed that it would be me, and it *was* generally cathartic. There was a rhythm and a calmness to the pattern of work.

I read the letters a little as I went, sometimes wishing I could travel through time to learn the things between the lines, the things that weren't said. For instance, did the formal language sometimes indicate naiveté or instead mask reticence and a world of secrets? Thinking of the letter that was scanned into Samuel's computer—*No one will ever know*—and the portrait tucked away for centuries in the attic, I suspected the latter.

I was drawn from my thoughts when, much later, I heard the house's other resident walk down the hall. Samuel stopped at the doorway of the library. Seeing us, he said in his typical irritable tone, "Chester has transferred his affections."

Drawing my mind to the present, I scoffed. I remembered countless times when the dog had been sitting with me peacefully and, upon hearing Samuel's car in the driveway, abandoned me completely and ran towards the door. "Clearly he has not," I retorted dryly.

Samuel forbore to respond. He was in a bad mood, likely annoyed again by my presence. I was, after all, here against his will and better judgment.

I set my letters down, drawing my protective gloves off. "While you're here... Do you have your aunt's DNA results in yet?"

"I received a notification that I should receive them tomorrow," he responded. "Will that be soon enough for you?" he asked with withering politeness.

I tossed him a look. Moving the box of letters, I shifted so that Chester's paw wasn't pressing into me. It *was* unfortunate, I reflected, that he had come to cuddle with me just as Samuel had returned. I took the opportunity to pat the pup, missing my own.

"Did you get the groceries?"

"Yeah," he answered.

He glanced at me. Our eyes met for a moment.

There was a long silence.

The fireplace crackled.

After a hesitation, he seemed to decide to linger, asking, "Did you ever get *your* results? It seems like it's been forever." Was he starting a conversation? I blinked, again surprised. He came to sit by me (I couldn't believe it), and...he smelled very nice. What had he asked? Oh, yes – the ancestry.

I glanced at him.

I'd had to resend my sample after ruining the stabilizer by trying to use it on Samuel. I did not report this, however. I said, "Mine was delayed, but yes, I got it." I stroked Chester's head.

"Any surprises?"

"Half Armenia, half Alabama," I answered. "Just as expected."

I was surprised to see genuine humor leap to his eyes. I hadn't seen that since... Well, college.

"You liked that, didn't you?" I asked, flaunting my comedic skills.

He nodded, looking at me.

After a moment, he asked, "*Apkarian* is your mother's name?"

I nodded. "Yes." I picked back up my cup, enjoying its warmth between my hands. Well, if we were going to be cozy... At this distance from civilization, I wasn't going to pass up an opportunity if someone would talk to me. I shared, "My father was in the military, and she was in school, and they met and... They never married, so I wasn't allowed to take his last name on my birth certificate. Anyway, they split up when I was three."

I had told Samuel a long time ago that I was from Alabama, but not a lot more. He stayed, looking at me, so I continued. "I lived with my mom then. She died of ovarian cancer when I was five. So young. Younger than I am now. My dad came and flew me back to Alabama. He'd struggled with addiction since he had left the military. He never had the help he needed." I swallowed. "They took me away from him when I was ten. My grandma got custody. She had a small farm, and she had to take care of both of us and the whole operation. He died of an overdose when I was thirteen." I could feel Samuel's eyes searching my face. The pain I felt when I talked about my father was acute. He had loved me, but he had loved his drugs more. He had wanted me, but he was a victim of his addiction. A victim who had chosen it every day.

"His name was Jonathan Andrews. He was very handsome," I said, reaching for my phone. The slightly brown-tinted photo I brought up showed him in his Airforce dress uniform, his golden blonde hair peeking beneath his cap. I moved my thumb right. "This is the three of us when I was two in Berlin," I said.

The corner of Samuel's mouth twitched just a bit. "You were giving them a run for their money."

I was. My mother was trying her best to hold onto me, and my father was reaching toward me to try to help. "'Trouble with a capital T,' as my grandmother always said," I replied.

He grew silent. Contemplative. I felt his eyes sweep over my face. Felt goosebumps. "It's amazing what you've accomplished, Maddie," he said finally, softly.

"It's because of my grandma," I replied.

"You were in child protective services, and you went on to teach at a Tier 1 university." His jaw clenched once, but tightly.

"Yeah," I answered softly. There wasn't really anything else to say.

I STARED at the eighteenth-century lady, sitting on my bottom in front of her. I didn't remove my eyes from the portrait. If I stared at her long enough, she would tell me who she was.

As I looked at the auburn-haired beauty again, my mind wandered back to my conversation with Jessie. Might this lady truly have been Sally Hemings's half-sister?

I considered the relationship between the two women. Martha's father had begun his relationship with Elizabeth Hemings after the deaths of all of his wives, including Martha's mother. We had some indication that Martha's experience with her stepmothers had not been pleasant. She had asked Jefferson on her deathbed not to remarry. Some thought it was a romantic gesture, but I think a woman dying deliberates practically. She was thinking of her three little girls.

One of the books I was reading mentioned there were clues that Martha's relationship with Elizabeth Hemings had been different from that with her stepmothers. When she had inherited Elizabeth and Elizabeth's children (many of them also her father's children), she had made the decision to bring them into her home.

I thought of Sally. She had been a small child when she had gone to live in her half-sister's household. Did she understand that she was owned by her sister's husband then? I think she would have. They were slaves. Few mothers would fail to prepare their children for all that could mean. The legal powerlessness, the uncertainty…

It seemed, from reports at the time, that Elizabeth was in Martha's bedroom when she had died. Sally, too, a child of nine years, had been there. Martha had given the little girl a bell to remember her by days before. What had it been like for Sally to witness death, especially the death of one too young, and to see Jefferson collapse at her bedside? It would have been scarring, I thought. At the very best, it would have left an imprint.

And years later, when she had begun her thirty-eight-year relationship with Jefferson, what were Sally's feelings? She was such a silent historical actor, the memory of her washed over in the tide of time, silence, and covering. Burying.

Let's say for sake of argument that she did have agency, that she was, if not happy, at peace with her decision to enter a lifelong relationship with Jefferson. Would Martha have been on her mind? I didn't have a sister, but... I couldn't help but wince.

And yet... Women were at such a disadvantage. In the past, it was almost guaranteed that they were going to be dependent on a man, whichever way they turned. It was only a matter of which man, and whether his personality would make life bearable. Sally, pregnant, could perhaps enter service in Paris as a free woman, with only her brother at her side. They could build a life, but it would be filled with uncertainty. And *hard* work. Or she could return to Virginia, be surrounded by her family, spend her life doing light sewing and looking after her children at Monticello— and end her life as a slave.

And just perhaps, given these conditions, she had made a clear-eyed decision without remorse. No one could fault her for that. Maybe not even Martha Jefferson.

I HEARD A NOISE AND JUMPED. I looked behind me and saw Samuel. "Hey." He really got the whole pants-to-shoe length/ratio thing. In other words, he dressed well.

Lifting my eyes from his feet, up his long legs, to his face, I responded quietly, "Hey." I sighed. "Do you think she's pretty?" I nodded toward the lady.

"Not really my type," he answered. I looked at him. A very slight smile was lingering.

What was his type? Well, let's consider. The only woman he had been thoroughly, uncompromisingly committed to the whole damn time I had known him—oh, excuse me! That was to say, Jenna. She was sorority blonde with that perfect, stereotypical ponytail. High maintenance, perfect makeup... In more recent pictures, she seemed to have been sporting a pixie cut. Blue eyes. Very stunning.

I looked back at the portrait lady. If Jenna was hot, the lady was elegant. More like me.

I couldn't think of a thing to say.

"I mean, she's a bit old for me," I heard Samuel say.

I cracked a smile—just. "But, objectively speaking..." I held his eyes. "Would you say she is beautiful?"

A pause. The gaze continued. "Unquestionably."

I broke eye contact. "I think so, too." I glanced back at her. "I don't think we ever will know." I tucked my hair behind my ear. "If she was Jefferson's wife."

He didn't answer.

I dusted off my hands. Got up. Returned to work. Felt his eyes follow me down the hall.

CHAPTER

FIFTEEN

"Put...aside vain regrets."
— *Thomas Jefferson*

It was March. I had been here two months.

I considered this fact as I walked toward the kitchen that night, wondering where it left me. Professionally, personally... I followed the smell of something cooking. Samuel was an adequate cook. Not adventurous, but then, neither was I. I opened the doors and entered.

He glanced up. Looked at me.

"I thought I might help," I said.

He nodded and vacated the chopping. I filled his place. Glancing around, I gathered that he was making a grilled chicken salad. I chopped the onions accordingly. That finished, I moved on to the tomatoes.

His eyes followed me, and my radar kicked up. I became very aware of him, too. Almost chopped my finger off. But I didn't, so it was all good. *Focus, Madeleine Ani.*

He put the chicken on the kitchen griddle, and the breasts began sizzling, filling the room with a pleasant aroma. He glanced at me, as if to measure how long until I was finished. *Chop carrot. Chop carrot. Chop the carrot.*

I had to break this tension. "So—"

He started speaking at the exact same time. "I was—"

I looked at him. He looked at me as if to say, "*Continue, please.*"

Clearing my throat, I said, "I like this brand of vegetables you bought. That's all I was going to say."

"Oh. Yeah." He flipped the chicken.

I made the bowls, piling cheese from his excellent selection on top. "What were you going to say?"

He cleared his throat. "Nothing."

The chicken finished, he cut it up and brought it over, topping the salads off. My stomach rumbled loudly. Embarrassing. He glanced at me, expression changing, a gleam in his eyes.

"Shut up."

He held up innocent hands. I had filled one bowl with slightly more cucumbers. I grabbed this one and went to sit at the bar, where he joined me.

"Aunt Millicent's results are in," he said as he sat, lifting his eyes upwards slightly. "It shows we're related in the right degree, which clears up some lingering familial questions about my great-grandmother."

A laugh escaped. "Good. That's good." Even though it might tell us little, I would be able to anchor Samuel's results with hers, checking relations and ancestries that appeared on the websites.

We talked about that for a few minutes, words flowing easily. Somewhere between the non-communitive side and the combative side, there had always been a collaborative side that flowed easily between us.

My phone, which sat on the counter between us, rang. I think we both saw *Bradley* flash across the screen. It jolted us out of some trance. I paused, heard Samuel shift. He looked away. Swallowing, I dusted off my hands, hesitated a second, and then picked up the phone and stood. I walked to the other end of the kitchen.

"Hey," I said, girding myself.

Bradley started talking. His tone was different than to what I was accustomed before the break-up, although I would have recognized his voice, of course.

I tried to focus. *Something about a book. A question about a research book that had been left on my shelf. He didn't have it. He needed it.*

"Yeah, I probably stored it," I said.

"I'll come get it. Or better yet, you could mail it."

"No, what I'm saying is, it's not there. If you left it there, it's in storage."

"I don't understand."

"I don't live there anymore, Bradley!" I clarified. A little too forcefully, but he was being dense. *A silence.* "I couldn't afford the rent." There was another pause.

He understood. Didn't ask where I was. Didn't seem to care. Just wanted to know if I could get it out of storage for him.

"No, I can't. I'm not in Massachusetts, even. I can give you the code and the address, and you can go get it. But, Bradley, all of my stuff is there. I promise you, you don't want to dig through it. You might as well just reorder the book."

"I can't. It's no longer in print. It's over four hundred dollars to buy from a seller on Amazon."

"Fine. I'll text the information to you."

"Thank you."

And...he was gone.

I stopped for a moment, burrowing my fingers in my hair. At some point, Samuel had finished and stood, quietly going to wash his plate and glass. He was listening, I knew. It was a little embarrassing to be so disrespected by someone who was supposed to have loved you. Like you couldn't choose any better than that! But I swear, Bradley hadn't always been such a prick.

Taking a breath, I turned around. Samuel leaned against the sink, looking at me, arms crossed casually. His expression was inscrutable. I gave a half-hearted smile and returned to sit before my salad that was suddenly less appetizing. A heavy beat of silence ensued. "Was it hard to divide up your stuff?" I asked. I cleared my throat because my voice had come out squeaky.

"Jenna has no attachment to material things," he said mechanically, like he was ironically quoting her. He grew quiet. I felt him studying me, felt his eyes touch the planes of my face. "You don't have to let him rifle through your stuff, Maddie," he said softly.

I met his eyes. "He lost his job," I answered quietly. "Received death threats. Lost a lot of friends. I don't think it's too much to say that I went a long way toward destroying everything he had built. He found a new job, and he'll recover before I ever will, but still. I can give him back a research book."

He surveyed me some more. "Does he call you Madeleine?"

I glanced at my phone. He must have heard the first few lines before I got up. "Yeah. Everyone in Boston does." I wasn't sure what that said about me.

A long beat of silence passed. He looked fierce, almost indefinably so, just something in the eyes and jaw. "I don't know what your relationship was," he said. "But if he even pretended to have loved you, I think he was a dirtbag for breaking up with you. A real man doesn't do that: leave a woman because the going gets too tough. He should have stood by you, no matter what."

I shook my head wryly. Pushed aside my food and straightened, drawing a breath. "You don't know what we went through. That is a level of heroism of which few are capable, Samuel," I answered.

"It is what I would have done," he insisted passionately.

I studied him. He wasn't very far away, and in the warm glow of the lights over the counter, I could see the stubbornness in his jaw. "Is it, Samuel?" I asked. "Because *I* seem to recall a young man, about eleven years ago, sending a breathtakingly sparse email to his partner, informing her that she was on her own, that she would have no further help, for something that was partially his responsibility."

He stilled. His eyes fixed on my face. There was silence for the length of several breaths. "What do you want me to say, Maddie?" he asked calmly.

"I want an explanation, Samuel." I stared at him, as fierce as he ever thought about being. He thought he was strong-willed? I could have ripped him from limb to limb on that day, and he wouldn't have known what had hit him. I know it made no sense now, but it was where we were. And I was owed an answer.

To my great surprise, he continued to regard me calmly. "You want an explanation? Okay: I loved you."

What?

It hit me out of nowhere. I felt like my chest opened, and the breath fell out of me. He paused another long moment, still regarding me, but with more emotion glimmering in his eyes now. "I had been with Jenna for four years," he said, still not moving. "We fell for each other so quickly. You know the ecstatic feeling of pairing up at that age? We did everything together, spent every waking moment... We made wild promises to each other."

He smoothed a hand on his face. "Things shifted, of course. For both of us. The difference in being eighteen and twenty-two is profound." He swallowed. "By my senior year, I was a man." He lifted a shoulder. "You blew into my life, and I learned quickly that a man's feelings were very different from a boy's."

Dear God. My heart triggered and seemed to catch, like it was about to gear up again and beat out an alarming staccato. I couldn't have moved if I had tried. My eyes were transfixed on his face, as if in permanence through eternity, in the manner of Lot's wife.

He finally looked away. "But the relationship was steady. We were committed. I know it sounds crazy now. We were so young, and we weren't married... But to break up with Jenna was unthinkable. I couldn't stay there a day longer. We exchanged our tickets with the airline and flew to Barcelona early."

He stood quietly, waiting to take my verbal pummeling. But I couldn't move. Couldn't speak. The thing was, it made sense. It was like what you *thought* was happening but would sound conceited if you said it or even if you adopted it as your most likely theory. Despite the fact that I had viscerally known it, I couldn't believe it. I stood still with my lips parted, wanting to run away dramatically, like a teenager.

"I'm sorry. So sorry. I knew what I was doing to you, and I hated it. But I don't think I was capable of seeing you again without doing something stupid."

I couldn't even fault him for his *feelings*. It was the most frustrating, scream-worthy experience of my life. And I couldn't move, couldn't react, because I didn't want him to know how deeply it all affected me.

It *was* eleven years ago. I said that to myself again. And repeated it.

I still couldn't manage any more than to walk away quietly, however.

***

"HE SAID *LOVED*. PAST TENSE," I pressed.

"Well, hon, but you have to think: why would he tell you now if he didn't think there was a chance?"

I sat on the floor in my bedroom the next morning, my designer jeans bending to accommodate me, my socks warm, and my head pounding. I was talking to Jessie. Obviously.

"Past tense," I repeated.

"With emotion," she said suggestively. "'*What do you want me to say, Maddie?*'" she mused, having memorized the script by now. I sincerely trusted he wasn't listening outside. "He has a simple narrative style. I like that part about being a boy versus a man."

Suddenly changing courses, she said, "Did he try to bring it into the here and *now*?"

"No. He answered my question."

"He could have lied if he had wanted to avoid it altogether. More like a man to have done that, honestly."

I swallowed, laying my head on my knee. The pressure felt good. "He could have, I guess. But I think I scared him. *I* would have been afraid of me right then. I demanded an answer out of nowhere. I'm not sure what happened to me."

"You're darn right. You were owed an explanation. And now you have it, hon. He was going to bang you if he stayed—"

"He didn't say *that*." I really wished she would find a different word. I thought of Aunt Enid, whose vocabulary was absolutely *replete* with different words. So, on second thought...never mind.

"Well, what do you *think* he meant? That he was so emotional he couldn't stand the thought of seeing you again?" she asked in a mock-romantic voice. "He's a man, Maddie. Get a clue. If he thought he couldn't control something, it wasn't his emotions."

Sheesh. My toes tingled. "All right. Fair enough."

"You see, they've got this thing called testosterone," she continued in an ironic reprimand. "You've been off the farm too long. Take Billy the Bull I've got out here. He wakes up in the morning, sniffs the air, and thinks: *sex*."

I admitted she had a point. Samuel said he had been in love with me. And he had indicated delicately that he had also been very attracted to me. Curling my toes, I said, "Well, I would not have been open to such a liaison."

Jessie made a dismissive scoff. "Yeah. Okay."

"I wouldn't have been!"

"We'll go with that," she conceded. "Does it make sense to you that he would have felt wrong breaking up with her?"

I considered it. "You know those kids who had been dating forever? Like even though they were just kids, they were on a trajectory? Practically married?"

"Yep," she said. "Youth group."

I smiled. Briefly.

"Well," she said, "this was a juicy tidbit."

"But it doesn't change anything, does it?"

"Sure it doesn't," she answered skeptically.

I DIDN'T KNOW how to go downstairs, how to see him. The thing was, all that had *actually* happened was that I had finally demanded an answer for his abandonment of the project, and he had answered me.

Just like all that had *actually* happened that last day in the library was that his hand had brushed mine.

Ugh. I moaned inwardly. But one must go on.

I descended the stairs a little late for breakfast, later than I usually got to work.

He was already out, probably communing with the sheep, thank goodness. I shoveled my oatmeal down and made a beeline for my research foyer. I would have preferred a covered hole or a cave, but you worked with what you had.

I tried to concentrate. I did not succeed. Finally, I decided I would haul up a few boxes that I had been meaning to add to my heap from the cellar. Setting aside what I was working on and removing my gloves, I walked toward the stairway door...and collided *smack*, hard into Samuel.

He grunted, reaching to stabilize me. "Maddie..." He sounded frustrated. He coughed, possibly because I had knocked the wind out of him. It was a hard hit.

"Sorry."

He threaded his hand through his hair. "That's okay. At least it's not in a bathroom," he muttered.

I flushed, cutting a scathing look up at him and reached for the door handle. He caught my wrist. "Are you okay?"

I looked up at him. His gaze was warm. Concerned. I drew a breath. He drew a breath. "I knocked into *you*," I said, swallowing.

His eyes searched mine. His hand had gone soft on my wrist. He blinked and looked down. "Yeah, but..." He appeared about to say something but changed courses and said something else. "You're like a reed. Too thin, and—"

"Too thin?"

"I could not opine as to that."

"You just did."

He pressed his lips together. Gazes locked in a battle of wills. He said, "What I *mean* is...I was afraid I had hurt you."

I took a shaky breath. My heart pounded. "I...was going to go get some more boxes from the basement." I turned, going down the stairs.

Samuel followed me.

Chester followed him.

"Chester. No. Stop it." Chester was escorted out.

I got a head start. Quickly, I found the early 1800s area. Okay. *Boxes. Boxes, boxes, boxes.* Bending over, I quickly skimmed through items, lifting lids, checking, unsnapping others.

"What are you looking for?"

"1827," I said shortly. I closed a lid. "Found it."

"Do you need help?"

"Nope."

I hefted the massive box. *Crap.* It was heavy. "I'll set that one aside. I think there's one more that I need." I shifted to look through another box. *Bingo.* I shoved it. It seemed to weigh perhaps a hundred pounds. It slid like two feet, no more, making an unsatisfying *thunk* as it hit something. I wanted to scream.

"*Maddie.*"

I looked up. Collided gazes with Samuel. He was *right there*. Neither of us moved.

I suddenly couldn't breathe. He seemed to be able to draw a breath, but that was about it. My lungs remembered what my brain couldn't, and I was able to take a shaky breath. He didn't touch me.

"Are you okay?" he asked softly.

"No, it...it's fine. It just surprised me." I cleared my throat, and I held my arms crossed tight over my cardigan.

He studied me. An eternity seemed to pass as he tried to work out my feelings. "I'm sorry I upset you. That's the last thing you need, after..." His voice trailed off.

I looked into his moss green eyes. "You didn't upset me, Samuel," I said softly.

He nodded once, holding my eyes. He looked away, brushing his hair back with his arm. He turned to lift one of my boxes.

Perhaps because I still felt some lingering irritation with him, I called as he went up the stairs, "You need a haircut!"

"If I want your advice, I will ask for it!" he fired back.

SIXTEEN

"Hope is the thing with feathers that perches in the soul/
and sings the tunes without the words/
and never stops at all."
-Emily Dickinson

What to do with Samuel? In all honesty, I avoided him the rest of the day, but I was prepared to move on. Did we have some difficult history? Yes. Did we have baggage? Yes. Were there going to be moments of awkwardness? Yes.

Where was I?

Ah, yes. The point was, we were two mature adults. If there was history, it was ancient history. And it didn't mean we couldn't continue professionally to do the job we had intended to do.

At least, this was what I told myself as I ambled into the kitchen the next morning.

I pushed open the door and jumped. Samuel was there.

I swallowed, playing with my hair. I felt his eyes following the progress of my hand. My skin tingled, my cheeks heating, and I stopped.

Clearing my throat, I said, "Are you...working today?"

I flushed. I shouldn't have said that. Why *wouldn't* he be working today, specifically? What was I thinking? *You're not, Madeleine.*

He looked at me. "Yeah."

Great. Noncommunicative.

But wait, no, there *was* something: "Are you?" He was doing that thing where he appeared to be just kind of hanging around, glancing at me surreptitiously from time to time.

"Yeah."

Happily, since this line of conversation was developing so incredibly promisingly, I heard nails clicking on the floor, and Chester Arthur Hayden entered the kitchen. He stopped to exchange amiabilities but clearly was interested in his breakfast.

"Come here, boy," Samuel called, going into a little side room and feeding him.

By the time Samuel emerged, I was getting yogurt and granola and sitting at the bar. He went to the fridge to get a bottle of water, presumably to take to work with him.

He glanced back at me. "You...slept well?" he asked.

"Um, yeah." I flushed. Again.

"Okay, um... I'll get to work."

"Okay."

Clearly, he was suspicious of my assurances that he hadn't sent me over the edge. As I looked at him, hovering in the doorway, I wondered about this.

I hadn't responded with any assurance that I had once loved him, too. I had just walked away, which, I suppose, he could have interpreted several different ways. Was he so sure of the bond that had existed between us, then, that he assumed it would affect me deeply? Well, he wasn't going to find *that* out from me. I was determined to give him no outward signs that I had ever felt anything more for him than passing notice.

Even if it wasn't true.

I ENDED up in the cellar. Right next to Samuel.

I had hit a dead end on cataloging the enslaved people of Hayden's Ridge, and I needed new material. Which, unfortunately, took forever to find during an endless file dig. Samuel, simultaneously, was searching for some letters from the same time period. Which meant we were at the same table.

I tried not to notice his trim waist and neat little butt. Those were matters which were entirely irrelevant. Especially for a scholar.

Tension crackled in the air. I'm not sure a basement was supposed to feel so charged. I was completely distracted. The only benefit to having him down here was that he lifted the massive banker's boxes for me when I asked, stopping with his work momentarily.

He glanced at me. I pretended not to notice.

But I caught him doing it several times over the course of the hour. I think he was as distracted as I was. My pulse was increased, my breaths short... It was like every nerve in my body was alive with awareness.

"Can you..." I indicated the box in front of me.

He looked up. "Where do you want it?"

"Just, um...wherever. I need the one below it."

He lifted it. In my state of being dazed, I didn't move. His back rubbed on my front—like, my breasts and stomach. He stilled. A good, long second.

Setting the box down, he turned. "Sorry, I..." He scratched the back of his head, looking absurdly guilty, given that it had been my fault.

I couldn't speak. I looked at him completely helplessly. "Samuel," I breathed.

Something flared fiercely in his eyes. Hope. Oh, no. It wasn't hope. It was *hunger*.

And suddenly we were kissing like...two people who had wanted to kiss for eleven years. *Badly*. The kiss...

Heaven... The exploration of his body and mine, his lips, performing beautifully, like I had always known they would...

"Maddie," he rasped, feeling or tasting my tears.

"How could you do that?" I whisper-cried, tears coursing down my cheeks.

"*Maddie...*"

"How could you just take a pass on what was between us?" I demanded fiercely between kisses, sobbing. My tears flowed over. But the kissing, the intensity, remained.

The physical force between us had once been like the highest-powered magnet. The intellectual chemistry like lightning.

And it was still there. It overcame personal devastation, depression, anger, and his sour temper.

His voice broke, though he didn't speak. His hand clenched where it was plunged through my hair, not painfully, but passionately. "What did you want me to do?" he demanded, pulling back, drinking me in. His eyes, in painful joy, touched my eyes, my nose, my cheekbones, my mouth... He looked back up, our gazes meeting.

Fresh tears rose to my eyes. His eyes were like a special dynamism; they could have softened the hardest iron within me. "I'm sorry." He shook his head. "I'm sorry. It was the hardest thing I've ever—"

Good enough. He didn't know what hit him when I began kissing him again. We kissed with our whole beings. And he was definitely up for the job. He was in the moment, like I was the only person in the world, passionate but purposeful, gentle but skilled.

It was like we knew instantly what each other wanted, and I had never experienced that in a kiss before. Maybe it was just the *enthusiasm*, because, goodness... Pent-up tension like that...like *teenagers...*

He slowed down, finally stopping, seemingly reluctantly, and laying his forehead against mine as we tried to catch our breath. His eyes flickered over my face. After a minute, they met mine, with the obvious question: *Where do we go from here?*

"WELL, *I* was prepared to proceed in a professional manner," I said, sitting a good two feet from him on the couch, just as a precaution.

He shot me a look. "It appeared that way in the basement."

I shot him a look back.

He, too, seemed to understand the need for space. I'm not sure either of us was thinking quite clearly. My heart was still pounding. I *wanted* him. I knew that would be a mistake, however. It was too soon.

I stacked a couple of pillows between us.

This seemed to amuse him, his mouth flickering as though hiding a smile. He met my eyes, and I flushed. I resisted the urge to slam one of the pillows against him. Because he did just get under my skin.

In every possible way.

"Why don't we...just see where it goes," I said. "I mean, just... continue with everything, keeping our minds open to the possibility."

He nodded. "I'm game."

SEVENTEEN

"The opinions and beliefs of men follow involuntarily
the evidence proposed to their minds."
-Thomas Jefferson

"Read this."

Samuel looked up from his desk, meeting my eyes briefly. I smiled, and he returned it. He then cautiously took the copy of the letter I handed him.

That previous letter from Alexander Hayden to his brother-in-law, William Wayles, where he had discussed the slave boy Jack, along with Etta Wayles Hayden's difficult pregnancy, was still gnawing at me. And I had a theory. It may have been crazy, however.

Samuel sat back, reading it. When he came to the end, he sat still for a moment. Blinked a couple of times. "I've never seen this letter," he said, his voice holding the weight that history sometimes brought. He scanned back over it once more before handing it to me. "How can he speak with such eloquence and tenderness over the loss of his own son and not see the obvious parallel with the Monticello boy he has bought?"

I shook my head. That had occurred to me, too. People could be callous. Unempathetic. I saw it in the way people spoke about drug addicts, for instance. Because it had affected me, such suffering pierced me to my core, but not others. At length, I said, "The truth is, Samuel, we're all like that. We only have empathy so far as it affects us, and to the extent we acknowledge the humanity of those around us. Until we let God heal us."

I felt him make a study of my face. "'I will remove from you a heart of stone, and give to you a heart of flesh?'" he quoted.

I loved that verse. "Yes. The thing is... I have a theory. You're going to think it's crazy."

He lifted his brows.

"What if Etta Hayden never produced a healthy child?"

He watched me, waiting for me to elaborate.

"I read this romance novel one time in which—" He rolled his eyes, appearing to be finished with the conversation. "*In which*," I pressed, "the lady of the house had severe fertility issues and was told she would never give birth to a living child. The husband's brother happened to have fathered the child of a maid, and they swapped the live baby with the dead one—"

"My God."

"—*and thus* continued the earldom."

"That's ridiculous."

"You have to admit it's possible!" I exclaimed.

"There are lots of things in life that are possible, Maddie," he said dryly. "That does not mean they are likely."

"Less likely things have happened," I retorted. "You're a historian. You know that fiction is never as wild as the facts."

He sighed, looked at me like he would very much like to bat away this conversation and move on with his life. Instead, he said, "Let's discuss the things that would have to happen." He ticked them off on his fingers. "Two women would have to get pregnant at exactly the same time, and give birth within, I would think, a

153

few hours of each other. The mother whose child was ripped away from her would have to stay silent—"

"Unless she agreed to it."

"Very unlikely." He continued. "The couple would have to bank on the notion that an infant's features and color would someday have no trace of its mother's ancestry, which I don't know how anyone *could* do with an infant—"

"Unless the child were something like seven-eighths white, like Jefferson's children. We know that two of them passed into white American society and were not, to quote their brother, '*known by the white folks to have any colored blood coursing in their veins.*' It was possible to 'pass,' Samuel. Many people did it."

"It was certainly possible, and many people certainly did it, some of them with more African ancestry than Jefferson and Hemings's children. My question is whether Alexander and Etta Hayden would bank on it."

I had to admit, he had a point: babies changed. I myself had possessed almost completely different coloring as a newborn, and I didn't imagine that was all that rare. Or that people wouldn't have known this as well in the early 1800s as they did now, even if they had never heard of genetics and melanin.

"If they were desperate for a baby, they might have taken a risk."

"The taboo, Maddie. You're not thinking like they would have thought."

I sighed.

"Am I wrong?" he asked. "Toss back a counter argument, if so."

"You're not wrong, in the main."

"Then I don't think this theory is going to work."

I met his eyes. Considered him for a second. "Do you think, Samuel, that you have an African American ancestor?"

He shrugged. "We can't know. You know that. There was a whole other family in that same Jefferson-Hemings DNA study you mentioned who had an oral history stating that they descended from Jefferson. They had reunions at Monticello. Then DNA testing proved there was no link whatsoever."

"Your point being?"

"Family stories are sometimes true, sometimes false. I can't, given my training, with blind arrogance and certitude, state that *my* family story is true."

I held his eyes. "I'm not asking for unimpeachable proof. I'm getting at your instincts as a historian and as a member of your family. I'm asking if you *think*, given the stories you have heard, the documents you have seen, and the knowledge of your family history, that you have an African American ancestor?"

He waited a moment. "Yes," he said, nodding once. To admit to believing an oral history with no solid proof as a matter of intuition went against his training and his proclivities as a person. And that was why I was putting so much stock into the theory. From day one, I knew that if Samuel didn't outright tell me the theory was bogus, there might be something to it.

"Then how," I said gently, but with the intense conviction of a lawyer giving a winning oral argument, "could the ancestor possibly have come into the line otherwise?"

He held my eyes for a moment, his wheels spinning. After a moment, he had that defiant look he got when he knew I had bested him. Which changed shortly after to grudging acceptance and even respect.

"We have proven that your male ancestors retained the original Hayden markers on their Y chromosomes. In your family Bible, from which your father constructed his family tree, we see the birth of a son produced from a marriage, right down the line. If there wasn't something very like a baby swap, with a Hayden male as the father, what else could it be?"

"I got it the first time," he said. "You don't have to beat a dead horse."

I leveled a look at him.

"Yes, okay? I see your point."

I lifted my chin smugly.

"Just no dead babies and back-stairs romances, please," he said.

I rolled my eyes.

He reached for the letter, taking it with a bit of sass, I must say, when I offered it. Then he got on his computer and went into the more extensive family tree I had been creating in a shared document with him. "Alexander Hayden didn't have a brother," he said triumphally. "He had three sisters, but no brother."

"It didn't have to be his brother's baby," I said, wishing deeply for that fire poker to brain him with. He was being difficult on purpose. If he wanted to knock romance novels, he could do it on someone else's time. "It could be his own baby, you know."

He looked up at me. "Abraham, Sarah, and Hagar-style? A plan?"

"It wouldn't have to be."

"No," he agreed.

Samuel was a Civil War historian. I knew he knew what I was thinking. Mary Chesnut, the South Carolinian Civil War diarist had made a few remarks on the matter. They stuck with you. "*The mulattoes one sees in every family exactly resemble the white children— and every lady tells you who is the father of all the mulatto children in [everybody else's house hold], but those in her own she seems to think drop from the clouds, or pretends so to think.*"

"There could have been a woman conveniently pregnant," I said, feeling difficulty even talking about that. What a position for a woman to have been in, completely powerless in any legal sense. And what a position for Etta Hayden to have been in, too.

"It would have had to have been, wouldn't it?" he asked. "If I'm a genetic match with Buckeye Hayden?"

I looked at his family tree. "Alexander Hayden almost undeniably would have been your (many-times) grandfather, yes," I agreed. "His father *was* still alive. But it's very unlikely it would have been his father's illegitimate child he raised rather than his own."

"You have a very kinky mind," Samuel remarked with distaste. I rejoined, but he did not respond or, indeed, appear to be listening. "Wouldn't you say the baby swap theory would be more likely if the Haydens were a bit older and never able to produce any children?"

"Yes," I replied.

He pointed at the family tree, looking smug now himself. I peered at it. "Baby John Hiram Hayden was born in 1827 when his mother was just twenty-six," he said. "Certainly too young to have given up all hope, given that they had only been married, what, two or three years?"

"That is a good point," I said coldly.

Gracious now in his victory, Samuel conceded, "This tree only has direct ancestors. If you could find that they never had any other children, it would strengthen your theory. She *might* have been told by her doctor that it was hopeless, or she could even have been recommended to practice abstinence, as some women were, for her health. Whereas, if you find that they went on to have several more children, the theory begins to look weaker."

I lifted my eyebrows. "I don't know why you say 'you' as if you're not going to be helping."

He looked wary. "I'm not."

"Yes, you are."

Etta Wayles Hayden to Mary Wayles, documented and preserved by Madeleine Apkarian, Ph.D., M.A., B.A.

April 17, 1827
Hayden's Ridge
My Dear Mary,

157

I have the most supreme pleasure of announcing to you the safe delivery of my son. Mr. H will scarcely let me lift my pen, but I could not keep you and my dear brother in suspense for another moment, nor could I grant the pleasurable task to another.

John Hiram Hayden was born yesterday morning at seven o'clock precisely, which leads me to believe he will be a very punctual young gentleman. I am well, and there were no complications. We can scarcely realize our joy and relief. The midwife pronounces him to be as healthy as any little lad she has ever seen.

I believe he favors your little Mary in some respects. He is not as fair, but yet still fair in most respects. He is very like his father, with the same contemplative expression, which leads me to believe he may be a balloonist, like his papa and uncle. I only trust he may never ascend in one!

Mr. H sends his love and bids me this very moment not to exhaust myself, so I will bid you au revoir, and send my love to your little family.

Yours With Love,
Ettie H.

SAMUEL GRUMBLED, but I did manage to get him to join my veritable archeological dig for more children of Alexander and Etta Hayden.

On the whole, it had been good for me to have to talk purely academically for like three hours. It reminded one that sex was not all there was to the world. I felt my face flush. By sex, of course, I mean romance and the relational drive that came from the instinctual, biological, evolutionary force. Nothing more. *Whew.*

I turned the page protector over in my notebook, pressing my lips together.

Chester Arthur, maintaining a well-trained distance from historic documents, kept us company. He panted in the corner, his eyes following Samuel with longing sadness, for all the world as though he were a beaten and neglected castaway, longing for the merest scrap of affection. This, because Samuel had been working for two hours.

Of course he would have a dramatic dog.

"They had another baby in 1829."

I looked up, hearing Samuel's voice. He was looking at his own page-protector-enclosed letters as he said that.

"What?" I breathed.

He nodded. "A daughter," he said, taking the missive out of the binder and handing it to me.

I got a sinking feeling. It didn't prove my theory was wrong. But it certainly didn't weigh towards proving it right, either. Samuel glanced at me. I guess he saw my reaction. "She could have been a fluke—I mean, an unexpected surprise or something."

"Or it could be a different couple who introduced a nonmarital baby into your line altogether," I said miserably. "This could take forever."

We kept plucking away, nonetheless.

Over the course of the afternoon, we found three more children, born every two years punctually, for a total of five children born of the marriage.

I didn't know where to go from there. Why was I researching Samuel's family tree again? If this was a dead-end, I was wasting my time. Precious time, really. And wasn't something else more likely to yield a massive find? The record of the enslaved people and their lives here, for one. That was where I should devote my time.

I sighed, going over to Chester. Kneeling, I rubbed his ears.

Samuel leaned against the wooden table where he had been researching. He looked at me. "History is frustrating work, Maddie. You know that."

I couldn't believe he was encouraging me in a project he had considered to be a useless endeavor from the start. I said, "I also know that sometimes you don't find the answers. I think I'm going to focus on cataloging the enslaved people of Hayden's Ridge. I should have that finished in a decade or so."

He smiled briefly.

"In all honesty," I said, "a historian has to know when he or she is on a rabbit trail. I think there's a reason your family hasn't been able to figure this out for about two hundred years. I'm going to shift gears and put this chapter behind me. If I happen to see something to link me to the portrait or the ancestry searches while I'm researching the other line of documents, all the better. But I'm going to move on."

CHAPTER

EIGHTEEN

"Should I draw you a picture of my heart, it would be what I hope you still would love, tho it contained nothing new. The early possession you obtained there, and the absolute power you have ever maintained over it, leave not the smallest space unoccupied."
-Abigail Adams

K*eeping our minds open to the possibility* was interpreted loosely.

I found myself making out with Samuel in the cellar several times over the course of the next week. What always started as a purely academic endeavor generally ended far more stimulatingly.

At some point, I'm pretty sure I was lifted off the ground, my legs wrapped around him. The feeling of his hair surrounding my fingers was captivating; the pure pleasure was unbearable. He seemed to find it likewise.

"You are really going to have to find a better place to kiss me," I suggested, teasing his lips.

"The cellar of a historic home is a perfectly romantic place," he responded. Though I felt his lips twitch.

"It smells like an open grave."

He laughed softly, something I hadn't heard in a long time. He said, "You are disgusting." But his actions would imply he felt otherwise.

I mused, "Although Enid would likely say that if your spirit is so moved..."

"Don't mention Enid," he groaned.

"*Que sera, sera,*" I continued, in a passable, sexy imitation.

"Don't speak Spanish to me."

I almost choked. Dear God, he never missed a chance for sarcasm. Imagine the audacity!

"The phrase," I said between kisses, "is composed of both Italian and Spanish words, superimposed on English syntax."

"Well, in that case..."

IT WAS HARD TO CONCENTRATE.

I did some meditation, found it wasn't enough, went back for some centered prayer, added in some mindfulness practices—and finally felt like I could read words on a page. Going down to the foyer, I spent three hours documenting and cataloging from the new, massive pile of boxes I had located in the cellar. I was following a *Geoffrey* and a *Janine* now, the first of whom appeared to have been whipped by an overseer as a boy in a manner he seemed to have described as "unfairly" to his owner. Sometimes a historian's work was not a pleasant task.

After I finished with that, I went back to my office to scan in documents. I was a bit sad that the genealogical project hadn't worked out. I loved matches and mysteries solved and *aha* moments. I would have loved to have found Samuel's elusive ancestor. I would have loved what that could have told us about American history. Having looked for this person for months now, I wanted to know about her life. But the taboo which had hidden the truth had defeated my attempts. Just as it seemed to have defeated every Hayden's attempt to ferret it out in the past.

———

WE SAT in the living room, the fireplace going, Chester Arthur Hayden asleep on his rug, and Samuel and I sitting on the red blanket that covered the sofa. I leaned into him.

That was new. He made it feel natural, however, like that was where I belonged.

He kissed me, slowly. It was tender, experimental, and a little bit in awe. And with these attributes, it heated up fairly quickly.

He took his time. I liked that. It boded well for...other things. Speaking of...I was going to have to be careful. This time felt different. Our tempos were matched. Our breathing breaks were sexy, our breaths just teasing each other. There was a piercing connection to it, giving a whole new meaning to the word *intimacy*.

I felt as though I could scarcely move outside the kiss. My whole world *was* the kiss. My hands trailed down his chest, and his passion kicked up a notch. I returned it measure for measure. His hands wandered slowly, reverentially, wondrously.

Bliss.

Ugh. Nothing in me wanted to stop. "Samuel," I whispered.

He stopped, coming to awareness, meeting my eyes.

I hesitated. "I've been off birth control for a while," I whispered. Comprehension flickered in his eyes. He got it. He nodded, his hand staying gently against my thigh as he moved slightly. I gathered myself to say the next part. "And my friend Jessie has been lecturing me about sex before marriage, so..." I glanced up with a slight smile. "I want to try it this way, if that's okay with you."

He nodded again. His eyes flickered over my face yearningly.

But he leaned over, kissing my forehead tenderly, so I assumed we were good.

I FOLLOWED THE SCENT.

I was surprised to find when I came out of my office that it was lunchtime. Samuel was cooking something. The aroma wafted to me first, followed by the clatter, and it was irresistible.

I entered the kitchen.

He stopped, our eyes meeting. I felt *alive*. The feeling swirled around us.

I needed some pillow barriers. "Hi," I said, heart pounding.

"Hi," he said. His voice was warm. Having known only grumpy, agitated Samuel whom I couldn't have, I hadn't thought about that: what it would be like to experience his tenderness. I wondered about that now, my mind exploring the possibility of what might be.

I needed like a whole wall between us.

I swallowed. "What are you making?"

"Vegetable soup," he said.

"Do you need help?"

"Sure." He handed me a stalk of celery and a knife.

"Having a good day?" he asked, glancing at me.

"No breakthroughs as of yet."

We put the soup together, and he closed the lid on the pot as I dropped the last of the veggies in. He looked at me, keeping his distance. But the air sizzled. He glanced at me again.

"That won't be ready until supper," he said. "I'll make sandwiches for now."

I helped him, and when we were finished, I asked, "Would you be able to come down to the basement to carry a box up? I think I've found one I need, and I could work on it in the foyer today."

"Of course," he answered.

We left the kitchen, walking circumspectly toward the basement door. He glanced at me. Caught me staring. I flushed.

He opened the door for us, letting me pass.

"Which one?" he asked as we came to the heap of boxes.

I took him to the one I needed and tapped the top. I had a good feeling about this box.

He lifted it, and I followed him up the stairs. After placing it on the table, he hesitated and then leaned across, framing my face with his hands and giving me a gentle kiss. I brought my hand up to touch his face, lingering a moment before getting back to work.

I DID FIND something of interest as I catalogued. A letter written in French.

July 1826
Ma Chérie,

Il est mort. Je quitte cet endroit mais n'allez pas loin. Je viendrai à vous aussi. Seulement quand il est sûr.

M

It appeared to be by the same author who penned the mysterious note about the Hayden baby, as well as the inscription on the portrait: *This monument of his love.* And it was addressed to Etta Hayden on the back near the remnants of a simple seal.

I went to my desk and put this into a translator. *My Dear, He is dead. I leave this place but do not go far. I will come to you, too. Only when it is safe. M.*

The person who had dedicated the portrait knew Etta Hayden. We knew that the French-speaking person had written a letter to someone in the house and assumed it was to Etta, but *this* was proof. My heart quickened. The letter Samuel had shown me about the baby ("no one will know") was meant for Etta as well. This person knew something about Etta Hayden's baby that the world at large did not.

Now, it could have been a friend, and she could have been talking about hiding something as simple as a birthmark. But I was beginning to be very curious as to the possibility that this *M* had been Etta Wayles Hayden's lover. I thought I had given up on this whole adventure. But I couldn't be completely on the wrong track, could I? I had put *so* much work into it.

And yet, I had committed to cataloging solely now.

If I should happen to see something while I did so... Well, that would just have to be.

TIME PASSED; our dance continued. Samuel wanted me as much as I wanted him; I was certain he was struggling. But he didn't push me to change my mind.

In fact, he seemed to assume nothing. I often caught him watching me cautiously, with the expression of a lover intent on pleasing, or at least on feeling his way through *my* feelings. We might know one another well, but we had never been *together*.

I liked the slight uncertainty. It kept him on his toes, and he needed that, I thought with a malicious grin. Not that he was a ball of nerves or anything. I almost rolled my eyes, thinking of how infuriating he could be.

Deep in the mire of cursive documents, I locked myself in my office. I needed space to think and I simply couldn't think when Samuel was around me. I never had been able to. And I was struggling to keep him at a distance. Hence, the lock. Samuel wasn't the type to break down the door if he was denied access. But still.

I had a task to do, and he was too tempting.

He did knock around lunch time.

I went to the door. Cracked it very slightly.

"What are you doing?" he asked.

"Working."

"In Fort Knox?"

"I need a mental barrier. And that is your fault. Don't look pleased! We *have* to pump the brakes, Samuel."

He cracked the door just slightly to see my face, his forehead crinkling. "Are you being serious?"

"No, of course not. I just need to clear my head, and I *can't* with you around."

"And I can't come in?"

"No."

"Why not?" He looked exasperated.

"Because I'm ovulating," I said boldly.

He lifted his brows. "I don't think it works that way. Proximity, I mean."

My lips quivered, despite myself. "Mother Nature tries every trick in the hat to encourage procreation."

He looked fascinated, glancing down at my body as if in awe and newly appreciative of the manner in which it could be his best friend.

"What you're saying is, if I come in there, you won't be able to keep your hands off of me," he said.

I eyed him narrowly. "What I'm saying," I said properly, "is that I have a healthy sex drive, and you—"

"Are very attractive."

"—just happen to be of the correct sex."

"Of course," he said, giving me a look.

I narrowed my eyes at him. But since I had been a little harsh, I gave him a demure smile.

He smiled back. "I'll let you get back to work, then," he said.

We shared a little secret smile. "Okay."

WE SAT at one of the town's few restaurants. Being in rural Virginia was peaceful, but often rather like I imagined living in the outer reaches of England and travelling to that one pub once a month. This one did have a tavern feel, with low beams, old wood floors, and a faint smell of beer on the air. The food was good, and we ordered, Samuel from memory. I imagined I would have the list of options learned soon, too.

"Why do I have a feeling you're no longer indexing?" Samuel asked after we had handed over our menus.

I looked up sharply. "I *am*."

"I see," he responded, looking infuriatingly skeptical. "In the office, away from all of the boxes, with only a clutch of relevant letters..."

I felt my traitorous face flush, even as I narrowed my eyes. "*Mostly*, I am cataloging."

He gave a faint smile, laced with victory. Dipping a chip, he said, "What are you doing?"

Giving him a glare as I considered whether to answer, I finally said, "I found—purely by happenstance—that *M* did write directly to Etta Hayden. Which almost certainly means that the letter concerning the baby that you have saved on your computer was to Etta. It...reignited my interest. And yes, maybe I have been following that trail a bit."

"Mmm hmm," he said, looking smug.

"Do you mind?" I asked.

He shook his head. "I want you to do whatever you want to do."

I tilted my head, studying him. "Is this sarcasm? *Do whatever you want...*?"

He met my eyes. "No." Reaching for my hand across the table, he took it. "I want you to do whatever you want to do, Maddie." He stroked the tender skin of my wrist. Gooseflesh rose on my arm. "Even if it's hair-brained." He smiled, holding my eyes.

My eyes smiled at him in return. "You used to would have kicked me out for going off script," I challenged.

"No, I wouldn't," he responded, before looking up and flushing slightly himself.

Ha. I had known that, had *felt* that, viscerally, at least.

We were positioned thus when the floor creaked and two people approached. "Samuel?"

It was a man and a woman. She appeared to be in her early forties, with brown hair and a scholarly demeanor, in baggy but elegant clothes, and possessing a nice handbag. The man who stood behind her I instinctively felt to be a professor as well.

Samuel looked up, sitting back. "Kathleen," he said, seemingly with some measured bit of surprise. He looked behind her, nodding at the man, as if he might be acquainted with him but didn't know him very well. "What brings you here?"

"I might ask the same question," she said exuberantly, glancing at me. "Oh, but your father's home is situated near here. I forgot!" Pointing at the man behind her, she said, "We're just on the way to a symposium in Williamsburg."

"Kathleen, have you met Dr. Apkarian—Maddie?"

She looked down at me, and as recognition of my circumstances hit, she smiled, but nervously, and said, "Ah...no!"

"Maddie, this is my colleague, Dr. Brown." Samuel also introduced the man, but I was watching the many expressions of Dr. Brown.

She pointed a finger between us, smiling brightly, and said, "You are together?"

I flushed. Samuel's eyes widened, almost with humor at her audacity. But since he didn't jump straight to irritation, I reasoned that he must have had a good working relationship with her. "Yes," he said.

"Oh, ah ha! How...wonderful!" She chatted to Samuel for a

minute or two warmly. I noticed she never said anything directly to me. She wasn't mean-spirited, I could tell, but she wouldn't touch the unclean either. And honestly, who could blame her?

Maybe there was a slight chance she was just an awkward person. The man, however, had definitely taken two steps back so that he was now logically associated with another table and could just be seen to be viewing his phone, unconnected to this table.

Though I'd been bristling (fundamental to my combative nature), I realized that probably Samuel didn't catch the undertones to the whole thing, some of which may have been purely female (she obviously had one of those harmless work crushes on Samuel), and I didn't want to do anything to put him on bad terms with his colleagues.

I mustered a smile as Dr. Brown wrapped up the conversation and left. Our bill came just after, and I also managed a smile as our waiter offered to take our plates. In the hubbub of paying and wrapping up lunch, time passed. I waited quietly in the foyer while Samuel paid. When he came out, he gave a gentle smile and threaded his fingers through mine.

We walked out to the car, and he came around to my side, opening the door. Just when I had decided that he had entirely missed the undercurrents in the restaurant, he hooked his fingers in my beltloops and drew me to him. His eyes skimmed across my face.

"You know you're actually one of the cool kids, Maddie."

I had been looking down, but I peeked up at him. His hands settled on my hips, and I hid a smile. "And they're all just jealous?"

"Exactly." He grew more somber, studying me. He gave a long sigh, before finally mustering a smile of his own. "Ready?" he asked, lifting one hand and giving my arm a squeeze.

"Well, Chester *will* be wondering where we've gone," I answered softly.

He kissed me, and I hoped Kathleen Brown saw through the windows.

CHAPTER

NINETEEN

"I like the dreams of the future better than
the history of the past."
-*Thomas Jefferson*

W*ho* was *M*?
I sat at my desk the next day, my pen against my lips as my eyes were unfocused in the distance. I liked romance novels, but at some point, I admitted to myself that *M* could be *anyone* rather than a lover. The person could be, for instance, a friend or even a female relative.

Whoever was referenced to have died, reading between the lines in the letter, there seemed to have been some degree of drama attached to the death. And whoever *M* was, he or she was in some measure of danger. Or at least, the possibility of danger if he or she acted in a certain way.

I scoured sources for evidence of any Frenchman in Virginia during the era and located a few but could find no one whom I felt likely to be *M*.

My phone buzzed, and I looked down.

Dr. Judy Carroll. My unmovable Bostonian fortress.

I answered the phone. "Hey, Judy!"

"Hey, kid. Are you staying at the family home of Samuel Hayden?"

"Yes, I am," I admitted.

"I thought that must be where you were holed up. That is one tight piece of ass."

My eyes widened, and I covered my mouth.

"We met once at a symposium of the Civil War. I propositioned him, but he wasn't interested. Married or something. Well, I imagine he's sorry by now."

"Um..." I had no idea whether she was joking. She wasn't as carefree as Enid, but she *was* deeply comfortable with sexuality. And speaking about it.

"Never mind. How have you been?" she asked, as if annoyed by the social necessity of pleasantries.

"Fine," I said, smiling. "Just sort of...moving on."

She said, "No good can come from dwelling on the past, I suppose. Listen, I've got you a gig."

"A job?" I asked, incredulous.

"No, kid, I'm sorry to say I still think that's a long way off." That was what I thought. She continued, "What I meant was, Rachel Goldstein—you know she left the *Boston Chronicle* for moral reasons and started her own Substack and podcast?"

"Of course I know who Rachel Goldstein is. She's one of my heroes, actually."

"Well, you're one of hers."

I blinked. My lips parted as I stilled.

"She wants you to write an article for her Substack on your experience, Maddie."

I brought my hand to my mouth again. Rachel Goldstein recently had been publishing big names whose careers had in some way been destroyed by intolerance, telling the other side of the story. She spoke from a place of truth and courage, with real empathy. When she spoke, people listened. To be honest, those stories had been one of the few balms to my broken heart.

My heart pounded. It could be a meaningful experience. It could give me the exposure I needed with the right people. But it could also open another can of worms. Backfire. At the very least, reopen the debate. At the worst, it could lead to another onslaught of vitriolic attention, which was the last thing I wanted or, frankly, needed.

"It might be a chance to tell the real story, Maddie. You know when free speech is threatened, women are threatened. Minorities. The poor."

"All of us," I whispered. At the university, John Granger, Judy Carroll, and I were all over the political spectrum. But that was something we had agreed on, whispering it in a little closet office in a meeting right before I left.

I thought of the things that had been written about me, things that were made up with no retraction ever offered in once-reputable sources. The way things were twisted out of all recognition. The assumptions that were made, the accusations that were thrown...

"Give her my contact information," I said.

"Haha!" I heard the satisfaction in Judy's voice. "It's going to be fine, Maddie. I think this might be just the thing."

I wasn't so sure. I was feeling a bit overwhelmed, both with the prospect of penning my story and with the idea of Rachel Goldstein even knowing who I was. I had been mildly academically famous before this storm hit. I had not been national-consciousness-famous. Or infamous.

I sat for a moment. Then I heard a noise and looked over my shoulder. Samuel had stopped in the doorway and was looking at me.

"You okay?" he asked, concern in his eyes.

"Did you sleep with Judy Carroll?" I asked.

He scowled. "Judy... That woman... She berated me for half an hour on how my statistical data didn't include enough women, which I *couldn't find* because it *doesn't exist*—and then she asked me to go back to her hotel room with her! She's older than my father!"

I laughed inwardly, my shoulders shaking. "I'm sorry to tell you that she's a close friend. Like an aunt."

"That's just peachy," he said grimly. "What did she want?" he asked, looking at me anew, a little curiously.

I took a deep breath. "She knows Rachel Goldstein." I met his eyes. "She wants to publish me."

He was silent as the weight of it settled over him. Something flickered in his eyes. "Maddie, that's a big deal," he said. The mood had shifted to a very serious one.

"I know," I said.

"Are you going to do it?" he asked.

I nodded.

He smiled. A one-sided, rare one. "I thought you would."

A MESSAGE from Rachel Goldstein *pinged* into my inbox on Monday morning. I spent most of the next week on a coffee high, drafting my article for her newsletter, revising it, throwing it in the trash, digging it out for more amendments, and generally driving myself crazy. Samuel helped me, offering advice when solicited, arguing with me when necessary (reminding me forcefully of our senior capstone days), and emboldening me when my courage flickered.

Kissing me whenever the mood arose...

Today, I sat in a high windowsill in a sunny room in the historic part of the house where we had been spreading out all of my drafts and paragraphs and themes. Samuel stood in front of me, kissing me senseless. He really was good at this.

"I'm still not convinced," I said, taking a breath, "that you are not kissing me to shut me up." We had been in an argument about the article's theme. I was winning.

"Do you mind?"

My fingers dug into the shoulders of his dark blue pullover, bringing him closer, closer... His lips worked their elegant dance. *Not at all.*

Even in the throes of passion, he never seemed to forget that he was kissing *me*. His fingers traced my jawline. His lips made an exploration of discovery. He was completely living his life in that moment, in that kiss, present, accounted for, and at attention.

I couldn't breathe, but I didn't care. My legs pressed into his hips, and my hand cupped his face. "Samuel," I whispered.

His passion increased. The intensity of the kiss seemed to be cosmic. His hand slipped under my shirt, skimming my spine deliciously. I sighed with pleasure. Just as we were heading to the point of no return, I said, "Samuel..."

He huffed, breaking away and taking a step back as he pulled his hand through his hair. "Would it be so horrible if I got you pregnant?" he questioned.

No. Please do. I mentally slapped Mother Nature. *Stop.*

He flushed, seeming to realize what he had said. "I mean, do you want children?" he asked, still a little red. But he held my eyes.

I couldn't help but smile. "Yes," I said, blushing now, too. "At least, *a* child. Do you?"

He gave me a little smile in return, nodding.

I held his eyes, biting my lip.

"I'll go," he said.

My eyes teased him. "That would probably be for the best. We will resume tomorrow."

He lifted a brow.

"With *the article*."

"No, *you* are impossible!"

This parry was lobbed at me vehemently from the other end of the library, where Samuel sat on the desk, arms crossed, handsome forearms on display (though this was quite beside the point). I was allowed to call *him* impossible, but honestly...

"How dare you! I am not stubborn, whatever you say." I stood by the large bookcase, my arms crossed inflexibly.

He looked heavenward. "You must show the personal side of it. Show what it meant for your private life."

I levelled a look at him across the lamplit room. "Do you really want me to go into that?" I questioned.

"Yes. Of course. People might not know what this sort of behavior does to people."

"Of course they know," I retorted. "It's the whole point."

"Yes." He held my eyes firmly. "But they don't have to sit in it, to see it before their very eyes and live it out. There's a coldness, a detachment, but don't let them get away with it. Show what it does to people's personal lives."

I studied him. "Do you really want me to talk about my relationship with Bradley?" I asked softly. He was driving me crazy right now, yes, but I didn't want anything to mess this up. I was trying to protect it so very carefully, and I wanted him really to think about what rehashing the end of my last relationship would feel like for him.

He considered me, more restrained now, but still feeling quite strongly. I could tell from the mouth and the jaw. After a minute, he said, "Look, Maddie... If you can live with the fact that I've been married, and...all of that... I can deal with the fact that you were serious with someone else—"

"With me writing about it publicly, and it being talked about, and probably tangentially gaining some measure of public interest and sympathy for it—"

"It's right. You *know* it's right to put this in there. Don't speak ill of him. Don't even say his name. But say that it caused the end of your relationship. The story isn't complete without it. You've written beautifully and meaningfully. But the article could be more effective. I don't want you to miss what might be your only chance to tell your side."

I studied him. Maybe it was because I had been snake-bitten, but I was wary. I hadn't seen the collapse of my last relationship coming. And I didn't know how to tell him, especially in the midst of him pushing me so hard, that I couldn't live without him.

I blinked, in the midst of him staring at me relentlessly, unsure when that had come upon me. It was a huge realization to have during an argument.

I drew a breath, crossing the room slowly. Giving him a look through narrowed eyes to let him know he had won, I snatched the paper away. "All right. I am going to go," I said, "shut myself in my office and revise."

He gave me the same mock expression. "See that you do."

I SAT AT THE DESK, a pen in my hand, notebook before me. I had been typing, but maybe handwriting—more personal, more connected to the written word—would bring forth the things I needed to say.

I didn't know how to talk about the emotional impact, about the loss of my career, my home, my boyfriend, without sounding bitter. I might be worthy of sympathy, but I would consider it beneath myself professionally just to write an article to gain sympathy.

So I cultivated humility, not taking myself or the things I had possessed so seriously that I couldn't see that there was a perspective to it all. I wanted to write as the person I was: Madeleine Apkarian, a girl from Alabama, orphaned—but there was a perspective to that, too—who had been very successful, very well-educated, and blessed. Someone who, fundamentally, had agency. Who was not a victim.

For the first bit of time I sat, I mostly tapped my pen against my chin, vaguely still irritated with Samuel, mostly because I knew he was right. Then there was writer's block, a dearth of narrative creativity. Then came deep thinking, which was real *work*.

Then there was a burst of insight.

Excitement, a vision of how words could connect... And then there was the taking of pen to paper.

TWENTY

"I have sworn upon the altar of god, eternal hostility
against every form of tyranny over the mind of man."
-Thomas Jefferson

Samuel listened, his hands clasped between his knees, his head cocked to the side, as I read him the article in its entirety. I knew when he didn't stop me once to correct a sentence that it was right. It built as I read it, the force of its words more and more impactful as they multiplied. Tears trailed down my face near the end.

I looked at Samuel. He nodded after a solemn moment. "It's right. It's good."

Simple words, but the highest praise from him.

"And you still don't think I'm crazy?"

"I do not," he affirmed.

I considered him for a moment.

"What?" he asked.

"Are you ready for this, Samuel?" I used my shirtsleeve to dry my face. He studied me. "It's going to get ugly when this goes to publication," I continued. "It's going to stir up a lot of good conversations, give some people pause for thought... But there will to be a lot of unpleasantness, too."

"I don't care what a bunch of trolls on Twitter say, Maddie," he said, scowling.

"The last guy I dated lost his job because of me. It seems like a fair warning to say—"

"Please. Stop."

I considered him. "It's beginning to be known in academia that we're dating. You could lose your job and standing. I mean that it could actually happen, Samuel. I want you to make that decision with your eyes wide open. I can't change who I am. I will always say what I believe, no matter how unpopular. But I'm here to tell you, it's a lot easier to say you'll stand firm now than when the whole world seems to hate you."

"My world is *you*," he said passionately, looking angry. He studied me as if he couldn't understand how or why I would say such things.

My lips parted at his words, and my eyes filled anew.

His expression softening, he came to me, wrapping one arm around me, and putting the other hand on the back of my neck. I looked up at him, and our eyes held a long moment. "It's not going to be like you think, Maddie," he said softly.

I stayed silent.

"It's not."

The insistence in his tone had me looking up at him. Holding his eyes, I nodded.

I kissed him.

Etta Wayles Hayden to William Wayles, documented and preserved by Madeleine Apkarian, Ph.D., M.A., B.A.

June 1, 1834
Hayden's Ridge
My Dear Brother,

All is set for the ascension on July 4. Alexander wishes me to tell you that the Poplar Lawn in Petersburg was confirmed by the city council as the site from which your balloon will depart. The field is adjacent to Jefferson Avenue. I can scarcely think of anything more appropriate.

There is a reason I told Alexander that I preferred to write to you. I have heard from I.J. He tells me that M. is to attend the ascension. I know that you are in contact with him. Please tell him not to approach me. Impress upon him that Alexander <u>does not know</u>, and that my marriage would be finished if he did. Tell him that much as it pains me, we must find a way to maintain the bonds between us in secret. I know he wishes to see the children. I wish dearly that he might. Sometimes when John Hiram laughs, he looks so much like M. that it steals my breath. Tell him that. Tell him that I love him.

What more can I say? I weep as I write this. The situation is impossible. Please give your two Marys my love.

Yours With Love,
Ettie H.

M WAS A MAN. Truly, he was man whom Etta Wayles Hayden was in love with. I didn't know any other way to read the last letter I had found while I was cataloging. It seemed that William and Mary Wayles's letter collection had been reacquired by Hayden's Ridge at some point and scattered at random throughout the other documents. This acquirement was hugely fortunate for me, since I didn't think Etta Hayden ever intended anyone at Hayden's Ridge to read that letter. An interesting insight into how little we know about people's lives in history just based on the clues they choose to leave...

Etta Hayden clearly believed her child to have been fathered by *M*. She couldn't be mistaken if John Hiram Hayden, in the midst of his laughter, looked so much like *M* that it stole her breath, could she? But that was impossible. Samuel's family tree showed him as descended from John Hiram Hayden, and the only way for Samuel to have the same Y chromosome as their distant colonial ancestor would be if John Hiram Hayden was fathered by Etta's husband, Alexander.

And what of the rest? Had Etta's love for Alexander, once so tangible it jumped through the paper, simply dried up? I didn't see that. She wasn't fickle. I knew her by now. The only way she would stop loving someone would be through years of betrayal or mistreatment or something of that nature. And Alexander Hayden wrote to his brother-in-law regularly, pouring out words of affection about his wife and children in a way that seemed to ring true, making such a thing improbable.

The door opened, and, my mind still whirling, I chewed on the end of my pen pensively.

"I think we should get married very soon."

I looked up quickly, my attention caught. Samuel had entered at the door. He appeared to have spoken the thought on his mind, passionately. His hand was raking through his hair again. I had true concerns that he would pull it out. Clearly, he was struggling with restraint.

Lifting my brows, I stood. I went slowly around the side of my desk, crossing my arms. "Is this a proposal?"

He made a dismissive gesture. "Sure, whatever." He looked at me like that was no big deal. Like he had been highly agitated in his own office, unable to think, and he had come in here to unburden himself.

Sometimes the man made my blood boil. Imagine coming in and just...declaring that! "Samuel..." I said in frustration. "No. That doesn't work for me."

I expected this to irritate him, but I began right away to see comprehension in his face that he had messed up. My words gave him pause, literally and metaphorically.

"You have been married before," I said, "so it may be no big deal...the whole process...but I haven't. You can't just...come in here and half-ass a proposal, or whatever that demand was. We're not going to casually do anything."

I thought he would offer some sort of argument. Instead, he looked chastened. He studied my face almost grimly, his own a bit red. He took a step back, like he was treading on thin ice. Then, meeting my eyes again, he nodded once and left.

THINGS WERE AWKWARD the next few days. There was an over-politeness, lots of little glances, and some stilted, well-mannered conversation. I think Samuel wasn't sure if we were broken up, and I wanted to keep it that way. Let him think on his sins.

By the third day, the tension was too much, and I decided to go into the city to get some groceries. Chester Arthur even seemed to feel it and begged to go with me. I asked Samuel if I could take him.

"Sure, but he'll have to sit in the car. The temp's fine, but he won't sit still."

I reluctantly parted with Chester's leash, acknowledging the wisdom in this statement. Samuel glanced at me hesitantly. "Do you need help with the groceries?" he asked finally.

"I'll be fine," I answered. Because he looked miserable, I tossed him a nugget. "I should be back before supper."

I stocked up and, since I was feeling generous, I stopped at one of Samuel's favorites to pick up supper. This seemed to cheer him. Upon seeing the bag, he looked up to study me, trying to discover whether a truce/forgiveness had been reached.

I turned my attention to Chester, who came up to me curiously. I *lavished* affection on him. "Who's a good boy, huh? Chester Arthur Hayden, that's who. I got you some kibbles, too, boy. Yes, I did."

Chester panted in my face. He had bad breath, but you would never tell that by looking at me. I rubbed his head. Samuel regarded us sourly, scowling darkly.

As soon as the groceries were up, we sat down to eat.

There was some more awkwardness. At some point near the end, I caught Samuel glancing at me. He looked so serious that the last vestiges of my frozen heart thawed. I covered a small smile and got up to clean my plate. I refilled my glass and walked back toward the counter, where he was still sitting, his eyes on me.

I leaned across, taking his sweater in my hand and pulling him toward me for a kiss. He gave a smile, looking up at me. "I will forgive you on one condition," I said.

He lifted that brow.

"Will you look at a letter with me?"

He sighed.

"No. This is a woman's handwriting. I will die on that hill."

Samuel, standing in his office with the recently-found letter between the Wayles siblings as well as all of the letters from *M* in his hand, had a certain stubborn look I knew well.

Sitting on the sofa, the fire behind me cozy and warm, I said, "Samuel, you know men's handwriting was more florid in those days."

"I'm good at this," he said. "This is a woman."

"Whom Etta Wayles Hayden thought to have fathered her son?" I demanded pointedly. He was losing this argument, no two ways about it. Ha.

"Maybe there were two "*M's*," he suggested. "One who wrote to her, who was obviously a woman, and another person, obviously a man, to whom she referred in this letter to William Wayles. People used initials all the time in letters. It could be two people."

"Is that likely?" I asked. "Two people mysteriously referred to by one initial, who seemed to need secrecy for some purpose, and who both happened to use the *same* initial?"

Samuel held my eyes. He knew it was not. His wheels were spinning, however, and he wasn't going to let a good argument get in the way of the answer this time. "What do we know of the *M* who wrote these letters in French?"

"We know this person knew about the portrait in your attic, was in on the secret, whatever it was, about Etta's first baby, given the 'no one will ever know' language, and also wrote Etta a letter referencing mysteriously a man who had died."

"And what do we know of this *M* who is referenced in Etta's letter to William?"

"That he was a man, who favored her son, John Hiram. That Alexander Hayden didn't know about the relationship between them, and that if he did, he would divorce Etta, or something drastic of that nature. That this *M* wanted to see her children. That she intended to maintain bonds with him, but in secret." When you said it like that... "That's an affair. It couldn't be

185

anything else." Samuel just stared at me. "What else?" I demanded.

He hesitated for a long moment. "An enslaved brother."

Our eyes held. I froze as I considered the possibility. My heart quickened. Long seconds passed. "It could be that. But, come on —Alexander would divorce her? Lots of people had enslaved brothers. Martha Jefferson did. Her daughters would later have them, too. If this were the case, Etta certainly wouldn't have been unique."

Samuel held my eyes still. "What if she was born enslaved?" he pressed softly.

The hair on my arms stood. "Etta?" I whispered.

I looked into nothingness as my wheels spun rapidly. *No one will ever know... Alexander does not know... The situation is impossible...* I thought of everything I had read. Etta's cloaked assurance to William's wife Mary that her son was fair. Etta's extreme anxiety during her pregnancy. My belief that she loved Alexander and hadn't had an affair...

She had "passed." My heart skipped two beats. Somehow, as soon as Samuel suggested it, I knew it in my bones. Etta Hayden was one of the numerous people throughout history with some African ancestry who had passed for solely European American.

I looked up. Samuel was watching me. For all his protestations that he didn't care about his family tree, I could tell this possible revelation had stunned him. "Why did I never think of that?" he almost whispered. "*You* never thought of that. We discussed an enslaved man or woman pairing somehow with a Hayden wife or husband, but not a *wife* being enslaved. It fits with the DNA. Alexander Hayden *would* have been the father of her children."

For some reason, I felt emotional. I never intended to stumble upon it here, tonight. There was no way to prove it, of course, but... Finally, things were starting to make sense.

I wiped my eyes, deciding to ignore Samuel's jibe about my never having thought of it. I took it as proof that he was trying to level the playing field, knowing that I was smarter than him. However, *he* had guessed this one, darn him, and I begrudgingly gave him credit for that.

"You are welcome," he said graciously.

I rolled my eyes. Taking a deep breath, I considered the hypothesis some more. "Oh, Samuel, what must that have been like for her?" I whispered. "To be born a slave. And then to marry one of the largest slave-owners in the state. To love him. To have his children. To have all of that uncertainty... I can't even wrap my head around it."

"What do we know of Etta and her brother William?"

"They came from the Piedmont. Their ancestral home burned. They lived in Washington, D.C., where they met Alexander Hayden while he was a U.S. Representative. They connected because the two men shared a mutual passion for ballooning." I considered what else I knew. "William married a woman named Mary and had a Little Mary with her. I think his wife must have been in on the secret. Obviously, she was a white woman, because William and Mary Wayles interacted with the Haydens, were very close to them, and that wouldn't have been possible otherwise. And if your theory about at least one of the *M*'s, if there are two, being a brother to William and Etta is true, William obviously acted as a liaison between Etta and *M*."

Samuel considered, deep in thought.

"Well?" I asked. "Any more brilliant revelations?"

"Only that the house burning is a convenient story. Which leaves two questions: how did they get to freedom, and how did they assimilate into wealthy white society so seamlessly and thoroughly?"

TWENTY-ONE

"One man with courage is a majority."
-*Thomas Jefferson*

Rachel Goldstein's editors emailed me with only mild edits and let me know that my article would run in two weeks. Cue an anxiety attack.

That aside, I was like a madwoman researching following the development of our new hypothesis. Nothing could hold me back, and I read through documents at warp speed, rather like a beaver intent upon demolishing an entire log by midday. There was a reason I hadn't thought of Etta Hayden as Samuel's ancestor with African heritage: I had never heard of it.

There were interracial marriages far back into American history, even among wealthy people. Adam Tunno and Margaret Bettingall in Charleston, for instance. But everyone knew Margaret to have been a woman of African descent. There were also many examples of lifelong partnerships. But those weren't marriages, weren't absorbed within the acceptable boundaries of society. I couldn't think of another instance of a woman having, somehow, escaped slavery, passed for a woman of only European descent, and gone on to become the most prominent woman in her community. Without her husband's knowledge.

The very uniqueness of the situation made this ground-breaking. The ripples in historical circles that it would cause would be enormous and long-lasting, telling us ever more about the past. Simply put, it was a story that, if I could find enough supporting evidence, needed to be told. And I couldn't deny that I felt certain it would save my career.

But I would never do that to Samuel, of course. His father had wanted privacy for the family. He didn't want them to be under academia's often-unempathetic microscope. Samuel wanted to respect that wish. And I respected Samuel.

MY ARTICLE RAN ON SUBSTACK. It was the first of May, and springtime was blooming at Hayden's Ridge.

And I was in the kitchen, panic-stricken.

I remembered walking onto campus the morning after the supposed "story" about me had broken. I remembered the protesters. The posters all over the bulletin boards in my building. The notes stuck to my office door. The chants. The campus security whisking me away and telling me not to come back.

I had only tried it once more, thinking that I wouldn't be intimidated, before I had realized it was impossible to be there safely. John Granger had packed my boxes for me when I had "resigned." And not long after, a lot more boxes had been packed. Bradley's.

I remembered what the full blast of being a pariah was like. The refusal of my academic colleagues to stand behind me, my superiors' decision to cut ties with me, my neighbors turning their faces away in fear of association... For someone unprepared for that, who was used to the normal social contract...it was the worst possible thing. It was dehumanizing.

Therefore, the fact that I was a bit nervous that I had gathered the temerity to tell my story was not unexpected. But it was nonetheless grueling. The story would hit other outlets later, but I watched as comments started coming in on the Substack article first.

I sat up, allowing a thin reed of air into my lungs. They were favorable. Some called me brave. That was good. I sucked in another slight breath.

Samuel was across the room on a barstool checking Twitter. Rachel Goldstein had five-hundred-thousand followers. She tweeted a link for the article with the caption, "This time last year, Dr. Madeleine Apkarian had a glittering career in academia. Then she defended the student body president's right to speak his mind. And she lost everything."

"It's been retweeted one-hundred-thirty-seven times so far," Samuel said. He looked up. "These are some pretty big names, Maddie." He got up and came over to me. My eyes widened as I saw some of the people from the media and academia who were sharing it with their own powerful captions.

Read and weep.

Terrifying.

If you think things like this can't happen here, you're wrong.

It felt vindicating, of course. As the morning went on, I lost count of how many people came out of the woodwork, saying that they knew me, and that I was one of the bravest people they knew. *That* surprised me. Or people I didn't know expressing shock over what was happening at universities and admiration for my stance.

I could have felt bitter. Where were these people when I was drowning? When I was a witch about to be burned at the stake? When I had death threats against me from people I had never met? When I needed help burying my dog, for crying out loud! I wiped away a tear.

"Don't."

I looked up into Samuel's green eyes. I lifted my brows.

"Don't pretend you're just one of the crowd. You're a pioneer. A torchbearer. These people couldn't speak then because they didn't feel safe doing so. Now that you've spoken, you've pierced the bubble, and they *can* speak about it."

I started to cry, and he tucked me against him, holding me a long time in the kitchen. He could really be a lot more tender than I had ever imagined, even in college. "I liked the one," I whispered hoarsely, "where the woman said she was going to tell her little girl about me."

"I liked the one," he said, "where your co-worker said Bradley had always been a dick."

I gave a choked laugh, burying my face against his shoulder.

I WAS INVITED onto like thirteen podcasts. I'm not sure if the number was an omen. But I took all of them. I took everything I could get. I wasn't going to lie down and let my career molder in the same flames which had brought it to the ground. Not if there was even a chance of salvaging it.

So in between video chats and phone sessions and a quick trip to Richmond, I also scanned furiously through hundreds of documents. The index of enslaved people at Hayden's Ridge which I had prepared was complete, and Samuel had no objection to that being published. In fact, he had already found a publisher. Being purely academic, it wouldn't bring me much money. But it would be a huge contribution to the field and colonial history in general. It would also be the first time a significant number of documents from Hayden's Ridge were made public. So, who could say? There might be moderate interest in it. And it was time to put it into the hands of editors.

But I had another project going, too. One might call it an obsession. I had to know about Etta Hayden's life. I had to know where she had come from. Who her mother and father were. Where she had been born. How she had broken free. If her husband had ever found out about her history. And if he had, whether their marriage had survived it.

"I'm sorry, but you're going to have to go over this letter with me again," I said, entering Samuel's office, where he was scanning documents. In actuality, I had in my hand every letter written in French by the mysterious *M*, but I planned to break him in easy.

He groaned. "Maddie..."

"I will make out with you later," I said (because I wanted to).

He wavered. Then he sat down at his desk. I handed him the copies. He glanced up at me. I tried to look innocent. He gave me a knowing look, but it was complete with an almost-smile. So I'm pretty sure he was thinking I was charming or sexy. This was good. Because I had a lot of questions.

"Exactly how good is your French?" I asked. I knew he had a working knowledge but wanted to know if he could catch nuances.

I thought back to college. We had both been required to attain a writing knowledge of a second language to test into our graduate schools. Mine was Russian. His was Spanish, and I knew that was how he had met Jenna, given that it was her major. But for it to have been Jenna's major, she had to have a writing knowledge of a third language, which had been French, and she had taught both at UVA. Before...relocating to Thailand.

Samuel sighed. "Working. Rusty, but...okay."

"And you said all of the endearments are feminine?"

"Well, of course, she was writing to Etta, to the extent she was referring to a person." He scanned over it. "So we can't base it on that. But socially, it reads like one woman talking to another."

"How so?"

He flipped back to the earlier letter. "She asks some pretty specific questions about her feminine health. I don't think even her husband would have done that in a letter."

Well, that was a good point.

He looked up at me. "How likely is it that any slave in Virginia would have had a writing knowledge of French during the early American period?"

"Very unlikely. You know that. Most weren't given a writing knowledge of English, even."

"Is it impossible?"

I shook my head. "Nothing is impossible." As Etta had reminded me. "The person could have…" I shook my head. "I don't know, been in a linguist's household, or a diplomat's? If we were in Louisiana, there could be a ton of options, but we're not even close to there. So while we wouldn't think of any slave/master dynamic in terms of leniency, if *M* was an enslaved person, that would have been how society then would have thought of him or her having a knowledge of French. At least, I think so. It would have required education, or at least proximity."

He looked back down at the letters. "Grammatically, it's not by any means perfect."

I lifted my brows. "Really?"

"It's quite rough, actually."

I leaned over, in full academic mode. "Show me the mistakes."

There were quite a few. Except for the French-speaking areas during that time, mistakes would have been the norm for most any American who knew French during the era. John Adams famously struggled during his time as Minister to France. Actually, even in English, perfect grammar could be an issue in writing. I recalled to mind a letter from General Nathanael Greene to his wife, Catherine, adjuring her to mind her spelling and grammar in her letters to General Knox's wife, a bluestocking, so as to avoid embarrassment. In other words, a lack of rank wouldn't neces-sarily be the only cause of poor grammar.

"Could it have been a Frenchman, given the errors?"

"I doubt it. French doesn't appear to be the person's primary language."

"Do you see anything else of note?" I asked.

Samuel scanned over it again. "I'm sorry. Nothing else leaps out at me."

I sighed, taking the copies back. "That's okay. Thanks for trying."

"My purposes were not exactly altruistic."

I smiled. I was rather looking forward to the evening myself.

———

WE DIDN'T MAKE it to evening. Midday, we happened to meet up in the kitchen. Who would have thought an old Virginia house could be romantic? Sometimes my connection to Samuel all but scared me. He made me feel strong, but my feelings made me feel powerless. Helpless. Once upon a time, I would have stuffed the feelings down, locked them away, too afraid to look them in the eye. I had lost a lot of people. And I was afraid.

But...I don't know. I was trying to *live*. And it wasn't going away, this feeling. It had never gone away.

Kissing complete, we walked in the afternoon sun out onto the lawn, holding hands. There was a slight rise that provided a breath-taking view of the James, and we stood looking out onto the river for a second.

I turned my head to watch a bird of some sort swoop down to splash a bit in the water. Then it turned and followed the bends of the river away. Farther down, a duck lifted its wings, joyously tossing up water as it bathed. A squirrel scurried away toward a tree, unnerved by the commotion. I looked up at the sky, blue and beautiful.

When I turned my head, Samuel had gone down on one knee.

My heart jumped, my breath catching. The look on his face was serious. He swallowed. His eyes didn't leave mine. I touched my throat with my hand. He hesitated. "Maddie... When I said that off-handedly about getting married... It wasn't because I didn't realize the significance of the moment, or because I meant to treat you callously." He searched my eyes, but the look turned into a caress. "It was because after we talked about having children... I realized that you were the woman I would have children with." My breath caught. "That either you would be by my bedside as I died, or I would be by yours." My eyes welled with large tears that dropped down my face, pouring like rivers. "And in light of that," he said, "all the rest seemed like a formality. I want to get started on this grand adventure, and that is why I'm asking: Maddie, will you marry me?"

I couldn't speak. I was crying, and I pulled him up, nodding against him so he could feel my assurance.

"You have to say *yes*," he croaked, a loving smile in his voice.

"*Yes!*"

Then he kissed me. I touched his face, holding it between my hands.

He pulled away, slipping a ring onto my finger. I kissed him one more time and then looked at the ring. It was antique. Art deco. White gold with a massive rock, hand-finished piecework, and a naturalistic motif of leaves and flowers. "It's breath-taking," I said, turning it over and over.

"It was my grandmother's," he said. "I went back until I found a marriage that had actually worked in this family."

I choked on a laugh, enveloped by the moment. I looked up at him. "It fits perfectly."

TWENTY-TWO

"These are the times in which a genius would wish to live. It is not in the still calm of life, or the repose of a pacific station, that great characters are formed. The habits of a vigorous mind are formed in contending with difficulties. Great necessities call out great virtues. When a mind is raised, and animated by scenes that engage the heart, then those qualities which would otherwise lay dormant, wake into life and form the character of the hero and the statesman."
-Abigail Adams

"Hey, hon."

Jessie had answered quickly, and I had been counting on at least a few more seconds to figure out what I was going to say.

I took a deep breath. "Jess... I was calling to ask if you...would come to my wedding..."

There was a poignant pause. "Only if you'll come to mine."

I gasped. "Did you get engaged yesterday?!"

"Did *you* get engaged yesterday?!"

We were both exclaiming and crying in seconds, and, when

Samuel came, looking concerned, I shut him out of the room. Wiping weepy tears, I said, "When are you getting married?"

"Next year. When are y'all?"

I winced. "In two months."

She gasped. "Madeleine Ani Apkarian! How on earth are we going to pull this off?"

"Well, we want to have a baby," I said, whispering. "I'm off birth control, and I don't want to go back on it. I want to wait until we're married to get pregnant, and to...you know... And I am on a short timeline here, because..." Might as well be honest. "I am just not going to hold out much longer."

"Well, I see that. He is *fine*. I like that he has the sheep." She sighed, apparently thinking of the sexiness of a man farming. "We want a big family, so we're going to get started right away, too."

"How many?" I asked, blinking.

"Oh, I don't know. Maybe five."

I laughed with shock, but joy, too. I could definitely see that: Jessie with a bunch of wild hooligans. And she was going to be happy. Well, she already was. She was going to have a partner, someone to walk through life with. My eyes welled up at the thought. "I'm so happy for you, Jessie."

"Hon, I'm so happy for you, I can't stop bawling. Go away, Dale, I'm not dying!"

I laughed again. "Okay, so we're in planning mode, I guess. I'll email you a list of stuff."

"You do that. I've already started a Pinterest board for you, hon, because I just had a feeling."

"Do you have one for you?"

"Yeah, but, I'm being reasonable about my wedding date, so that can wait," she responded smugly.

I shook my head. "Alright. Talk to you later."

"Later, alligator."

My phone buzzed. Pulling it out of my back pocket, I rose to my full height, answering it. "Hello?"

"Are you with Samuel?"

I was surprised to hear Enid's voice.

"Um, no. No, I'm not. He's outside, and—"

"No, I mean, are you *with* Samuel?"

"Oh. Yes, I am."

Enid heaved a great sigh. "Thank heavens for that."

I smiled. There was something priceless about being accepted by the family of one's future mate. "He was going to call you tonight. We...got engaged, actually."

"That's wonderful. It should have happened a long time ago, of course." I flushed. I had no idea she knew. "But that is beside the point." I was beginning to be concerned. Her tone was tense, and she hadn't mentioned sex once. "As it happens, I am very glad his own love life is evening out. My dear, I need you to find him. I have something to tell him, and I would like for you to be there for him when I do."

My heart escalated as I headed toward the back door. "Is something wrong with Aunt Millicent?" I winced. "Or his mother?"

"No, no." That was all she would say.

I walked out toward the barn, where I found Samuel. He was working with a sheep but looked up when he saw me. He smiled, which warmed me down to my toes.

"Okay, I'm here with him," I said.

"Put me on speaker phone."

Samuel, frowning now, was walking toward me. He stopped just next to me.

"Hello, nephew dear."

"Hello," Samuel answered suspiciously.

"Listen, darling, there's something I have to tell you, and there's no easy way to do it: I'm married."

Samuel blinked, and then rolled his eyes. "Well, it's not exactly like this has never happened before," he said sarcastically. "How did it come about?"

"Well, you know we were planning on France this summer... We decided to go earlier, and we're here now. One thing led to another, and I am the new Mrs. Taliaferro."

I saw Samuel pause. Tilt his head. "Mrs. *Landon* Taliaferro?" I knew that tone. It was not good.

"Yes."

"He *graduated* with me! He was my *friend*!"

"And now he is my lover. Yes. It is all very difficult to process."

Samuel looked, as he often did with Enid, like he was going to have a convulsion. "You are *disgusting*!"

"Landon doesn't think so," she said naughtily. "I am the Brigitte to his Emmanuel."

The look on Samuel's face... Purest outrage, gravest disgust, and perhaps impending illness... "What the *hell*? How long have you been dating? I guess this is why you've never told me a *name*!"

"Indeed, that is true. We agreed it would only upset you. Your uncle says hello, by the way."

"Tell my *uncle* that he can—"

I took the phone off speaker and angled away, trying not to laugh. When Samuel looked annoyed with me, I muted the phone and said, "You need to calm down. She's gotten your goat, and you will hate yourself for that tomorrow."

He stared at me like the bull again, breathing through his nose, a sign that he was boiling. But he knew I was right.

I put it back on speaker phone. Enid was saying, "...and I can't think why you would deny me such pleasure when you have embarked upon a course of recreational gratification and bliss yourself!"

"Don't speak of Maddie like that in front of that bastard!" he said, for all the world as if I were a virginal Regency heroine. "And *we* are the *same age*!"

"Don't call your uncle a bastard."

Samuel gasped. Amused as I was, I was afraid either he would have a stroke or I would betray myself by laughing. "Enid," I said, "I'm going to let you go, okay? Talk soon." I ended the call.

I let Samuel breathe in silence for several minutes.

Then I said, peeping up at him, "Are you worried he's in it for her money?"

"He has more money than she does," he replied shortly.

"Well, then," I said brightly. "That's a relief, then."

Samuel gave me a look. After a moment, he said, "Why *did* he marry her?"

Enid had mentioned it was for the sex, but I wagered that would not be the right thing to say just now. So I said delicately, "Samuel... I know she's a mother figure to you—"

"*Older* than my mother."

"Indeed. But... She's a very attractive woman." He looked down at me. I had his attention. "She has an electric personality. Is it just possible that there is something real...or real*ish* here? If he is or was your friend, I can't imagine he's a bad person." I moved in closer, touching his chest. "And if he makes her happy..."

He covered my hand. "He had better."

I smiled. He gave me a peck on the lips, his other hand moving around my waist. I pressed against him, kissing him again.

"You're like a siren," he said. "I'm very angry, but I can't even think clearly when you do that."

"I know," I commiserated.

This surprised a laugh out of him. He kissed me with gratefulness.

WEDDING.

Wedding, wedding, wedding. There were endless details. We

decided we would hold the ceremony behind the house on the hill overlooking the river. That was easy.

As was the dress. I drove to Richmond and video chatted with Jessie while I picked out a gown. It was simple but pretty. Very much my style. Strangely, the shoes were harder to choose, but I ended up slightly stretching the budget on a pair that caught my eye. I ordered the veil online, wanting Italian tulle but being unable to find it in the stores.

I sent Samuel and his best man (a friend from Charlottesville) links for their suits, which I had picked out because they didn't care. They planned a day to go for fittings. Jessie was searching for a lavender dress for herself. Another friend of Samuel's had two little girls who were going to be our flower girls. I met the mom for the very cute fitting.

We talked to a florist, a caterer, and a deejay. I almost forgot that we needed a cake, so that required another quick trip into the city. I knew it would come together eventually. I wanted the wedding to be nice, and it would be. I had just never expected to care so little about the details. I decided, however, that this was a very good thing.

I WORKED on edits after they were returned for the index. Actually, I *drowned* in edits. My book was large, memorializing every enslaved person, along with every detail I could find about them, who had ever lived at Hayden's Ridge. Every word was based on a primary document, which had to be cited and quoted. Then also, there were suggestions on the arrangement of the documents to be waded through.

Samuel had agreed to write the forward for the book, and when he submitted it, I was impressed. It hit just the right notes. Solemnity about what had happened here, at his ancestral home, without navel-gazing. Sorrow without false modern confessionals.

Awareness of the depth of the lives lived and of his own family's part in the history. And of the profoundness of time and the people who lived before us.

We didn't mention what we knew about Etta. She had a story to tell, but it was separate. And part of me prayed that I would get to tell that story, too.

I was calling myself the editor of the collection since it was gathered entirely from primary documents. I liked our names together on the cover which was sent to us. *The Enslaved People of Hayden's Ridge: A Complete Guide to the Lives Lived. Edited by Madeleine Apkarian. Forward by Samuel Hayden.*

"Very pretty," he approved, looking at the mockup. We sat on a blanket on our little ridge overlooking the river. I assume the water flowed, but it was too deep to tell today.

I looked up at him suddenly. "My name. I hadn't thought. What am I going to do?"

Samuel looked down at me, the wind tousling his hair. "That's your call," he said.

I studied his handsome face. I thought for a long moment because I wanted to get it right. It was every woman's prerogative to decide it because it would be for a lifetime. "I think I'd like to be *Hayden*," I said softly.

He nodded gently, holding my eyes, a slight smile on his lips. It might not be modern to admit he was pleased, but I could tell he was.

My phone rang. We both looked down. *Bradley* flashed across the screen.

I studied the phone, confused. I couldn't imagine what this was about. I glanced up at Samuel. "Do you mind?" I asked seriously. I wasn't going to answer if it would upset him.

"Whatever, but if he's rude to you—"

"I'll sign off," I promised.

I stood, walking a few feet away. "Hello?"

"Madeleine." His tone was different. I could tell in an instant.

He had come down off whatever heights he had been on. There was a long pause. "How are you?" He sounded human again.

"I'm fine," I answered. "Are you?"

Another long gap. I could almost feel his emotion. "I read the article."

I bit my lip.

"You didn't say I abandoned you. Or that I ditched you like everyone else," he said, voice heavy. "You talked about me in terms of a victim, about us as a casualty of the mob."

My throat burned. "It's true," I managed.

"Thank you for that," he said. "But it's overly generous."

I swallowed. A long, understanding silence developed between us. Forgiveness.

"Look, Madeleine, I know we're finished. But I wanted you to know...I'll treat the next woman better. And I wanted to say I'm sorry. I had hate built up inside of me, but your article...saved me."

I blinked away tears. People had no idea how powerful an apology was. It soothed and healed and plunged down deep to wash away bitterness. It was like all of mine for Bradley evaporated. My dad had apologized to me not long before he had died. He had owned up to what he had done, and how he had failed me. That was no small part of the reason I was able to have healthy relationships with men now.

"Thank you, Bradley," I whispered. "That means a lot."

WE PLANNED a dinner with Enid and Landon, which rolled around all too soon. Enid had suggested this forerunner meeting to me as a means of keeping Samuel and Landon from killing one another at the wedding. As this was something I also had an interest in, I bent my powers of persuasion upon Samuel. He was not very persuadable.

Luckily, I had a trump card. I kissed him, obviously. When that didn't suffice, I looked sad, which made him crazy, and he acquiesced rapidly.

That settled, I set about planning the meal, the first which I would host in the old dining room at Hayden's Ridge. Samuel and I roasted a chicken and vegetables, whipped an old tablecloth into place over the dining table, and coughed from the dust as we dug out the china and silverware.

Samuel looked like someone on death row as we went to answer the door, both of us a bit dressed up.

We opened the door to reveal the happy couple. Enid wore a lovely dress, her slim arm twined through the expensively clad arm of her husband. I looked at the man.

Yep. Samuel's age.

He was handsome, with blonde hair, a wide smile, and an eye for a suit. He had colonial roots back to Italy, Enid said. But, given that the Taliaferros were one of the first families of Virginia, he looked more English than anything.

Enid handed me a bouquet of flowers, which broke the thick tension.

"Oh, thank you!" I said. "How pretty. Samuel, will you go put these in water?"

Samuel stared at Landon gravely.

"Samuel?"

"Sure." He reluctantly took the flowers, walking off.

I led the guests toward the dining room. Enid looked touched that we had gone to so much trouble, and she hugged me. "Let's see that rock," she said.

I extended my left hand.

"Beautiful," she approved. "When my sister, Celia, was lady of the house here," she said, "she had an antique pearl, encased in diamonds. It was from the eighteenth century, I believe."

"Ah, yes! I have seen it in a portrait of one of the ancestral ladies. Well, let me see yours!"

Enid extended her hand to reveal a tasteful ring, which suited her perfectly. I looked at the groom. "Well done."

He smiled. "Hello, Maddie. You're beautiful, just like Enid said. Is Samuel very mad?" he asked, as though it were a foregone conclusion.

"Yes," I answered bluntly.

He sighed. "What can I do?"

"Just give him some time. He'll come around. He's brusque, but he is actually very open-minded."

"I know," he said, nodding with a sigh.

Samuel walked in then, and we all straightened up. I shepherded everyone to their seats, and we began the meal.

I initiated a conversation, which Samuel joined only in short, clipped statements. I was skeptical of the couple at first, but...I don't know. They had an easy way with each other. It didn't strike me as one of those crazy, infatuated flings that ends in disaster months after it began.

Samuel and I got up to prepare the dessert in the kitchen, and as soon as we were behind the closed door, I said, "You have got to give an inch, Samuel."

"No, I don't."

"Well, this is awkward," I said firmly. "*You* are making this awkward."

"He married my aunt."

"Yes," I said, putting the whipped cream on the counter. "And she is of sound mind."

"She has never been of sound mind," he retorted sarcastically.

I pointed the spoon at him. "You are going to be nice." I raised my eyebrows, daring him to contradict me.

Looking at the spoon, he demanded, "Or what?"

"I have not decided," I said grandly. "But you will not like it."

He gave me a challenging stare.

The desserts were prepared in silence.

As we were about to go back out, I caught him, bringing him

to me. His eyes rested on me as he looked down. "Hey," I said gently. "So your family's screwed up; whose isn't?"

A slight smile played about his mouth, the first of the night I had seen. Encouraged, I said, "She means a great deal to you, Samuel. I can't tell you how wonderful that is. I don't have any family, so I know."

His eyes changed. Lifting my hand, he kissed my fingers, right below my ring. "You have a family, Maddie," he said.

I smiled. Reaching up, I stroked my fingers over his hair at his temple. "Are you ready to go play nice?"

He gave a slow, slightly rakish grin. "I'm far from ready for that," he said, pulling me against him.

Laughing, I let him kiss me. When we were finished, we weren't even sure which room we were in, let alone who our guests were or what our grievances with them were.

"Ice cream is melting," I whispered.

Going in for just one more, Samuel afterwards helped me carry the desserts out to the dining room. Our guests must have noticed immediately a change in him. I wouldn't say he was downright hospitable, but he was much more benign. And we thereafter actually had a pleasant conversation and a really lovely evening.

CHAPTER

TWENTY-THREE

"I never considered a difference of opinion in politics, in religion, in philosophy, as cause for withdrawing from a friend."
-Thomas Jefferson

As our July nuptials neared, two thoughts occurred to me: first, that it was a very bad month to have an outdoor wedding in the South; second, that our loved ones were on a well-charted path to drive us crazy.

It was going to be a small wedding. Friends of Samuel's were coming—he had a nice collection of them from high school, college, grad school, and the university where he now worked. Aunt Millicent would be ceremoniously driven in from her Kensington Palace-esque assisted living home. Aunt Enid and Landon would attend, as well as Jessie, of course. From my side, the only others I had invited were my professor friends, John Granger and Judy Carroll.

I got a call from Judy on June 25th. She refused to fly and damage the environment, so she had commanded John to drive her down to Virginia in her Prius. The thought scared me. I was

207

afraid they would argue politics all the way from Boston and wreck or something.

"He's bringing his wife," Judy said. I felt relief at that. She would provide a much-needed buffer. Poor Anna. "Do Conservatives *have* to travel with their wives? Is it a law?"

"Now, Judy. She's a very nice person. You know that."

"Well, I'm not sitting in the back."

"If not for you, John and Anna would be flying. They are being kind. You could be grateful."

She huffed.

Two days later, I got a call from John. "Listen, Madeleine, Judy's killing me."

I tried to restrain a smile. "Oh?"

"She asked me to drive and then accused me of sexism for assuming that I would be driving." I tried not to snicker.

"Do you know the distance from Boston to your fiancé's house?"

"I'm not sure—"

"Eight hours and fifty-four minutes."

I winced. "Maybe you can listen to podcasts?"

John answered darkly.

A week later, it went from bad to worse: Anna happened to remember a previous engagement and would be unable to attend. Wise Anna. I didn't blame her one bit. But it did lead to every likelihood that we would hear of a murder on I-95 South.

WE HAD a lot of people flying in, and I tried to keep tabs on their flights. I called Jessie an hour before she was supposed to board just to check in with her.

"Hey, is everything on time?"

"We are walking through the airport doors now."

"You and Dale?"

"No, Dale's not coming. Somebody's got to watch both of our farms. He sends his congrats, hon."

I frowned. "Who *do* you have with you?" I thought maybe it was her mom. That would be fine. I could add a place card for her at the reception. The caterers had planned for a few extra plates.

"I'm bringing Dan."

My eyes widened. "Your *bull*?"

"Maddie, honestly. His name is Billy!"

"Oh, yeah..." I mused in confusion.

"Dan? Your father's best friend in the whole wide world? Who went up to New Hampshire to watch you graduate? Well, you need someone to give you away, don't you?"

My eyes filled with tears. "Yes," I whispered. "Yes, I do." I could barely speak. "Thank you, Jessie."

"You got it, sis. This TSA officer is staring at me suspiciously, so I'm going to sign off now."

I pocketed my phone, breathing deeply in order to avoid tears. I prayed Jessie wouldn't get arrested, and then went to call the caterer.

HAYDEN'S RIDGE WAS *TEEMING*.

It was the day before the rehearsal dinner, and Jessie was due to arrive any moment with loaded-down carry-ons full of supplies she had been collecting and her maid-of-honor dress. The ribbons of the perfect color for the bouquet, which she had tracked down, were the only items I could think of currently that she had, but I knew there were a lot more. I honestly didn't even know who I was anymore. I was regretting, just the tiniest bit, my declaration that we would not do things casually.

Tomorrow night, the dinner would be fancy, but tonight was

informal. We were having a barbecue. The smells were delightful, but the bugs and heat were not. "I swear, if I get a bunch of mosquito bites before my wedding..." I grumbled ominously.

"I told you to put on bug spray," Samuel said crankily.

"Judy thinks it kills the environment," I whispered. "If she smells it on me, I'm toast." I didn't even have a lot of skin covered in my sundress. I had lived in New England far too long.

"I know. It's slightly toxic to birds, fish, and aquatic invertebrates," he intoned. "She's already lectured me. We'll see who's scratching tomorrow."

Ever more fearful that it would be me, I gave him a look.

A rental car pulled up, and Dan and Jessie got out. Seeing them, my heart swelled, and tears rose to my eyes. I ran down to them, hugging them emotionally. Then I introduced them to Samuel. He was very welcoming to Dan. When I got to Jessie, it was a bit awkward between them. There was a long pause. "Yes, we've talked," Samuel said.

My brows drew together. I couldn't imagine when. But since Judy yelled out that she needed more wine, and John told her she'd had enough, I decided I needed to go referee.

"WHAT WAS THAT?" I asked in the kitchen. Jessie was helping me wash the lettuce, her blonde, frizzy hair springing here and there, her tomboyish clothes *so* her. My heart squeezed, despite my growing curiosity.

"What was what?"

"You and Samuel."

"I think that was him not wanting to pretend we'd just met because he doesn't like to lie to you," Jessie said, lining lettuce up on a platter with unconcern.

My brows drew together. "You've talked? Did he call you for my ring size or something?"

A hesitation. I stopped what I was doing, and she did, too.

"Now listen, Wildcat, I don't want you to tear my eyes out when I tell you—"

"What on earth? You're scaring me. Did you sleep together in a past life?"

She snorted, then sobered. "No." Drawing a breath, she said, "The last time I talked to him, we were twenty-two years old."

I sucked in my breath. I held her eyes, my wheels spinning. "When I was in college?" I asked.

She nodded slowly. "I got his number. The details are unimportant. I knew he was going to marry her, Maddie. I have a strong intuition, and I was right. And I also knew that if y'all ever had a conversation about it, it would break you when he ultimately chose her. A girl can lose a lot of men and recover, but not the man she's meant to be with." She took a breath. "So I decided to save you as much heartache as I could. You had called me to tell me about the awkward moment in the library. I was afraid something was going to happen. The tension was at the brink. So I called him and told him if he cared about you at all to get on that plane as soon as humanly possible. He agreed. He had already been thinking about leaving, and I just provided the tip to the scale, so to speak."

I studied her a long moment. "Thank you for that," I whispered finally. "I never understood, except just to generally think for some reason I had fallen short of her. When he explained how he had felt, it finally made sense." I could admit things like that to Jessie. She would never call me crazy.

Jessie picked up a tomato. "He's a good man," she said. "I liked him then and thought it was a shame." She grinned a little meanly. "What's his worst fault?"

Surprised, I considered. He was moody, but I actually found that kind of sexy. Sharp-tongued, but I'm not sure how our dynamic would work without that. "An almost insane degree of loyalty," I said with a little laugh.

"You call that a fault?"

I laughed more fully. "No." I wiped my eyes, and it wasn't just the onion I was cutting.

"Well, then," she said. "That says it all."

I SAT at a round table outside under the stars with Samuel, Jessie, Judy, and John. Dan was showing some of the others the proper way to barbecue as they looked on, entranced. He seemed to have taken on the duty of educating the poor city slickers with noble equanimity.

We sat around, having a comfortable, trusting conversation about my professional prospects.

"A lot of influential people are calling for the university to apologize and reinstate you," John said. "Is that something you would want, Madeleine, if possible?"

Frogs chirped and crickets sang. Samuel, his cup in hand, studied me.

"I think there's too much baggage there." That was an understatement. It would take a generation before that campus and I could meet each other tranquilly, of that I was sure.

"Have you gotten any offers from Tier 1's?" John asked.

I shook my head. "None."

"What about good Tier 2's?"

Judy scoffed. "Madeleine's not going to a Tier 2."

"Well, at this point, I would be grateful for any offer," I said honestly. "I don't mean that I would *take* any offer, but I can't be uppity here."

"Don't sound so defeatist," Judy interjected.

I looked at her. "I'm not. I just don't think I will ever teach at a Tier 1 again."

Judy shocked us by slamming her cup down on the table.

"No," she said fiercely. "I did *not* pour concrete into the toilets at the state capitol for a female professor to be bullied out of her job by a delusional mob!"

We all stared at her, eyes wide. Wow. This was a revelation.

"I don't know what the heck you're talking about," Jessie said, "but I like your tone!" Judy and Jessie were getting along like a house on fire. That, frankly, scared me.

The men were still trying to recover from the concrete in the toilets. Ultimately, John said, still alarmed, "Well...maybe Madeleine is just being a realist. What do you think, Dr. Hayden?"

"I'm not sure. I don't think this can last forever. This type of political extremism usually fizzles out."

"Or turns into a world war," Judy mumbled grimly.

"Or that," Samuel agreed.

THERE WAS a knock on my bedroom door. I opened it.

Samuel stood in front of me. He appeared slightly guilty.

I lifted my head up and pinned a look of mock remonstrance on him. I stepped back for him to enter and closed the door so we wouldn't wake our guests. "I'm sorry," he said. "I wasn't deliberately keeping it from you that Jessie had called me. It completely slipped my mind. I didn't want you to...get the wrong impression."

"Samuel...I didn't."

His shoulders loosened. "I left because I loved you. Just so we're clear. Not because Jessie threatened me."

I smiled. "We're clear." I gave him a peck on the lips.

He looked down at me, his eyes heavy with longing, his hand on my shoulder.

"What is this?" he asked, fingering my silk robe.

"Pajamas."

"Easy to remove?" He took me in, every inch.

"Yes."

"I have to get out of here."

I laughed, doing him a favor by being the one to break away, pushing him out the door.

TWENTY-FOUR

"Lovers don't finally meet somewhere.
They're in each other all along."
-Rumi

I was surrounded by women.

Aunt Millicent had been driven in from Richmond. She observed the placement of my veil with a critical eye. Enid reviewed with me the undergarments most calculated to bring pleasure on a honeymoon. Judy made finishing touches to my bouquet. For all of her protestations that marriage was an outdated institution, she had *insisted* that I have a floral arrangement made to the precise specifications of Kate Middleton's Royal Wedding.

"I think it's about time," Tom's wife said, corralling her little girls, who were looking adorable and already spreading flowers in our changing room.

My heart pounded. I hadn't expected it to feel so serious, the moment.

It wasn't just another day, was it? I swallowed.

"All right, all right, let's line up, ladies!" Jessie demanded, securing her wrap and handing me my bouquet.

Dan waited outside, I knew, and it was time for those not in the wedding party to find their seats. I heard the second-to-last song before the wedding music was to begin.

"You clean up well," Aunt Millicent said, pausing in front of me before going to find her escort. I smiled. As compliments went, I would take it.

Judy made one last tweak to my bouquet before she left, admonishing me to remember that my heterosexuality was the greatest bar to true feminism, and to adjust accordingly.

"*Knock boots*," Enid whispered, kissing me and then departing.

"I love you," Jessie whispered, tears in her eyes. She kissed my cheek, took the girls' hands, and headed out.

PEOPLE SAID that love was finding your other half. But we were two fully formed individuals. Complete. For me, it was like coming home. A lighthouse to a ship. Or as Shakespeare put it, "*the star to every wand'ring bark.*"

It sounded cliché. But my home was with Samuel. Wherever we were together. And there wasn't any getting over that. If we had fifty years together, or some time less, that would always be true. He was my last.

My mother believed that a bond between two souls was ancient. Not the people, but the bond. That if was there was love, it had always existed, and always would exist.

My grandmother had not been so sure about that. She had thought it sounded a little pagan. *But let me tell you something, Maddie, if you can find what I had with your grandpa, and grow old with him, you won't regret it.* Her plain-spoken way of saying the same thing.

I *brimmed* with love. Samuel worried about me, but I cried all

216

the time these days. Not from unhappiness. It was like the fullness had to spill out somehow.

My dad had loved Zelda Fitzgerald, a fellow Alabamian. I remembered him reading a quote to me. *'Nobody has ever measured, even poets, how much a heart can hold.' And that's how I feel about you, Maddie. How I felt about your mom, too.* I knew now what he meant.

I walked down the aisle. My betrothed's eyes locked on mine. I had never seen such a serious expression on his face. He wasn't afraid. He was in love, well aware of the profoundness of it, and struggling fully to encompass it. He hadn't even looked at the dress, but I didn't care.

As Dan handed me over to him and shook his hand, the groom still didn't remove his eyes from me. He took my hands, swallowing, chin wobbling with emotion before he got it under control and tightened his jaw. I pressed his hands, and he brought mine to his lips and kissed them. The minister made a joke about waiting for that until the end, and it broke the tension, overwhelming feelings laced with joyful levity now. We both smiled.

And I pledged my life to Samuel Hayden.

THE RECEPTION WAS in full swing. A stringed band played, caterers served from a tent, and the crowd mingled.

I was looking rather fabulous. I had changed into a semiformal white gown, partially backless with tiny straps and a formfitting silhouette. It would be surprising for everyone, I feared, given my normal cool-girl, modest academic style.

Samuel's expression had been arrested. Then...hungry.

I floated around a bit, mingling, making sure Aunt Millicent had everything she needed, for one. She sat at a table looking formidable in her pearls, with a cane nearby. Enid had been looking out for her and had gathered everything possible for her comfort. "It was a lovely ceremony, my dear," Millicent said. "My nephew couldn't take his eyes off of you." Changing courses, she said, "Now, I didn't say anything the last time, but the Hayden name *must* be perpetuated."

I almost smiled. I had wondered if there was anything of the old world lingering around here. It would appear there very much was.

"Now, you don't have to answer, and that is all I am going to say. It would just be a shame, is all," she said, nose in the air. "Run along, my dear."

I found Samuel for our first dance. We did every old-fashioned detail: toasts of the wedding party, cutting the cake, throwing the bouquet.... I had never considered myself traditional, but I loved it, every last detail.

I surveyed our guests. John and Judy. Jessie. Dan. Millicent. Enid and Landon. Samuel's best man, Tom, and his other friends. And it occurred to me... These were my people. I had people. An inner circle. A support group.

Leaving Boston, I had felt like I had no one. But that is never as true as it seems.

We were about to do our walk with confetti or rice being thrown at us, or whatever Jessie had concocted. For the sake of John's ride home with Judy, I hoped it was made of biodegradable material.

My hand was comfortably in Samuel's as we watched everyone line up. Sunlight glinted off Landon's golden blonde hair, and Samuel snarled as we looked down on the guests from the doorway.

"I can't believe he's *married* to her," he said.

Watching Enid (who looked stunning in a light blue tea gown), bend over Landon to receive a strawberry from his fingers into her mouth, I could imagine that the disgust was genuine. They joined the other guests, and then the lines were formed well enough that we were ready to walk through them.

Samuel stopped, looking at me. "I can't believe I'm married to *you*," he said.

"I'm assuming this is meant in a different tone," I said, smiling.

"It's the embodiment of a dream, Maddie," he said soberly.

My smile slipped. Eyes filling, I touched his face and kissed him.

I always knew he could make me deliriously happy. That may sound crazy, given the arguing and his crabbiness. But life didn't always make sense. His lips lingered, and our guests started cheering, making us both smile. I flushed, because it had been a pretty steamy kiss, but Samuel took my hand, and we ran through their confetti, laughing and wiping it out of our hair and ears at the end.

Aunt Millicent waited at the car, too dignified to throw rice. She kissed Samuel's cheek, whispering something to him. She took one each of our hands. I thought I saw emotion in her eyes. "I think you'll be very happy," she said softly.

Samuel pressed her hand gently, emotion in his eyes.

She studied him for a moment. "Talk to your mother," she whispered.

He held her eyes for a long moment before looking down and nodding. Then he kissed her cheek, looked up at me, smiled, took my hand, and opened the door for me.

TWENTY-FIVE

"The best feeling in the world is kissing someone for the first time when you've really wanted to kiss them for a long time."

-Anonymous

I woke up in Samuel's bed, the sheets rustling as I turned. His arm was around me, an incredulous look in his eyes as he surveyed me in the morning light, his wife.

"I'm glad we waited," he said. "*Now*."

I smiled, looking up at him mischievously. "You like the consummation aspect, do you?"

"I do." His eyes darkened with passionate remembrance. "I very much do."

It was an otherworldly experience. The pleasure, yes, but the *connection*... I didn't feel that words could even begin to plumb the depths.

I studied his face, this close angle, the stubble I never saw... Our souls knew one another, but our bodies... It was a very fine education, an exploration of the highest order.

Where was I?

I looked around. *Not* in Samuel's bed, it seemed. Oh, yes. We had spent the night at a fancy hotel in Richmond. Not the one I had first stayed in, but one very similar. I had scarcely noticed it the night before, but it was nice to wake up to.

"We should probably order breakfast," he said.

"We should," I agreed.

Our gazes held. He kissed me. He leaned up, changing positions with me until my head was on the pillow. My fingers laced through his hair as I returned the kiss. My sleepy morning feeling evaporated into thin air.

And breakfast was entirely forgotten.

BACK AT HAYDEN'S RIDGE, we settled into a new rhythm. We would have liked a proper honeymoon, but we also felt like we were under a time crunch with getting the documents sorted. Samuel would be going back to work in a little under two months.

I would not.

Since publishing the article, I had received offers from a few small colleges. One of them, particularly, was a Christian university that had an excellent reputation. Not Ivy League, but it was nonetheless solid. Part of me wanted to start over humbly. Part of me wasn't sure I wanted to re-enter academia at all.

"You don't mean that."

Samuel and I had carried the portrait—*that* portrait—up to the attic. We couldn't find any more information about it. It had survived in mint condition under a drop cloth up here for who-knew-how-long. And, let's be honest, we were both afraid Chester was either going to drool on it or knock it over.

I rose to my full height after tucking the cloth. "No, I know."

He held my eyes, hesitating.

"What is it?" I asked.

He waited another beat. "I have a spousal hire under my contract."

Geez. He really was a high-ticket item at his university.

He studied me. I guess he could tell how I felt. "I almost didn't say anything. I just thought I should mention it."

I tucked my hair behind my ears. "Yeah. Thanks. I just..." I was top of my class. I had offers—actual offers—before I had even graduated. I'd had a career. A good one. A prosperous one that was making waves. I could stand shoulder to shoulder with the best of them. It wasn't arrogance; I didn't think of it that way. In academia, you were a commodity. Like Samuel: a high-ticket item. Well, I had been the highest. The cream of the crop. To get a job under a spousal hire... It wasn't what I had worked for, to say the least.

"It's beneath you, Maddie," he said, voice scraping. "We both know that." He moved forward, putting his hands on my waist as he looked down at me, like he wished he could take away the hurt, the ignominy.

I wiped a tear.

"But that's life sometimes," he said. "I don't want your mind to be wasted. And I don't think you would be happy doing anything else, would you?"

"If it's like it is now, I don't want it," I said miserably.

"It won't be. Because people like you are going to see to that." He held my eyes steadily.

I drew a breath. I took his hands in mine. He was right. There was hope. I nodded. "But I won't do a spousal hire. I will stand on my own two feet. That's who I am."

The corner of his mouth lifted in a half-wince. "A spousal hire is not exactly the kind of thing you pour concrete down toilets for, is it?"

I choked on a laugh. When I had recovered, I said, "That it is not. I'm going to fight for my career. I won't take it lying down. I haven't, and I don't intend to start now."

He nodded. "That sounds like you. Stubborn."

"I'm glad you're not stubborn."

Ignoring me, he continued, "There's a position open in my department. Apply for it, then."

I held his eyes. Drawing a breath, I nodded.

WE SAT on the sofa in the living room, a summery candle burning, Chester Arthur Hayden lying on the rug, and Samuel's arm around me. I, being an excellent wife, had given him popcorn for supper.

"Just don't get used to it," I said.

"You know perfectly well that *I* cook most of our meals," he countered.

His words sounded crabby, but he was smiling. It was amazing how well we had gotten along over the past week. I knew normal interactions would resume sometime. For now, he had a vested interest in being compliant.

"But with such efficiency?" I questioned.

"There you have me," he quipped.

The idea had been to watch a movie. The TV was turned off not long in, however. The kissing was still top-notch; the only difference was that Samuel was tenderer, if possible. Maybe more *reverent* was the word? I knew the feeling.

His tongue grazed mine. Would that never fail to excite me? I gave back measure for measure. His hand cradled the back of my head. I trailed kisses along his jawline, intentionally enticing him. I felt his heart, under my hand, pounding.

His hands broke free and wandered delectably.

"Not in front of Chester," I protested in a whisper, still kissing him.

He stopped. "Are you serious?" He looked at me. We both looked at Chester. He *was* watching with interest.

Samuel started kissing me again. But he was distracted. I had psyched him out. He broke off. "No. I can't do this."

I laughed.

"Come on," he said, taking my hand and starting for the door.

I put out the candle and blew a kiss to Chester.

TWENTY-SIX

"Every human being must be viewed according to what it is good for. For not one of us, no, not one, is perfect. And were we to love none who had imperfection, this world would be a desert for our love."
-*Thomas Jefferson*

Samuel

He picked up his phone, looking at it a moment before dialing a number he hadn't in a long time, if ever. It rang three times.

"Samuel?" The voice was breathless, surprised, unbelieving.

His chest pinged. It sounded like Enid. He always forgot that. He bit his lip. "Yeah."

A pause. "Congratulations on your wedding," his mother said in a neutral tone. She had made the mistake of using an endearment once somewhere when he had happened to see her out. It hadn't happened again.

"Thank you," he said, as impersonally as possible.

Another long pause. "Are you calling because your Aunt Enid told you I wanted to...to talk to you?"

Now he was the one who let silence grow. "Yeah," he said at last.

He heard her swallow. She took a long breath that she maybe thought he couldn't hear. "When I heard that...Jenna had left... I couldn't have felt more guilty if it were me who left you all over again. I was afraid you would think something was wrong with you."

"That's generally why you don't abandon a seven-year-old."

She let the silence grow for a second. "Well, anyway... I know that's not really at issue now, but... I owe you an explanation, Samuel."

He remained silent.

She began. Solemnly. "When your father and I married, I went on the pill. It happened not to suit me. I tried it for a year or so, and it made me absolutely crazy, so I had to come off of it. Then we decided to have you. I began having depression before you were even born, and after, I had the typical postpartum depression, in the worst kind of way. It went away, and I had a little reprieve, and I loved you so much. We were happy, I think, for a while. But your dad wanted me to stay proactive about taking care of myself, and I just wouldn't, and we did argue some. I had always struggled, hormonally speaking, and then, because of some problems I was having, I had to have a total hysterectomy before I was even thirty. After that, I just sort of...spiraled. I had no sense of life, no enjoyment, and really no will to live." He heard the emotion in her voice. Felt it in himself.

"The simple truth is that I felt nothing. I knew I was supposed to love you, and I wanted to, but, as far as *feelings* go, I felt nothing, not for you, not for anyone or anything. I was in...a bad place. I was driven by selfish desires, by a need to feel alive again, and by taking care of what *I* needed. I know that sounds terrible. It *is* terrible. Understand me when I say this, Samuel: I *did* make a lot of mistakes that had nothing to do with my health, and I *was* selfish. I am not making excuses, because there aren't any. I'm just trying to tell you how I got to the point that I could walk away. As time passed and the dust settled, I wondered how I could have left my little boy." He heard her crying as she said the last two words. "I did love you so."

He tightened his jaw, fighting the prick of emotion behind his eyes.

"But your dad said that you don't get a second chance with kids, and he was right. Dead right. He asked me to stay out of your life until you were grown, and I agreed to his terms." She paused. "We stayed in touch, you know."

"I know," he said, voice rasping.

"He wanted us to reconcile, you and me, but he didn't want to push you, and I don't either."

He didn't know what to say. He wasn't cruel. He couldn't *not* address the things she had said. "I didn't know any of that. At least, not anything that I couldn't see for myself."

He almost heard a smile in her voice. "I imagine your dad didn't feel comfortable talking to you about hormones and hysterectomies."

"He did tell me not to hate you," he said. He felt the need to tell her how generous his father had been. "He told me that you had been through a lot."

She didn't respond to that, but he did almost palpably *feel* her response. He knew she was crying again, even if silently. He looked toward the ceiling, trying to restrain his own emotion. A long time passed, but he didn't think either of them considered getting off the line.

Finally, she whispered, "Enid says she's really great. Maddie."

He could tell her things, things about how he had struggled throughout his life that would curl her hair. But somehow, the desire to do that had dissolved. "She's...yeah. She's great." That

227

wasn't the half of it. He tried to imagine Maddie going through the things his mom had, and his heart softened by several more degrees. He honestly couldn't imagine.

"Do you want to talk about Jenna?" she asked softly.

"I wish her well. But there's nothing that needs to be discussed now."

"Easier to move on when they're not your soulmate."

"Mom..."

"Just saying..." she said almost playfully.

She wasn't wrong.

"Not so easy when they are," she added, more seriously. Sorrowfully.

He didn't know what to say. If his parents had felt for each other what he felt for Maddie... Him being left wasn't the only tragedy here.

"I will always love him," she said.

He swallowed. "I think he always loved you." Finally, a tear spilled over and tracked hotly down his cheek.

"Then let's try this, Samuel. For him."

He paused to think for a long moment. "Okay," he answered finally. "But slowly."

"I can do slowly," she breathed.

He nodded, well aware that she couldn't see him. His voice scraped. "Talk soon?"

"Talk soon."

I READ through Etta Hayden's endless stack of letters. At some point, a Hayden family member or secretary had been pretty vigi‑ lant about regaining possession of the family's letters, so I had a deep collection through which to sort. Etta had a vibrant social circle, of course, with constant correspondence. The type to send a historian looking for clues as to the woman's ancestry into a panic. The correspondence was simply endless.

It was clear that I would never get through it all. It would take years. Etta was intensely prolific as a writer, and very well-reasoned and eloquent. Her handwriting was beautiful, but difficult to read, so I was lucky if I translated five full letters per day. That was why I gravitated mostly toward her letters to her brother and her sister-in-law, the two people whom we suspected knew her secret.

"What are you doing?" I heard Samuel's voice and looked around to the entrance of the room, where he leaned against the doorway.

I sighed. "Just researching."

"Researching?" he said in a passable imitation of Enid. "Is that what they're calling it these days?" His eyes smiled as they rested on me.

I smiled with him, my eyes dancing. His spirit had been lighter since he had talked to his mom. I enjoyed this side of him.

He came over to me, putting a hand on my shoulder. I felt him read what I was reading. After a time, he said, "We're never going to get through all of this, are we?"

"Honestly? No. What we need is a team of about ten undergraduates assisting. That, however, isn't very likely here."

"At the back of beyond?" he asked ironically.

I smiled. "Precisely."

He sat down, reaching for a stack. "Well. I can help today."

TWENTY-SEVEN

"There are no secrets that time does not reveal."
-Jean Racine

The end of summer was bliss. We researched most waking hours, but there were lunch picnics, long walks with our resident Labrador, interesting daily finds, even more interesting nights...

I felt like I was going to have to get a stronger prescription for eyeglasses, which, as I told him, I blamed entirely on Samuel. The original agreement was to help him catalogue, while I would be able to use selected materials for a career-launching project. While this was, technically, what had happened, I somehow felt that I got the rougher end of the bargain.

"And then to throw you *in the mix, as something I got, too..."* I had said with mock despair.

"A raw deal, certainly," he had responded with typical sarcasm.

As this bickering had led to an interlude of kissing and rather more intricate familiarities, I conceded that it wasn't such a raw deal, after all. And in truth, I was as committed to the project of preservation and classification of the documents as was Samuel.

Mostly, it was because he needed me. But a little bit, it was because I would always wonder about Etta Hayden—how she came to be where she was, and where she had ended up—if I never completed out her story.

And that was why I read on.

Etta Wayles Hayden to William Wayles, documented and preserved by Madeleine Hayden, Ph.D., M.A., B.A.

May 17, 1863
Hayden's Ridge
My Dear Brother,

Alexander knows. I fear all is lost. I will write more when I have more information. Please stand in readiness to receive me in Maryland if necessary. I do not yet know the status of our children and grandchildren. We have not spoken, my husband and I, since the truth was revealed. This, after nearly forty years of commu- nion and constancy between us.

I have borne five children, the eldest of which is thirty-six years of age. He is in constant danger in his colonelcy, as are my two younger dear ones. The girls, thank heaven, are safe with their husbands' families. And yet, I cannot be sure their father does not mean to disown them. He has not spoken on the matter or even mentioned the children. I suppose he can scarcely imagine that the grandson he bounced upon his knee the night before last has African ancestry in his veins. You know Alexander. You know that he is a good man. But tell me, is there a Virginia planter alive, who could treat his children the same with such knowledge? It was our lives' earliest lesson, was it not?

In this terrible flanking maneuver on Fredericksburg, which led to the battle at Chancellorsville, we determined it was too close, and that if the Federals broke free through Richmond, it would be only a matter of moments before they made it to us. Given that we have several of the grandchildren here with us, and Charlie's wife Lucy is with us and in a delicate condition, we determined to go to Alexander's hunting lodge deep into the Piedmont, almost to the mountains.

We also determined to take with us our most precious belongings, which Alexander immediately perceived to be all of the family's letters and documents dating back to before America existed. This took several days, and it was mostly he and I who did the actual work of locating them and storing them in crates. At the same time, the rest of the family and servants were preparing our other belongings, asking, of course, the mistress of the house a dozen questions per hour.

In this chaos, Alexander stumbled upon my letters to E. All of my letters to M have either been burned or carefully stored in places no soul could ever find them, in the portrait of our aunt that the other M brought to me so long ago. Most of the other M's letters are there also. But my letters to E... I had completely forgotten such existed. I can scarcely believe he has been dead more than ten years now.

My husband, seeing them, had pause, and then great consternation. He could think of no other meaning behind such intimate letters with a man other than you but that type of correspondence which exists between lovers. Oh, Bev, when he looked at me... It was not anger, but complete devastation. And you may say that I am a coward, or a traitoress, or a weak woman. Indeed, I feel all of those things. But I chose my marriage, Brother. Over every other consideration of danger to so many. I told him that I had not one brother, but three. And when he did not believe me, I told all.

I can scarcely realize my loss. I am sixty-two years of age. I have known early America, and I have experienced its disintegration. I wonder what M would think. Sometimes I think she would be proud of me. Sometimes I think ashamed.

Despite everything, despite all that it would mean to my children, and the life I have lived…I do feel hope. Hope that the conclusion of this great misery of our nation will mean that so many in bondage will not have to make the same difficult decisions as we and half of our ancestors have made down through the generations.

I do not know if this letter will reach you. There is nothing else for me to do but write to you. It is what I have done since we left home, in every crisis. I do not know if I might come to you under a flag of truce. The fact remains that you and I are on opposite sides of a civil war. I must bear up and face the truths in which I now live. In any event, my nerves feel more orderly for having spoken to you, even if only by a letter.

Yours With Unending Love,
Etta

I LEAPT FROM MY CHAIR, my heart pounding. My feet carried me by rote, hammering on the hardwood, toward the back stairs.

The attic. I had to get to the attic.

I could barely think. Etta had just confirmed my suspicions. She *was* born a slave. M was her and William Wayles's brother, as was a man named *E*. The other *M* almost certainly was their mother. But that wasn't the half of what I suspected.

My hands trembled. If what I believed was true...

I felt lightheaded. I paused, pressing my hands to my temples on the stairway. Was I *crazy*? But the portrait... It was Etta's *aunt*? The slip, in her emotional consternation, of calling William *Bev*? I pressed my fist to my mouth, shaking inwardly.

Finding a new burst of energy, I bounded to the top of the attic stairs, where I flung open the door. I saw the portrait behind its cloth, and, with mental apologies to Samuel, I went down on my knees and half uncovered it.

Then I began taking the backing off. Not with abandon, of course. I exercised as much caution as a person with trembling hands and raging adrenaline could do. Finally, it popped out of its setting, and I carefully maneuvered the backing out.

A packet *plunked* to the floor.

I stared at the parcel. It was a stack of letters tied with ribbon. My breath caught. I took it in my gloved hands, hearing them crinkle. Dust motes showed in the beams of light from the tiny windows. I turned the letters toward the light.

They were *from* Etta, written in French. To her mother. *M*. Of course. *M* for *Mother*, or *Mama*. I drew a breath. Turning them over, I looked at the direction. They were encased in an outer sheet of paper with another person's handwriting marking the direction.

They were addressed, not with a typical direction, but certainly to a place. A very famous place. To Monticello.

I screamed.

"MADDIE, WHAT THE *HELL*?"

Samuel came up to the attic at break-neck speed. Upon seeing me on my knees in the floor unharmed, he developed that sort of rage that thinking someone you love is harmed, only to find out that they are not, can give. "There better be a freaking anaconda up here to justify that!" he yelled, still breathing heavily.

I held his eyes for a long moment, not apologizing. I wasn't going to have to when he heard this. "Etta Hayden's mother was Sally Hemings," I said.

He stared at me, stock still, uncomprehending. When understanding set in, and he grasped it, I think he then fully understood the scream. "Which means that her father was..."

"Thomas Jefferson."

He didn't even react, obviously in shock. At last, he blinked. "What have you found?" He whispered, going down beside me. Upon seeing the state of the portrait, he cut me a look.

Heading off criticism, I said, "I did tell you I thought there was something back there."

He didn't respond, reaching for my gloves, which I took off and handed to him. He read the letter that I had, with the help of a translator app, just finished reading.

1822
Washington City
My Dear Mother,

*We are settled and all is well. Beverley has secured gainful employ-
ment, and I am keeping house. I can scarcely thank Mrs. Trist
enough for agreeing to be our emissary, through her letters to
Father. I miss you with all my soul and want nothing so much as to
see you. In lieu of this, these letters must suffice, and I thank God
for them.*

Your Loving,
Harriet

Samuel looked up at me, his face drained of color, bewildered, his eyes giving away his awe. He handed me back the letter with a hand that was not quite steady. I tucked the missive back in its place and, pulling another pair of gloves from my pocket, coaxed out another letter.

It was in French. From *M* to Etta. I swallowed. From Sally Hemings to Harriet Hemings. Of course. Sally had learned French in Paris, and it was likely she had learned to read and write in French as well, while she may never have been taught the same in English. It also provided an extra layer of confidentiality. I handed the letter to Samuel for translation.

1826
Charlottesville
My Dear Daughter,

I bring you this portrait for safekeeping. It is fortunate that your husband did not think it unusual that you should be visited by a woman you claimed to have been your nurse. I am so grateful to have looked upon your face again. I imagine the story about it having been your aunt and salvaged from your burned home will suffice as an explanation.

And after all, it is *your aunt. He burned their letters after her death, for privacy's sake. But her portrait he preserved. Still, he did not wish her to be the subject of public conversation and felt this were to be a less likely contingency if no image of her were ever found. He asked his daughter, Mrs. Randolph, to find a place of safekeeping for it.*

Why she has turned the task over to me, I could not at first imagine. She scarcely remembers her mother, I know. I thought perhaps she meant it as a punishment for me. Mrs. Jefferson was my sister, yes, and sometimes, oftentimes, over the years, I have thought of that. And perhaps that is why now I have gone out of my way to preserve it. You have the means to protect it, and I know it will be safe in your hands.

Let this be a monument to his love, then. You are a monument to mine, along with your brothers. To everything I hope for the future and cherish in the past of my family. His promises were fulfilled. My children are free. That is all I ever desired.

Your Loving,
Mother

SAMUEL LIFTED HIS HEAD, and his eyes locked with mine for a long moment. There was nothing that could be said. We simply stared at each other in the silence.

CHAPTER

TWENTY-EIGHT

"The earth belongs to the living, not to the dead."
-Thomas Jefferson

We had an argument that night. Our first one since the wedding.

"We have to talk to Monticello," I said, while we, both still a bit numb, sliced veggies for a stir-fry.

Samuel, his shirtsleeves rolled up as he chopped the onion (because I hated chopping onions), glanced over at me, maintaining his silence.

His promise to his father.

Taking a breath, I lowered my knife, resting it against the carrot gently. "Samuel," I said, shaking my head, "you know this is not something we can keep to ourselves. We know what became of Beverley and Harriet Hemings. We have a letter in the handwriting of Sally Hemings. We have enormous illumination on her life. We know what Martha Wayles Jefferson looked like." I crossed my arms. "No one else in the *world* knows these things besides you and me. In the whole world, Samuel."

"You act like it's simple," he said, frowning, face pained. "My dad made me promise I wouldn't put the family story out there. That may sound crazy. But we were close. I don't make promises to people I love lightly."

"Your dad didn't know these things, Samuel. He wasn't operating with all of the information when he asked that of you. This type of information belongs to everyone," I said passionately. "This belongs to the public, to the public debate, to the annals of history!"

"Why?" he asked, equally fervently.

"Because it's American history, in which Sally Hemings is a very vital player. Because it concerns elucidation on the life of a Founding Father. And because you're a damned historian, Samuel!" I exclaimed. "I shouldn't have to tell you this."

"All of those things may be true. It may be a famous story. But it is *still* my family story," he retorted with heat. "Which my father asked me to protect from public scrutiny. Don't you think that was what Sally Hemings and Harriet Hemings Hayden would have wanted, at the end of the day, too?"

"I think they could not have imagined a world in which their status and race would not be the first thing that people see. Or in which the general public would care about their lives in a sympathetic manner. But that is where we are. When you are sitting on something of such colossal importance, Samuel, like this information, like this house, like the whole of the Hayden's Ridge collection, you cannot keep it to yourself any more than you should conduct an archeological dig in Egypt and proceed to take home your loot!"

"It is not loot; it is my family!"

"You know what I meant. You know I don't mean to devalue that. But honestly, Samuel, you are not thinking clearly here."

"Not thinking clearly? Is that what it is?" he demanded. "I made a promise to my father. Like I've made promises to you, Maddie. I would never think of breaking them. I wouldn't be who

I am if I did. And if you want me to, I don't really know what to say to you."

"Don't paint me in the role of someone who believes breaking promises is fine," I countered, tears of rage starting to my eyes. "In almost every case, I believe we never should."

"Just in this case...?" he questioned ironically.

"I am arguing for rationality. That has to come in here somewhere."

He dragged a hand through his hair, releasing a pent-up, emotional breath. "I'm...going to go feed the sheep." He put down his utensils, and without another word, left the kitchen.

Etta Wayles Hayden to William Wayles, documented and preserved by Madeleine Hayden, Ph.D., M.A., B.A.

April 30, 1865
Hayden's Ridge
My Dear Brother,

Well, it is all over, my much-beloved brother. The war. Slavery. The killing. We are safe here, and we have made it through with all of our sons alive. That is a matter which puts a great deal into perspective.

I am sorry to have left you in suspense since my letter of two years ago, but it was found to be simply impossible to get correspondence through to the North.

My marriage has been a struggle. Alexander could not do as any gentleman in his position would want to do without destroying the family name and putting our children at risk. He is not without sympathy. In time I think we may restore our bonds completely. But trust was broken, and trust takes a long time to build. And you and I know better than most the abiding prejudices which makes it impossible to fathom being married to one of my status.

He does not tell me that I cannot write to you. But he has asked me to break bonds with M completely. M's status, as you know, is different to mine and yours. He is legally free, and yet publicly known to have been born a slave. He does not hide it. I have written to him of the dangers to my children of our continued correspondence. I have received a terse response. I only hope he does not hate me. I know that he has a son who died in a Confederate prison camp. My heart bleeds for him, and for the brother I shall have no more. But thus were my choices.

God bless you, my brother, and your two Marys. We are just about to sit down to supper. I have a great deal to be thankful for. I look now to the future.

Your Loving Sister

I ate supper alone.

Finally, I went back to our living room, which was generally cozy but felt cold somehow tonight. I sat at the desk, going through my emails. I saw one from UVA and blinked blindly as I read it, my heart sinking.

Swallowing, I set it aside and went through the rest of my emails. There were a few requests for appearances on podcasts, several for articles, and a couple of speaking engagements. A lot of them had hefty financial offers attached. I would parse through them tomorrow and accept or gratefully decline.

I clicked through social media, smiling when I saw that Jessie had won some sort of prize for her bull and was broadcasting that fact loudly. Enid and Landon were on a yacht somewhere. Judy was sharing a radical feminist article.

The door opened, and I looked up. My heart rate escalated. Samuel, looking sheepish, came in. Eyes sweeping over me, he said, "Maddie...," in a torn voice and walked toward me. I got up, going to meet him halfway, and his arms came around me.

"I'm sorry," he said, kissing my cheek. "I was such a jerk."

"No, you weren't," I responded, laying my head on his shoulder as his arms tightened around me.

His thumbs stroked me, but his expression was distant, as if he were considering something deeply. At last, he focused on me, gaze flickering over my face. "If I agreed to allow the collections to be made public, we would get a substantial preservation grant, and there's no one I would trust like you to manage that process. If we let it be known what you've found here, your reputation in academia would be established again, and on a level few people ever see."

I held his gaze. "That made up no part of my arguments to you earlier, Samuel," I said with great firmness. "I would never forgive you if you made the decision to go public for that reason. That's not what this is about."

"You came here to save your career. I can give you that. How could I not?"

"Not like this. Not on this scale. I came to develop something along the lines of the index, and that's in the hands of the publisher. I'm serious, Samuel. Do not play with the idea of doing that for me. If you do this, it's going to be because you want to."

He sighed, kissing my forehead and tucking me against him. "I want to agree with you, Maddie," he said softly. "As to the argument. I know you're right about the history. I just can't get my dad out of my head on this."

I smoothed my hand on his chest. "Have you ever considered that your dad made that decision for *you*, Samuel?" I asked softly.

He looked at me, confused. It was funny sometimes how little one could see about one's own family. This seemed obvious to me. We were talking about a man who had remained in touch with an ex-wife who had deserted him. Who raised his son not to hate her. Who took great care to ensure the same son had female role models. This was not a man who cared about the family story staying private, the secrets intact, for his own protection.

"What do you mean?" he asked softly.

"Well, you're an American historian, Samuel. You do Virginia history and the Civil War. He knew any negative publicity from Hayden's Ridge could only damage your career. He knew you would want to take the collections public as soon as they were in your hands. And he knew that could be detrimental to your career. He didn't want you to sacrifice all you had worked for in order to tell the family history."

He looked at me, a sort of blinding perception seeming to hit him. He grasped at once the truth of something that had, apparently, been hidden from him, just out of sight. I kissed his jaw, considering that I had given him enough to think on for tonight.

WE LINGERED IN BED. I could scarcely consider my career, or the future, or anything from history of very great importance when Samuel's arm was around me. My head laid against his chest; I could hear his heartbeat. I loved that.

His hand, which had been resting on my hip, came up to brush my hair back. He tucked his chin to look at me, and I smiled. His thumb traced my lips, and I kissed it.

His eyes lingered on me. "I want to go public, Maddie."

I lifted my brows, just before raising myself up. "What?"

He held my eyes.

"Is this because of last night?" I asked.

He gave a short ripple of laughter. "While you do create a very unequal contest with such behavior—"

"That is not—"

"—I arrived at this conclusion because of your earlier, persuasive arguments." He held my eyes.

I gave a little smile.

"Which happen to be correct," he added.

Well, well, well. "Do you feel at peace?" I asked. I really never would want to persuade him to act against his conscience. I hoped he knew that.

He nodded. "When you said that... It was like you knew my dad."

"Well, if that was how he felt, he might have had a point. You could be cancelled over this, you know."

"For the crime of being born?"

"Precisely."

He looked at the ceiling for a time. "I think I may have gotten into the wrong company... But I'm starting to say *public opinion be damned*."

I smiled, and as we kissed, I could feel him smiling, too.

TWENTY-NINE

"In matters of style, swim with the current;
in matters of principle, stand like a rock."
-*Thomas Jefferson*

I may have bitten off more than I could chew.

The press was intense. We started with just informing the right boards and organizations, with which we worked to formulate a press release. The story hit the news and went viral within two days of Samuel's decision to go public.

We were asked to go on news outlets, radio shows, and podcasts. We didn't see each other, except brief snatches, for days. The world just as fascinated by Harriet Hemings Hayden (or Etta Wayles Hayden) as we were. Her story was finally told, and at a time that the world was ready for it. There was no small degree of interest in the portrait as well.

On the upside, my purely academic book hit the bestseller list. The public at large spoke my name at their dinner tables, something I couldn't quite comprehend. Academia was thawing. But an iceberg doesn't melt overnight.

I thought about this as I watched my husband lower the curtain on the portrait in the grand foyer at Hayden's Ridge. Not Martha Jefferson's. Hers was in its rightful home again. But we had unearthed the portrait of Etta Hayden and given it a place of prominence. This lady of the house, matriarch of the family, daughter of a Founding Father, a brave woman, and many times great-grandmother of Samuel.

We were hosting an event to thank the boards who had helped us take our findings public. The guests clapped as many of them saw Harriet for the first time. I don't think the fascination with her life would ever cease.

We milled.

There were cocktails and hors d'oeuvres. There were academics. A lot more interest in our research... Samuel's eyes met mine across the crowd sometimes, a peaceful smile in them.

When it was all over, we crashed on the sofa, his arm around my shoulders. "Chester is going to be angry," he said. "He's been in his crate for more than an hour."

I smiled. "Spoiled pup."

Samuel closed his eyes briefly. "No more interviews," he said.

"No," I agreed.

He opened his eyes, looking down at me, friendship, fondness, and love in his expression. He was happy.

My smile slipped. I hated to, but I had to tell him something more sobering. I bit my lip, holding his eyes. "UVA turned me down, Samuel."

There was a moment's pause. His lips parted. "What? Maddie, no..." He looked anguished as he gathered my hands, squeezing them tightly, and it soothed my battered heart. His hand then cradled my face. "When did you find out?"

"The night we had that argument," I said.

"Why didn't you say?" he asked softly, eyes flickering over my face.

"Because I needed to decide what I was going to do. I hope

you don't feel excluded, but I don't think that's the kind of decision anyone can really help you make, do you?"

He shook his head. His eyes softened. "What are you going to do?" he asked gently, pulling me into his lap.

"I'm going to accept the offer from Brighton Christian." Surprise flickered in his eyes. "It's a good school, and I'm fortunate to have an offer from them. They've proposed a good salary, and I'm going to give them their money's worth. And it's a thirty-minute drive from your house in Charlottesville," I added.

He smiled, his reaction seeming to be pleasant. "That's very Maddie," he said, pleased, eyes glancing over my face.

"What?"

"Starting from the bottom and *showing* all of those imbeciles."

I laughed. "That's not—"

He stroked my hair. "You're extraordinary, Maddie," he said.

I smiled, smoothing my hands down his chest. "I know. I have it on excellent authority from Jessie that I'm just about the smartest chick she's ever met."

That made him smile. He hovered closer, kissing my forehead. But my mind whirled with all there was to be done. "There will be travel in our future, you know," I warned him. "I'm not sure we really *can* avoid all of the news shows..."

His eyes smiled tenderly. "I would be happy anywhere with you." He kissed my cheek.

"And our weekends will be spent here, of course, getting the collections public."

He kissed the corner of my mouth, teasing, causing my pulse to accelerate. "Naturally."

"And it will be really busy, getting started with our fall semesters."

"Terrible." Our lips touched.

"And getting Chester settled into your house in Charlottesville..."

"Maddie?"

He stopped, giving me a pointed look. Smiling, I wrapped my arms around his neck and returned his kiss. Pretty soon, nothing was remembered except the rhythm of two bodies, the matching of two souls, and the joining of two hearts.

THIRTY

There is an old Armenian saying: *The sun won't stay behind the cloud.*

I didn't remember much about my mother, but I remember her saying that. It means that the truth will not remain hidden forever. It *will* reveal itself. To me, it had been like a promise over the past year, reverberating in my mind, presenting itself in moments of hopelessness.

But it had been a promise over my life, too. In English, the quote resonates like an assurance that the sun will come out after a rainy day. I would say it to myself as a child. Sometimes through the fog, you can't see the sun. But you can remind yourself that in some imaginable future, things will be different. Better.

I was happy. I'm not sure in my life I've ever been brave enough to say that, or that it would have even been true if I were. I knew there was an element of chance to the whole thing, of serendipity. But as summer blended into autumn, I also knew that more than half of the reason was Samuel.

In my bedroom, I put my blazer on and slipped down the stairs. Going into the kitchen, I saw Samuel standing at the island, preparing my lunchbox, meticulously folding, sealing, packing. He was in his dress clothes, ready for work.

I couldn't believe sometimes that I had him. But our Craftsman-style house in Charlottesville with the charming sidewalk swept clean of leaves attested to the fact. The pillow beside mine that smelled like him attested to it. The smile in my heart that nothing could seem to dim attested to it.

I looked back him, packing my lunchbox. It was my first day.

I felt nervous but also eager. My classes had filled up and were already waiting-list-only. It seemed there were students eager to learn. And I was ready to teach.

I sidled up to Samuel with a peck on the cheek.

He glanced down at me with a slight smile, eyes running the length of me. He dropped what he was holding and pulled me to him. I let him kiss me as long as he wished.

I had him to see in the morning, and him to come home to. I had a job, friends, and hope.

My promise had not failed me. The sun beamed radiantly.

<hr>

The End

AUTHOR'S NOTE

In 1873, Madison Hemings sat down with the *Pike County Republican* to give an interview. His words were unemotional and spoken with simplicity—his life story. They nonetheless had the potential to be explosive. In the interview, he revealed his family history, including the bargain struck between his parents, Thomas Jefferson and Sally Hemings, in Paris, as well as the names of the children of Sally Hemings. I encourage you to read the interview in its entirety.

His interview was largely lost to history. Historians who did address it wrote his story off as untrue, the words of someone seeking to increase his importance. But most everything Madison said has since been proven. Even without later overwhelming proof, the words have a note of authenticity to them. He merely mentioned Thomas Jefferson—aware of his national importance, of course, but like anyone else would speak of their father when giving their life story—and then proceeded with information about his maternal ancestry, mother, siblings, wife, children, and career.

Sally Hemings had four children who lived to adulthood. We know a little about her two youngest, Madison and Eston, due to the interview. Beverley and Harriet have never been found. They left Monticello in 1822, lived as white American citizens, and disappeared from the record. There is no question that this was by design. Jefferson could not free them without calling attention to their status, so, even while physically free, they lived the rest of their lives as technically, legally enslaved. They have been lost to history.

But there were tidbits... Tidbits that had me wondering what the most likely scenarios for Beverley and Harriet were, based on the facts. And thus, this novel was born. A discovery may be made tomorrow that will prove all of my guesses wrong. I very much hope there *is* a discovery about their lives. But there is a chance there never will be, and so I made artistic choices based on the historical evidence we do have.

In the interview, Madison, an older man by then, relates that Beverley married a "white woman from a family in good standing" and had a daughter "who was never known by society to have African blood coursing through her veins." Something about his phrasing when discussing Beverley led me to believe that he and Beverley were on good terms. On the other hand, I suspect that he and Harriet (or the fictional Etta) had a falling out around the time of the Civil War. He relates that they had not spoken in ten years.

Why, I wondered? We know that when Beverley and Harriet left Monticello with Jefferson's permission and some money, they lived in Washington, D.C. at least for a time. Madison says that Harriet married a "man of a good family whose name I could give but will not for prudential purposes." He was protecting Harriet, obviously. But I also think he might have been intimating that we might know who her husband was if he told us. He didn't say the same about Beverley's wife, although from his clues we can gather that she was likely from at least a middle-class family. Because of these things, I imagined that Harriet may have married into a very wealthy or prestigious family.

Context clues also hint that Madison may have been bitter about his and Harriet's possible falling out. He indicates that he doesn't know at the time of the interview if Harriet is dead or alive. The Hemingses were deeply concerned with family ties. They kept up with each other. Named their children after each other. Why, then, this distance? I reasoned that the most likely explanations would be that Harriet had turned her back on Madison due to his more public, visible manner of being freed (through Jefferson's Will), or because they fell on separate sides of the Civil War. Or both. If Harriet had chosen to sever ties with Madison abruptly only in their late middle age, a plausible reason would be if her husband had found out who her parents were only then and asked her to do so.

I wove fact with fiction based on a likely interpretation of documented facts. For instance, Sally Hemings did go to France while Jefferson was Minister to Paris and did learn the language, although we do not know if she had a writing knowledge of it or if she learned to read or write English either. She and Jefferson did begin there what appears to have been a thirty-nine-year relationship.

I express no opinion in this novel as to the nature of their relationship. Some have imagined Hemings as an entirely unwilling participant, a victim of prolonged rape. Some have posited that, even if no violence was involved, due to the power deferential between Jefferson and Hemings, she could not have said *no*, which would also indicate a forced relationship of rape. Others have noted that when the relationship began, Sally was in France and could have taken her freedom legally but chose instead to reach an agreement with Jefferson and return with him to Virginia. Of course, in Virginia her status returned to that of an enslaved person; this would mean that if her decision changed, she would be without recourse then. Some have imagined theirs as a long-term, devoted relationship of love. I didn't want to take a position in that discussion because only Sally

Hemings could tell us how she felt. And history has left her in silence...

The only position I did take was that of Sally strongly wanting her children to be free. In the interview, Madison Hemings tells us that she extracted a promise from Jefferson that he would ensure the freedom of any children they would have. He fulfilled that promise, and Sally Hemings did accomplish her objective of delivering her children from slavery.

We do not know the precise nature of familial interactions between Jefferson and his children with Sally Hemings—only tidbits. In a fictional letter I crafted from Harriet (Etta) to her mother, I had Harriet call Jefferson *Father*. I believe there is enough historical evidence from indicators in Madison Hemings's interview to have made this a possibility, at least in private. One senses from Madison's tone that there was, in his belief, some degree of difference in the outward display of affection from Jefferson between his children with Hemings and his legal grandchildren, of whom he believed the latter were the greater beneficiaries. But there is also some evidence that Jefferson spent a lot of time with his sons once they were artisans on his properties, and that he passed on a passion for music to his son, Eston.

Beverley, on the other hand, may have favored him in his interest in science. A man who was enslaved (and later freed) at Monticello, Isaac Jefferson (also known by his family surname, Granger), mentions that he went to the launch of "the balloon that Beverley sent off" in Petersburg, Virginia. It seems, therefore, almost certain that Beverley took an interest in, and may have made a career out of, hot air balloons. There was, indeed, a newspaper advertisement for a balloon ascension in Petersburg on July 4, 1834, Independence Day.

It was the mention of Petersburg that made me decide to set Hayden's Ridge east of there on the James River in Virginia. In my fictionalized version of their story, I have Harriet meeting her husband because of his shared interest in her brother's ballooning hobby. Since we know Beverley lived in D.C. and later Maryland, Petersburg seemed an out-of-the way choice for a balloon launch. But nothing in history is random. So I decided to make it because the place of launch was near his brother-in-law's home. But there could be other reasons for choosing Petersburg, as well. At the time, Petersburg had a large Free Black population, and we do know that at least one former enslaved person from Monticello (the said Isaac Jefferson) was living there and that he followed Beverley's life progress to some extent. The only reason we know about the balloon at all is because of Isaac's memoirs, so he may have been at least part of Beverley's impressive day at the ascension. Isaac Jefferson also says that Madison Hemings came to watch. [Citation for some of the listed facts (not my choices or opinions) regarding the balloon in this and the previous paragraph: *Gordon-Reed, Annette. Thomas Jefferson and Sally Hemings: An American Controversy. Charlottesville and London, University of Virginia Press, 1998, p. 151.*]

There is no known portrait existing of Jefferson's wife, Martha Wayles Skelton Jefferson (who was often called Patty, but I use her formal name, Martha, in the book). In 2014, the White House Historical Association commissioned John Hutton to craft a modern-day portrait of her, which I did not know about until I had already researched references to her appearance pretty deeply for my own literary portrait. I think Hutton's portrait hits the nail on the head. It was almost exactly as I had imagined her (Google it!).

Those who have visited Jefferson's gravesite will know that the current monument covers the graves of Jefferson, his wife, their two daughters who survived to adulthood, and one son-in-law. This is not the original monument. On Martha Jefferson's side of the current monument, there is a similar inscription to the one described in the book. However, it does not include the more passionate language of Jefferson's original epitaph for Martha, "This monument of his love is inscribed," nor a Greek inscription

ப.ıginally included which translates to, "Nay if even in the house of Hades the dead forget their dead, yet will I even there be mindful of my dear comrade." I hope readers will forgive the artistic license I took to use the original language in this book.

If you are interested in reading good fiction based on the life of Jefferson's eldest daughter from his marriage, Martha Jefferson Randolph, as well as an exploration of the facts and possibilities of the life of Sally Hemings, I would highly recommend *America's First Daughter*, by Laura Kamoie and Stephanie Dray. I found the book to be very well-researched.

But of course, if you are interested in learning more about these topics, the bulk of what I would recommend is history itself. There are many historians of Jefferson, and their amazing body of research, particularly works by Annette Gordon-Reed, Jon Meacham, and Peter S. Onuf, were invaluable in my efforts to piece Jefferson's world together enough to bring the people of the past to life for this book. Meacham's biography of Jefferson, *Thomas Jefferson and the Art of Power*, illuminates Jefferson with such vivacity that you feel like you know him. It certainly deepened my interest in studying him. Gordon-Reed's research on the relationship between Hemings and Jefferson and the Hemings family (in *Thomas Jefferson and Sally Hemings: An American Controversy* and *The Hemingses of Monticello: An American Family*) were reference points throughout the writing of this book. There are simply no words to describe the level of research and analysis Gordon-Reed undertakes in those two books, or of their contribution to the body of Jefferson studies.

While I do lean heavily on the research of multiple historians for this entirely fictional novel, any mistakes or differences in interpretation of the history presented are entirely my own, and I present the views of no other person but myself. By the same token, while I have undertaken quite extensive research for this book in order to weave a seamless narrative and get the facts as close to accurate as possible, I do want to acknowledge that the actual historical foundation was not by any means my own original legwork. I relied on historians for that. I want to state also that the endorsement of no historian has been given or sought because this is a work purely of fiction.

For more on the historical choices I made, visit my blog at: www.TaraCowanBooks.com.

MANY THANKS TO...

My parents, for giving me an interest in history.

My sister, who helped me out of several thorny manuscript issues and encouraged me to publish this book next. I couldn't have done it without you.

My brother-in-law, Ryan, for checking the French passages for me.

Hannah Cowan Jones, Pam Cowan, and Beverly Crouch. It's a joy to share the book first with you and receive your valuable feedback. Thank you!

My heavenly Father, for telling us that He has not given us a spirit of fear, but of power, and of love, and of a sound mind.

BOOKS BY TARA COWAN

The Torn Asunder Series

Southern Rain

Northern Fire

Charleston Tides

Thank God for Mississippi

Secrets of an Old Virginia House

ABOUT THE AUTHOR

TARA COWAN is an author of Southern fiction, including *Thank God for Mississippi* and the *Torn Asunder Series*. She loves history, travelling, reading good fiction, watching British dramas, and spending time with her family. An attorney, Tara lives in Tennessee and is busy writing her next novel.

TARA holds a Bachelor of Science Degree in Political Science with minors in English and History from Tennessee Tech University and a Doctor of Jurisprudence from the University of Tennessee College of Law.

TO CONNECT with Tara, visit her website at www.TaraCowanBooks.com, follow her on Instagram, or find her on Facebook or Twitter.

Made in the USA
Columbia, SC
18 January 2025

52048394R00162